FO-KISSED

FO-KISSED

A TALE OF A STRUGGLE, DECEIT, DRUGS, MUSIC, MURDER, LOYALTY AND TRUE LOVE!!

CHRISTOPHER R. BROWN

iUniverse, Inc.
Bloomington

F0-KISSED
A tale of a struggle, deceit, drugs, music, murder, loyalty and true love!!

iUniverse books may be ordered through booksellers or by contacting:

iUniverse
1663 Liberty Drive
Bloomington, IN 47403
www.iuniverse.com
1-800-Authors (1-800-288-4677)

Because of the dynamic nature of the Internet, any web addresses or links contained in this book may have changed since publication and may no longer be valid. The views expressed in this work are solely those of the author and do not necessarily reflect the views of the publisher, and the publisher hereby disclaims any responsibility for them.

Any people depicted in stock imagery provided by Thinkstock are models, and such images are being used for illustrative purposes only.
Certain stock imagery © Thinkstock.

ISBN: 978-1-4759-4446-4 (sc)
ISBN: 978-1-4759-4447-1 (ebk)

Library of Congress Control Number: 2012914605

Printed in the United States of America

iUniverse rev. date: 08/13/2012

CONTENTS

This book is dedicated to Reine and "Hurricane Ivan", Grain, Jim, G.I. Stone, and most importantly Gee Gee for keeping me focused and for all their support.

Lil Man felt he was at the end of his rope, and something good definitely needed to happen in his favor and it needed to happen fast! Things just weren't working out for him growing up. School work was a breeze, but having good grades and graduating would have only taken him but so far. The Hip Hop era was all over the air waves all around the world. Kids all over were coming up with new dances, and even dressing according to the music. But Lil Man never got caught up into all of that, he wanted to work. He wanted to be a part of something positive.

But with a knuckleheaded rap sheet and sporadic work ethic, the economy would definitely prove to be a tough one to break through to. And to top that off, those weren't the only factors holding Lil Man back and keeping him off of his would be road to success. There was something else much more special, something inside of him that we wouldn't find out about until later. This is his story . . .

GRADE SCHOOL DAZE

Growing up Lil Man had loads of fun, if society would allow him to call it that. For the only child at around the age of three he remembered how much fun it was to read! And living in the Logan section of Philadelphia, the 'hood' was like nothing more than a huge playground for everybody in his eyes! Who would've thought you could be part of a real live army throwing "dirt bombs", small balls of hardened dirt that exploded on contact into little clouds of dusty smoke. Yea, even the dirt was friendly back in the late 70's it seemed.

The firehouse was only a few blocks away down on Louden Street, so around Halloween time it was always on and poppin! Being dressed up as Dracula with fangs and a cape with fake blood dripping from the corner of your mouth, while bobbing for apples wasn't bad at all. Especially while Michael Jackson sang "Thriller" in the background. These days were to be considered the best. Even his first crush in the second grade had the patent leather "MJ" jacket with all the zippers. So it was only right mom got him one to, the reversed color . . . black and red outline while hers was red and black.

Man! We put the rug in 'rug rats'! Second grade was where he experienced his first up close real live animal encounter. Our school, Birney Elementary had brought in some farm animals from The Philadelphia Zoo. Horses, pigs, ponies and sheep. We got to take some sheep's wool home in zip lock bags as souvenir's. Sheesh that was a horrible smell if you think about it, but back then it was the sweet smell of kids just having fun.

These were definitely the days to take in and cherish, and could probably slip away in the blink of an eye, if you let it. But it was all good. Hip Hop music that would be considered 'Old School' nowadays stayed playing on the radio, and those tunes mixed with grandma's chicken and rice aroma made for a positive upbringing. Grandma and grandpa were cool as ever, so it seemed. Not too old and weren't too young. They had the right amount of energy and patience to keep the family together. Lil Man and his mom lived there with them in their house for a while. Coming from the south, the grandparents had the hospitality it took to help raise us all, along with some quick discipline!

No getting out of line 'round here', not at all! Talk back, ass on fire. Those were pretty much the rules. A lot of people from the south could be considered generally friendly, so it was up to Lil Man to develop his own little world of troubles and worries. It didn't take him too long to develop his own attitude of 'I know what I'm doing', and finding things out some of the hardest ways possible.

Dark Clouds Forming

It wasn't until about the fourth grade when Lil Man started to see his own dramas. All the fun he was having begun to diminish as it became historical news that the Logan homes began to sink. Lil Mans grandpa was the backbone that kept stuff together in the scrawny adolescent's eyes at the time. So being a steady worker who drove trucks for a living, grandpa was able to move them to a quieter neighborhood over in Penrose around southwest Philadelphia, near the Philadelphia International Airport. And here is where Lil Mans grades in school started to slip a little. Nobody knew or even bothered to inquire about what troubled this young man.

Truth was that deep down he missed his pop, who wasn't around of course because Lil Mans mom and pop were still so young themselves and still living at home with their parents. And that absence of his parents started reflecting through school work and mischievous behaviors. Not to point the finger, but in their absence he'd get away with much more than usual.

Fights in school soon became the norm as Lil Man grew tired of always seeing others' family functions take place where usually both parents would attend, while he had just his mom. Maybe the grandparents understood this, and tried to compensate as much as they could through gifts and some down home acts of kindness. But mom, who was his closest friend as a "youngin" really couldn't relate, as she was still very young herself, having given birth to Lil Man while she was only 16 in the winter of 1979.

One of his first after school fights probably began the addiction, because nothing else seemed to hold his interest anymore. Not to mention the fact that no one had really gotten into Lil Mans ear about the potentially dangerous and destructive path he was on. It was in fourth grade science when he asked for a hall pass to go and use the tiny gentleman's room. He had no idea his life would probably never be the same again after this innocent trip to just go and drain the "main vein".

Upon entrance, there was definitely something different in the air . . . "Wassup Lil Man!!??" He had found himself greeted by three of the schools sixth grade bullies who clearly already had problems of their own, which was obvious by the smoke filled air and cans of spray paint openly bulging from their pockets. The paint had just been put to great use all over the stalls and walls of the poorly lit room.

"You look like you could use a puff or two lil homie". Lil Man had found himself approached by T-Ricky, the largest of the group of three, while B-mone and Pete puffed on the last of their cigs. Lil Man was determined not to show any fear, although these guys second home was in the Principals office just about every day.

"Nah man, I'm ok for now. I don't smoke. Plus that stuff smells way too strong, we'll never get away with it." Lil Man didn't exactly say just no. He didn't want the guys to have second thoughts about him not partaking. "Well, you just make sure you keep your mouth shut bout this aight Lil Man? We don't want to have to come back and see you bout this if you know what I mean!"

T-Ricky had a habit of trying to sound extra cool whenever he spoke. He was noticeably covering up the fact that he was a bit of a struggler when it came to literature. And keeping B-Mone and Pete around made him feel even tougher, like he had his own gang. "No sweat man, I won't say a word. But you just be sure you never threaten me again or you'll have some big fourth grade problems to deal with! Got that?"

Lil Man had said this out of his mouth without even thinking T-Ricky and his crew could just jump him right there on the spot. And what he really wasn't expecting is what the head of the "tough" crew said next . . . "You know what Lil Man? You're alright wit us man! Keep your mouth shut bout this and you can hang out with us whenever you want! Man we get all the girls and all that . . . You can be part of our crew!!"

Lil Man thought to himself how cool that could be. It would be great! He had only came to pee and finally got himself a whole entire new crew to run with. He was so spoiled and bored from his games and routine at home, that he felt like it was time for some new action anyway. Not to mention mom having a newborn on the way about to steal the show. He gladly accepted. "Alright man. I'm gonna roll wit y'all, but right now I gotta get back to class. We can just meet up later."

"Aite Lil Man, later!!" All three dudes said at once. Lil Man went strolling back to class just knowing he had a new crew to hang out with now. With no pop around and the new baby about to take over, he thought this should fill the void quite easily.

TIME FOR SOME ACTION

It was after lunch time later that afternoon and while Lil Man was looking forward to running with his new crew, he was hardly prepared for the note that he had just received while sitting in art class. It was from B-Mone, and the note read: "afta school you gon get it Lil Man, we gon beat dat ass!!"

And just like that, Lil Mans new found joy was swept right up from under him. And only by a note that had been passed to him by the very same girl he had plans to impress with his new older buddies. Her name was Veronica, but everybody had called her Lady V or Vernie. She had a pretty face and was over developed for her age. Rahim thought she was even that much more special because she was the only girl in the entire school who wore light grey contact lenses.

To be a red bone with silver eyes, she had to be the flyest girl in the whole neighborhood. Every young boys crush. And now for Lil Man to get this threatening note from her, the very girl he had plans to approach and maybe even get a kiss from soon, ruined his entire week! And it was only Monday afternoon. Lil Man felt confused, perhaps even a little intimidated.

"Girl! What the hell are you doing passing me this note!? You crazy or something!!" Vernie didn't understand, nor did she really care how she just ruined Lil Mans entire world. He was just puzzled and salty all at the same time. "You read it, my boyfriend gonna kick ya ass after school today so you betta be ready ya lil punk!!"

Vernie had said all of that while rolling her eyes, shaking her head and twirling her hips like she was the sassiest and most untouchable girl on the planet. And at that moment in Lil Mans mind, she was. But none of that even mattered, because the whole class had stopped and seemed to have frozen in this moment of time to see what was going on. The class had stopped to hear Vernie check Lil Man loud and clear. "Rahim Bowman!!" His teacher shouted out frustrated from being interrupted by all the excitement, using Lil Man's full name. "I let you go to the bathroom and this is how you repay me? Now take another hall pass and march yourself to the principal's office young man, now!"

The teacher scolded him in front of the entire class, including Veronica, who still had her hand on her hip which was fully cocked to the right and tapping her foot and rolling her eyes as he walked out. All Lil Man could hear behind him were snickers along with 'oohs and ahhs' as he had to go and get dealt with some more in the principal's office.

What Lil Man couldn't figure out was why somebody sent him a note through Vernie saying it was "on" after school. He hadn't let out one word to anybody about the bathroom situation. He was sure to keep that under his hat as it was his main ticket to a new found freedom away from the drought and lack of activity at home. Already embarrassed and frustrated, Lil Man couldn't believe what had happened next. As he walked into the principal's office, all he saw was none other than T-Ricky, Pete and B-Mone getting reprimanded in a far corner of the office.

The three were sitting on a bench facing toward the entrance of the office where Lil Man had just walked in. Between them and the bench where Lil Man sat, were all the busy faculty members in the office filing papers, talking on phones and typing at computers. The office was very busy at this point in the day, especially with three of the schools most troublesome tyrants sitting over on the other side who had just gotten busted for smoking in the school.

But it wasn't too busy for Lil Man to tune in to what was going on the other side. He heard it all, and realized that the calls that were being made were to the parents of the bathroom culprits. They were being expelled. And in the midst of all the commotion, Lil Man noticed the boys across the room staring him down, awaiting eye contact. Making faces and balling their fists, Pete, T-Ricky and B-Mone were going out of their way to make it obvious they couldn't wait to get their hands on Lil Man.

On top of that, after the calls were done the three were allowed to go back to class and finish up the day. On the way out, they made it clear that Lil Mans fate was sealed after school, by bumping shoulders and winking. T-Ricky whispered the evilest line he could muster up grinning, saying "see ya later Lil Man."

Lil Man felt like he was done for sure, only because it was three of them all with plans to pay him back for droppin a dime. Meanwhile, it was his turn in the hot seat at the office. "Mr. Bowman! Care to explain why you caused all that commotion in Miss Tyner's class today? Lil Man was all lost for words. Troubles on his mind from home combined with this new found drama weren't making for a great day at all. "I'm having a bad day that's all Mr. Clooney, it happens to the best of us. Didn't really mean to disturb the class." Lil Man was trying to keep the situation as simple as possible, because he knew he had more drama to face.

His mom was called about disrupting the class, and he was scheduled for an after school melee. Mr. Clooney handed him a pink slip and reminded him he was scheduled for detention for the next three days. The rest of the afternoon seemed to have lasted an eternity. While sitting in a daze from so much on his mind for a fourth grader, Lil Man sat through last period science class wondering why the prettiest girl in school passed him a note total opposite of a love letter. Why did his new hope of friendship get crushed in an instant? And how was he gonna explain all this to mom? Lil Man was just planning his way home safely. This was all way too much for an inexperienced fourth grader to go through in one afternoon, but it was Lil Mans reality.

Once the 3 o'clock bell rang for dismissal, the halls flooded immediately with hundreds of kids eagerly and disorderly rushing to the exits to get home. But the noise and ruckus in the halls were nothing to the sounds of the pounding coming from Lil Mans own chest. He had no choice but to blend in with the rushing crowds and keep up the pace as he headed for home. Going down the second flight of stairs almost near the first floor exit, all Lil Man could hear was a mob of kids yelling out "**Fight Fight Fight!!!**"

He was thinking to himself "damn, they couldn't even wait til I got outside! Not to mention nobody had even swung a punch at me yet. My peers are really crazy!" But just then he realized that the focus of attention wasn't even on him. Not even close! Just then further down the hall he noticed a swarm of kids gathering around a rumble already in progress. And not to his surprise, it was B-Mone and T-Ricky going to town beating the crap out of none other than . . . Who? It couldn't be. It was Pete! All curled up in a fetal position next to a water fountain in a pool of his own blood, receiving what had to be the beating of a lifetime. Punches to the face and kicks to the body and back were all anyone could see being delivered to Pete if you were close enough to look his way.

A few other by standers were even taking part and joining in on the beat down. Damn, Pete was getting 'rolled on', and heavy to! The extras on the sideline were only adding their hits in hopes of gaining favor with the already expelled bullies. The beating lasted for a full four minutes, which could be compared to forever in ass whuppin time. But it died down as the shrilling sound of referee whistles blew louder than fire truck sirens.

The angry mob surrounding Pete began to thin out as kids started darting and scattering in different directions to get outside to safety in hopes of not getting recognized by school security guards. But T-Ricky and B-Mone were two of the last few to disperse as they got in their final couple of blows. Lil Man was stunned, and taking it all in as this ass whuppin was surely supposed to be for him. But it had gotten delivered to one of the crews own members. B-Mone yelled at T-Ricky "aight man, that's enough!" as T-Ricky was still tryna get in his last few stomps.

As security came closing in, T-Ricky broke down one end of the hall while B-Mone darted in the other direction, right past Lil Man. Opportunity knocked. Not to be a hero, but to find out why his name had gotten caught up in all this mess, Lil Man decided he just had to take action. As B-Mone attempted to fly by, Lil Man stuck out his sized nine Reebok classic and tripped him up something awful!

B-Mone went diving face first toward the staircase scrambling and reaching for something or someone to break his fall, but nothing was there but concrete wall covered with posters and flyers for the school. After that impact knocked out all of his wind, B-Mone slowly staggered up to his feet and turned around only to get a face-full of Lil Mans book bag filled with today's homework and heavy text books. "Lil Man! What the hell you think you doing cuz!?" B-Mone was out of it and gasping trying to catch his breath as he tried to speak. But it was too late for answers. School security rushed down the hall fast and Lil Mans arm had gotten yanked in the direction of the double doors heading towards outside. It was a bloodied up and battered Pete, catching his breath while hunched over and limping. "Come on man, let's get outta here! I gotta tell you what's goin on!" The two started to run for the doors together, and once outside and clear for home Pete began filling Lil Man in on the scenario.

What's the Skinny?

On their way home still crippled from the earlier match-up, Pete laid out everything for Lil Man. "I'm sorry man, but I was the one who told Mr. Clooney about the smoking in the bathroom. I tried to make it look like it was you to T-Ricky, but Miss Tyner sent that note Vernie gave you back to the office. Everybody saw that it was my hand writing." Pete was so shaken up from the brawl, that he had no choice but to be sincere and come clean with Lil Man. The two of them were alone now, so he figured if another beating were to occur, he might as well get it out of the way now. He thought it couldn't get much worse, but he was just a hair short of being wrong.

Lil Man snapped and hemmed Pete up against a car that they were next to. "Man! You can't go around lying like that!" Lil Man had the wildest look in his eyes and cocked back a punch that was sure to put Pete's lights out. But seeing how terrified Pete was and so bruised, he was satisfied and decided not to let'm have it. Plus, a battered Pete had more beans to spill. "B-Mone was mad because it got back to him that Vernie like's you man. She's in your class and all the girls be talkin bout you. So B-Mone and T-Ricky really wanted to get you already. They just used smoking as an excuse to do some bullying. It was only a matter of time. They were jealous bullies."

Pete was telling the truth, and Lil Man could sense it. And it wasn't really a surprise that Vernie was stirring up trouble around the school by making older kids think she was their girl. Yeah, Vernie was trouble alright. It was her looks, mixed with being an immature fourth grader. More than half the fights in school were over her. And most of the guys in the school were too young to even realize it. But it all made sense now that Pete had come clean. Now all Lil Man had to do was figure out how to explain all this to mom without getting his turn at a beating at home. Though she was young, Lil Man's mom along with the help from her parents had tried to keep Lil Man focused on schoolwork, and what they thought should be the innocent lifestyle of a boy in the fourth grade.

They really had no idea what Lil Man was going through. Especially since the school had only called home to say he had only disrupted the class, he hoped. So to make himself feel a bit better, Lil Man decided not to mention any extra events that had taken place besides a little talking in class. Other than all that, Lil Man and Pete had some of the same things on their minds. They had developed a bit of a bond. Pete came clean with Lil Man, and earned his respect. And Lil Man sort of came to Pete's rescue when he wasn't able to get up right away from the beat down. Pete was most certainly thankful for that. All in all, the two became close after that unfortunate situation.

Lil Man had no idea that the main reason T-Ricky kept Pete and B-Mone around was because they were afraid of him. They did anything they were told by the overgrown sixth grader. Pete told Lil Man that they all started hanging together after T-Ricky robbed them of their lunch money all the time, and made them not snitch. They got used to doing this until they just brought him their lunch funds on a regular basis. That had actually gone on for a few grades, up until Pete's beating in the hallway.

When Lil Man got home, he walked right into the first degree. "Boy! Where the hell you been all this time!?" his mom started. "Mmm Hmm! And what's with your clothes!?" continued his grandma. Lil Man hadn't realized he had gotten blood all over his sleeves and jeans from helping Pete. And his new white sneakers his mom had bought him just a couple weeks before were all scuffed up. After the school had called and he came walking in late, they were both hot with him. Lil Man hated lying to the ladies he loved so much, but he just had to try and maintain his innocent appearance.

"We were playing football at lunchtime in the schoolyard mom." The fib had come out so smoothly that he even believed himself for a moment. But he hadn't counted on grandma reading his body language so well whenever anything was out of place. Her sense always did shine the light. Grandma then shot eyes at him as if she stood by him in school all day.

"You sure bout that young man!? You know they called dontcha?" Damn, the school must've reported the fight he thought. He just knew he was busted. Then his mom added "You just couldn't start the week off right could you? I'm taking all of your games, toys, and no t.v.!" Wow, they really had him cornered now. He just knew Mr. Clooney had given his mom the entire scoop. Lil Man was worried about his routine at home becoming more of a drag then it already was. He cracked and ratted himself out.

"It was just a little fight mom. And it wasn't even me! I was helping another kid who got jumped after school." Grandma jumped in and cut him off immediately. "Hmph!

So you **were** up to no good today huh?! I knew I smelled trouble all over you the minute you walked in here boy!" They didn't know a thing, except that he was to report for detention the next three days. But their reverse psychology mixed with his guilt gave it all away. Mom had finished up the meeting.

"Go to your room and do ALL of your homework now!! And I had better not hear a peep out of you or that t.v. got it!!??" Lil Mans rough day had proven to turn even more sour once he had gotten home from school. But in an attempt to keep things running as smoothly as possible, he decided to just take it all on the chin and replied with a sorrowful but respectful "yes mom". Once up in his room, all he could think about was how things went wrong one after another today. He thought about Vernie, and how a chick so pretty could be so much trouble for so many guys in one school.

But on a lighter note, he decided that even with some detention to face, at least no one had gone to the bush to break off a "switch" to whip his behind with. Of all the troubles in the world, nothing seemed to top a whuppin' with a fresh "switch" on a young boys skinny legs and behind. Tired and worn out from a long day, he quickly fell fast asleep, realizing how lucky he was to get through the day untouched.

BROKEN SILENCE

Not much to his surprise, after dozing off Lil Man was awaken by what sounded like arguing coming from downstairs. "That boy gettin into more and more trouble by the day! Y'all better get control of his lil ass or it's getting shipped off to boot camp some damn where!!" Grand pop was downstairs snapping! The head honcho had come home and got an earful about Lil Mans chaotic day. It was just an add-on to the list of household issues that set Gramps off. He was already cranky just for being the only steady bread winner. Grandma didn't work, just always preached about the bible and how everybody's days were numbered. And mom was pregnant again, so she had sided with whoever had gotten the loudest in an argument just to try and save face.

She always faked the funk as if she knew what she was doing as a mother, but the truth was she was really too busy sneaking out of the house all the time to be with Lil Mans dad. Either that or off to a Tina Marie or Michael Jackson concert somewhere. Rahim's dad rarely even interacted with him that much, just came around to take mom away for a while. But Grandpa's thundering words had shaken the walls and echoed through the house, so Lil Man could sense things were about to start changing from the vibe he felt.

But he was still too young to really understand exactly what would change. All he knew was that grandpa sounded mad, madder than he had ever heard him sound before. And on top of all that, in the midst of all the fussing, Lil Man heard his own name through it all . . . Yep! It was safe to call this a bad day. And for Lil Man, it was only still just the beginning of a new world of shit. He decided to just try and go to sleep and try and forget it all.

The next morning, Lil Man came across Pete on the way to school. They chatted about the day before, and decided it was best not to bring it back up in school. They knew people would still be buzzing about it. Especially since the presence of the bullies was gone. Most kids in school seemed far more chatty and cheerful than usual. Even Vernie had a new found confession for Lil Man during third period.

"I was really trying to be **YOUR** girl Lil Man, but B-Mone stayed in the way all of the time. He was extra jealous whenever he thought somebody liked me besides him." Vernie's words came out with a deep exhale, with a sigh of relief like tone. Everybody in the school was acting brand new and funny, now that the terrible trio was gone. So she felt this was the best time to get it all out. And with Lil Man looked up to for his deed's, this was part of Vernie's immaculate game.

Lil Man had been the only one to step up on Pete's behalf, and with that he noticed a new buzz surrounding him now. In class, during recess and lunch, everywhere he went! But something felt eerie about all the attention, so deep down he really didn't want to welcome it. He knew it would lead to more drama, but he felt he had to please the audience to a certain extent. He just decided to try and capitalize on Vernie, who had so much to get off her chest all of a sudden.

"I don't like it when you be out here fightin Lil Man, it makes me all nervous and I can hardly concentrate on my classwork." Lady V was lying through her pretty little teeth. But she had to have some game for the new most popular guy in school. Vernie really just loved trouble. Commotions lit up her eyes and face the way an emergency flare would light up a dark cave. "Girl, just yesterday you were rolling your eyes and shaking your head. Now you care if I fight? What happened to all the rolling and shaking and tapping of the feet?" Lil Man was trying to play it cool, but he really couldn't believe he held the attention of the girl everybody wanted for so long. "All you had to do was talk to me you know?" Lil Man and Lady V chatted throughout classes and became an item that day. To everybody it looked like they had become inseparable.

And the whole time during the school year, all that had stood in their way were the would be bullies and some shyness on Lil Mans part. "What you doing later after school Lil Man?" They never usually had plans other than just walking home with friends or stopping by the comic book store to get some junk food and candy. But Vernie had something else in mind today. "Meet me at the store and we can go to my house if you don't mind walking a different way." Lil Man's face lit up. "Ok, that's cool. But you gotta give me a minute, I have detention." Vernie didn't seem to mind at all. "Uh huh, I'll wait. You just be sure you meet me."

Her face was so gorgeous that Lil Man hadn't really given it a second thought. He'd be there! After detention, he had a date! The rest of the day flew by quickly, and when the final bell rang Lil Man headed back to his homeroom to do his twenty five minute bid of detention. There were only about fifteen other kids in there that day. Anyone in the building who had detention was to report to the same room. But it became a reunion when he saw Pete in there. Pete was relieved, although a little embarrassed and sore from the day before still. Seeing Lil Man walk in was like having a warm blanket put over him on a chilly night.

"I'm just tryna hurry up and get outta here man. I gotta go meet up with Lady V after this." Lil Man knew Pete had hung out with Vernie before. She always used to tag along with the former trio of bullies. So Lil Man brought her up to try and get the scoop on her. "Yea, she sure is pretty! But I don't see why everybody keeps trying to talk to her. Her dad is up here almost every day fussing over that girl. And he's crazy!" Lil Man didn't really pay Pete's statement any mind. He was just eager to get on with the date. He was so bored with everything else that he didn't even care. He was becoming a thrill seeker, and getting involved with Vernie seemed like the perfect idea, at the time.

After detention let out, Pete and Lil Man finished up their chat and parted ways. Walking down the Essington avenue strip, Lil Man spotted Vernie in front of the store. She had her hand on her hip while tapping her foot, rolling her eyes and popping the bubblegum she had just bought out of the store. "Boy what took you so long!? You ain't know not to keep a girl like me waiting??" She came off as an adult who knew exactly what she was doing. Lil Man was just glad she hadn't stood him up. "I'm Just now coming from stupid detention. We had to finish at least one homework assignment before we were allowed to leave." Before Lil Man could say another word, he heard car doors slamming behind him.

"Hey baby!" Vernie was smiling hard at who was coming towards them. And before he turned around, Lil Man already had an idea of who it probably was. It was B-Mone, along with T-Ricky and two other guys he had never seen before. He was set up. 'Another situation too good to be true' he thought. But before he could even think about his next move, Lil Man felt himself being shoved into the entrance of the store. The four guys had him surrounded inside the store and decided to do him in there, out of public view. "You thought you were getting away with playing hero Lil Man?" B-Mone was the first to start talking his trash. He felt extra little after being smashed with Lil Mans book bag. Plus his girl was watching. Lil Man had it set in his mind that however this went, he would be sure to make the point that he wasn't just going to get beat down without dishing out some pain to.

The odds were definitely against him though, four on one inside this tiny one and a half room sized comic book store. And they were all larger in height and weight compared to the scrawny built fourth grader. He even felt smaller when he noticed Vernie looking in from outside the window over one of the dudes shoulder as they closed in on him. All he could do was make the best of it. Lil Man grabbed B-Mone's jacket and swung him into an old 'Double Dragon' arcade machine, knocking it over.

He felt the hood of his jacket being yanked as one of the unknown dudes turned him around and delivered a blow to his ribs. "This lil fucker don't know when to quit do he!?" He pushed Lil Man towards T-Ricky, where he received a crack to the chin. Lil Man noticed that T-Ricky could have hit him a whole lot harder, but didn't. So he did the total opposite and quickly returned the favor to T-Ricky's nose, breaking it. T-Ricky crashed into a rack of potato chips, alerting the attention of the small shop owner who had been in the back putting over stock away.

"Hey! You boy's had better get the hell out of here tearing up my damn store!" The loud and deep voice of the man had startled all of the boys at once and caught them off guard. All but Lil Man, who was recovering from his rib and chin shot. "Nah man, I owe this lil punk a beat down." B-Mone was feeling like he needed to get some payback, especially with Vernie outside still watching. But little did he know, Lil Man shared that very same feeling! T-Ricky and the two unknown older goons adjusted themselves in a hurry, and made a break for the door to get outside.

They ran straight past Vernie and jumped back into their car, leaving Lil Man and B-Mone still inside. It hadn't shown right away, but Lil Man noticed that B-Mone was shaken up and nervous with all his help gone and being alone with a kid who was a fighter. B-Mone now knew that Lil Man wasn't bothered or afraid at all. He wanted to try and save face in front of Vernie, so he attempted to negotiate with Lil Man in a low voice. "Hey, look Lil Man. I never wanted to come in here and mess with you. Not here in this store. It was T-Ricky, he made us come in here and get you."

Lil Man already knew it was all lies. Pete had run it all down to him in detention. B-Mone didn't like Lil Man the entire school year. And everybody kind of knew Vernie had liked Lil Man from all the girls in school talking about him all the time. The only one who was really unaware was Lil Man, and that was mainly because he didn't care. He was focused on school work and not getting his behind whupped by grandma for not having good enough grades. Lil Man was a grade freak geek, a nerd. Lil Mans greatest fear at the time was mom's belt, so all the trouble among other students in school was next to nothing. He was almost totally unaware of any dangers in the world besides mom's purple and black leather belt that he only saw on the weekends or whenever he had gotten a bad report in school.

Nothing could really tame Lil Man besides the thought of that belt. He drew back and punched B-Mone dead in the mouth the moment he stopped speaking to put in his request. He didn't even really want to do it, but the message had to be sent to leave Rahim Bowman aka Lil Man alone! T-Ricky had seemed to get the message loud and clear, but being watched by Vernie made B-Mone hard headed. He was dizzy and dazed, so a final three punch combination, two lefts to his ribs and a powerful jab to his jaw laid him out flat.

B-Mone was out cold up against the counter of the store. When Lil Man stepped over him to walk out, the store was a wreck. And the old man was furious, cursing and threatening to call the police. But Lil Man's only true worry was still his mom finding out about him getting into more trouble, that and the pictures of the purple and black belt in his mind. He got outside, and the expression on Lady V's face said one thing . . . "I feel so silly and sorry." There were no need for words, her eyes had shown her true guilt and shame. But Lil Man knew she would be nothing but more trouble, so he just walked right by her and headed for home without saying a word.

At that point, Lil Man felt exhausted. He just wanted to vent to his mom and grandparents everything that was going on in school. He figured if he let everything out to the people he trusted at home, everything would be alright and he could get through this. But lady luck was just not willing to be on his side just yet. There were more dark clouds and storms developing up ahead.

New Surroundings

When he finally reached home, Lil Man was relieved to smell grandma's cooking. It comforted him like heated socks on cold feet. "What you making Grain?" He tried to maintain his innocent role by coming off as just a curious child. He had always called his grandma Grain since he was two years old, but nobody ever knew why. It just stuck with her. "Oh nuffin. Just frying some fish and got some creamed corn and mixed vegetables to go with it. Ya mom is baking a cake in the oven, so no stomping around!" She hadn't let the cat out of the bag just yet, but grandma already knew about the drama in school.

He couldn't hide it if he wanted to. Not only were the signs written all over his face, but his clothes were those of a kid who had just fought off a pack of wolves. She hadn't hinted towards it being his fault, but Grain had to let him know. "We're moving again, and probably this weekend. We found a bigger place on the other side of town, and lord knows we need the room." Lil Man could sense by the way she had said 'bigger place' that she knew something about his afterschool troubles. They had planned on moving to try and keep him away from drama.

Grandpa had gotten off of work early, and decided to go pick up Lil Man from school. When he saw his little Rahim talking to Vernie, he felt proud and fell back to watch him in action. And when the guys went in the store, it made him want to watch even harder. Grandpa had caught a glimpse of Lil Man taking action into his own hands, and now figured his grandson could handle himself. Lil Man had no idea he was being followed or watched. Especially not by his own Grandpa, who knew he had some things troubling him, but couldn't pinpoint exactly what it was. And seeing him rumble at the store had given him some clues, but Gramps still had no idea how far off he still was from getting to the truth about Lil Man.

It felt kind of weird as a kid moving around all the time. But it sort of heightened Lil Mans senses and gave him an edge over other kids his age. He had gone through a lot, and so early in life. Lil Man was going to have to adjust to a new school again. A new neighborhood. And new attitudes from the adults around him that he didn't quite yet understand. His mom and grandparents had their problems as well and he couldn't see it all the time, he had been in school. They tried to keep things as positive as possible but the truth was that times were rough, and it trickled down to the soon to be teenage Lil Man.

He thought about Pete, and how their differences made them see each other in a different light for who they really were. But moving away to the other side of the city probably meant they wouldn't be seeing each other too often anymore, if at all. And even though she had her weight in drama with her, he knew he would be having thoughts of Vernie. He tried to convince himself that she was probably best kept "out of sight, out of mind."

The next two days at school went by in a slow drag, as Lil Man tried to mentally prepare for the upcoming move. He decided not to goof off or disturb any classes, and finished up the week pretty strong. He spent spare moments rapping to Pete, as he was sure they'd be departing for good. They were in an era where guys didn't call guys on the phone. It just wasn't considered to be a cool thing to do unless it was about a party or some girls getting loose after school. But through their conversations, it was obvious they wanted to stay in touch.

But oh well, Lil Man wasn't calling. And Pete was embarrassed and being hard on himself for getting beat down. So he wasn't picking up the phone any time soon either. The new friendship was about to be put on ice just as quick as it had begun. But life goes on.

Moving Day

Saturday morning woke Lil Man up to a bunch of noise and commotion. The moving truck was out in the driveway, and Lil Man could hear his grandpa giving instructions to the movers about how to arrange the appliances to make fewer trips. But there was a whole entirely different story unfolding in the living room. Lil Man went from his bedroom window to the top of the steps to get a closer listen.

"I don't owe you a damn thing! You're the one leaving not me!! And you better get that finger outta my face before it winds up broken! I'm not playin with you!!" It was his dad, fussing at his mom. He didn't have a thing to be mad about, he was the one who was never around and was a dead beat. This was just the perfect opportunity to try and flip things around and make it look like it wasn't his fault. Nobody was buying his lame story though, he was a true character. Their bickering had the baby crying on the couch. The morning was already busy and Lil Man hadn't even gotten all of the crust out of his eyes yet. At least breakfast was going in the kitchen, thanks to grandma. She was in their pretending to be busy so she didn't have to tend to the argument while grandpa was outside with the movers. Then just as mom turned to go and pick up the baby from off the couch, everyone's morning had been suddenly interrupted. (**POP POP POP POP POP POP**

POP!!!) Gunfire had erupted and filled the air of the entire neighborhood. No one in the house knew what direction the sounds had come from, but they were immediately followed by screeching tires.

Grandpa came up from the basement in another rampage. "See? That's exactly why we're getting the hell from around here!" He lit a cigarette and turned to his wife. "Those kids don't need to be around here wanting to go outside all the time with that kind of stuff going on!!" He was referring to the shots they just heard, so Lil Man felt a bit relieved to hear their moving wasn't entirely over him. "You can't even plant your garden in peace without bullets flying through the roses!! These kids are too damned crazy!"

Grandpa was being as serious as a heart attack, but Lil Man couldn't help chuckling to himself at the way the old man went rambling on and on. Even though he was cool, grandpa was coming off as old and funny right now to Lil Man. "Well, are you gonna at least tell me where you guys are moving to??" Lil Man's dad was still trying to get answers out of his mom. "I already said I don't know! And even if I did I'm not so sure I'd tell you with that attitude!!"

She was rolling her eyes and mom's tone of voice actually had reminded Lil Man of how Vernie was acting in school, just when he was trying to forget all about that girl. The smell of breakfast became irresistible, and Rahim found himself drawn to the kitchen table. Just as he pulled his chair back to sit down, Lil Man heard the shrilling sound of about three or four police cars speeding in the wrong direction on his one way street. They must've been responding to the shots everybody had just heard, in pursuit of that car with the screeching tires.

Yeah, Philadelphia always had something going on. So now was just as good as time as any for Lil Man to ask . . . "Where we moving to Grain?" His mother was in the other room trying to tune in on his question, especially to get away from dad and all his arguing. Truth was, grandma didn't really have an exact clue as to where they were going either. Rahim's mother had come into the kitchen to chime in on the conversation. Even though she had two children of her own, she was still sort of viewed as a baby herself in grandma's eyes. So she wasn't always up on all the family affairs either.

"We're moving uptown near the Fern Rock train station, near Broad Street and Olney Avenue. The neighborhood has a park with a recreational center, and there's also a pretty decent school nearby." Grandma wanted to throw in as many perks as she could to make the new place sound nice, but that's all she really knew about it from what her husband had told her. And for the most part, it was a pretty decent place at first. But for Lil Man, trouble was sure to surface its ugly head sooner or later.

JOY RIDING

A few years have gone by since the family's last move, and Lil Man was still finding himself adjusting to the new neighborhood. He saw that Fern Rock and Olney were totally different from any other places they had lived. There were a lot of different ethnicities and cultures all living mixed together and near one another. Everyone from Indians to Koreans, Japanese to Chinese, Cambodians to Africans, Jamaicans and Russians. If you could name the nationality, chances were you could find them here in Olney. Lil Mans new class in school had an "Esol" program, where foreign students who couldn't speak English well went to study and practice the language.

But overall, this was becoming a social handicap for Lil Man, which he figured was all part of his families plan to keep him out of trouble. But as it turned out, things for Lil Man had gotten worse. He was a teen now, and even though his state of mind was maturing, all this really meant was that after school fights would no longer satisfy his boredom. Lil Man was seeking new action and needed it quick!! For the first time in a while, he felt like he really didn't know what to do with himself. And nobody seemed to really care. He thought, 'what better to do than to go for a drive?'

This might not have been his greatest idea being sixteen with no license, but mischief became an overwhelming drug. So a drive seemed the perfect risk to take. Lil Man found himself speaking out loud with no one around, "I'll just grab grandpa's keys when nobody's looking and make my move." And why not? He felt he had become too big for video games and toy's, and was still too young for the woman he kept having dreams about. There weren't any girls in his neighborhood his age, none who spoke English anyway. And nobody around here knows you. It'll be perfect!

Yup, Rahim had a whole talk with himself about why and why not he should do it. The final answer popped up in his head . . . "You've never driven a car before!" This was thrill seeking at its best he figured. Before actually sneaking the keys away, he tried one last time to debate with himself. "You'll just get caught. What if somebody sees you? That would be fun, wouldn't it? You're not scared, you're a man! Let's go! This will be great!"

Lil Man gave himself every excuse in the book to go through with stealing his grandpa's car. Before grabbing the keys, he went to the living room window to scope out where the '93 Marquise had been parked. There was nothing special about the car, just extra clean and ran as great as the week it was first built in. Lil Man was scoping out where and how the car was parked so he'd know exactly how to make his move. He then did what he thought was slick, just remove the car door and ignition keys and leave the rest. After getting dressed he waited around until nobody seemed to be paying any attention and then slipped out of the back door of the house, opposite of where the car was parked as to kill any suspicion.

He then walked around front up to the beige colored Mercury as if he owned it. Once in the driver's seat with the door shut, Lil Man knew there was no turning back.

All he could do now is quickly rehearse the thousands of times he had watched his grandparents drive in his head, and now it was time to act it out. He started the car, and put it in drive while holding down the brake. He then released the brake and pulled right out of the parking space so smoothly. Lil Man was so impressed with himself on how easy he made that feel and look that he secretly began feeling excited. But he was determined not to get goofy or show any signs of inexperience. But then after a few blocks of smooth sailing, Lil Man encountered his first major problem on the road . . . he had absolutely nowhere to go! Sitting at a red light on the intersection of Broad Street and Wagner Avenue, Lil Man noticed he wasn't far from where his older cousins had lived. He had three cousins who he hadn't seen in years, and figured that he might as well go and check them out. Lil Man couldn't let anyone he knew see him driving though, so he parked about a block and a half away from his cousin's house before going to see them.

Walking down his cousin's block brought back a lot of old memories. Back in the day he remembered going around there hanging out with his older cousin's where he had caught some of his most memorable moments and aroma's coming up. "Wassup cuz! We ain't seen you around here in a while man! Whatchu been up to!!??" Lil Man's cousin Stoop Head was all hyped up when he saw him! He liked him because he had reminded him so much of himself when he was younger. Stoop Head especially took a liking to Lil Man because he had heard how he could handle himself if a situation were ever to arise. "Nothin much man, I go to a new school and walked instead of taking the bus that's all." Lil Man was smooth with keeping anybody off his tail. He had to keep his extra cool about having the car. Lil Man had paid special attention whenever around his older cousin's, because they always had a signature way of letting him know he was being observed. This secretly kept him on his toes.

"Come on in man! We bout to crack open a few cold ones!" The invitation was irresistible, but Lil Man couldn't stand the smell or taste of beer. After that sentence from his oldest cousin Stoop Head, he knew he wouldn't be staying long. Once inside, already on the couch in position were Lil Mans other two cousins, Rocky and Maze. Maze was the second youngest under Stoop, and Rocky was a couple years older than Lil Man. They were celebrating because Maze had just gotten out of Juvenile detention for about sixteen months for a robbery he hadn't committed. He never said anything to the police about what he may have known, so he sat for the entire year and a half strong without giving anybody up. He got his name from pretending to be lost all the time, when the time was right.

And Stoop Head whose real name was Jason, had gotten his nickname from the shape of his head resembling a flower pot on the stoop, were they lived all their lives, was the most troublesome of the three. He just had never been caught for anything. He was also known for getting into and out of a jam without anyone ever catching wind of it. It was safe to say Stoop Head was Lil Mans favorite, he always kept close and made sure nobody ever said anything too crazy whenever Lil Man was around. He looked after him.

About an hour went by and without even noticing Lil Man had knocked off about three 16oz cans of beer. "Ya mom ain't gonna whup dat ass is she?" Maze always blurted out something to make sure Lil Man was awake and sharp on his toes. Even though he was a bit older know, they always made sure he left in his right state of mind. "Naw man, I'm cool. My mom not gonna say nuffin." They chatted over their beers for about another hour or so, and Lil Man had noticed Rocky and Stoop taking turns coming in and out of the back door. 'What's that odor?' he thought to himself. It was weed. The smell wasn't too familiar to Lil Man's nose. But he knew from the strength of the smoke and the funny look on their faces that he had better not touch it. He was already nervous enough about taking the car.

"Yo man, I gotta roll. Too much schoolwork and y'all know how my mom be trippin." Lil Man was just ready to get outta there and go and face the music back at home. "How is she anyway?" Stoop Head was trying to analyze Lil Man's look in his eyes before he left. "She's cool man, just give her a call sometime. But yea, lemme get outta here before it gets late aight? Im'a see y'all later." Lil Man was determined to leave on a cool note. He didn't want his cousins to know he had the car, and he didn't want anybody at home to know he had been around there. Lil Man walked out and started up the street towards where he parked his grandma's Mercury. "Yo Rah, wait up!" Before he could get a whole block he heard Stoop's voice calling out to him. "Yo, make sure you come back around tomorrow. We're gonna have some girls over and I know you will like them." "Alright cuz, cool. See ya tomarrow."

Lil Man already had his mind made up that he wasn't going to smoke or drink with his cousin's, but to just chill out and kick it with whatever girls were coming over sounded like a good plan. He wasn't going to drive again, but he definitely would be back to chill with the chicks. He was bored and felt he really needed something to do.

When he was sure the coast was clear, he walked right up to the car, got in and took off. He knew he was gone long enough for his family to notice the car missing. But he couldn't worry too much about it, he had to face his people one way or the other and just go home.

Lil Man knew to expect some type of trouble, but he wasn't sure what kind. All he could do was drive the car home as carefully as possible and hope the same parking space would still be there. He finally made it back to the block, but there were definitely a couple of surprise's waiting for him. Even though he was impressed with himself on how well he could drive, the two things he noticed when he pulled up had brought his nervous feeling back. The parking space was gone! And on top of that, his family had been lined up on the porch watching him pull up like a panel of judges watching an accused criminal being brought into a courtroom.

He still had in mind how he had driven through three entire neighborhoods without a single scratch. But those points soon vanished as he came to a slow stop, smashing the passenger side front end into another car parked right in front of the panel of judges! This trip instantly switched from a joyride into a nightmare for Lil Man. "Dammit!!" He shouted to himself inside the car. He knew his life was over now. Even though he crashed very slowly, at about three miles per hour, the situation brought on an embarrassment that made it feel like a high speed chase coming to a horrific ending. He tried to make himself feel better by flashing back to how well he had just been driving, but it wouldn't work.

The lightweight impact had pushed the parked car up onto the curb, smashing in its tail lights and driver side bumper. When Lil Man put his grandma's Mercury in park, he looked up and noticed that his unintended target had belonged to their next door neighbor. He felt like just melting away as his family stood there staring. His grandma put her head down and turned and walked into the house. Grandpa looked on with his eyebrows and forehead scrunched in fury, while mom headed towards him with the infamous strap wrapped around her fist.

Lil Man jumped up out of the car before she could reach him, and ran around the car in the opposite direction of his mom yelling out . . . "I'm sorry!!" He didn't know what else to do. While this may have looked a bit humorous to the general public's eye as the scrawny teen ran, he really felt like he was in grave danger. He didn't know the measure of his punishment, so he figured he'd make it as less severe as possible by apologizing. He ran around to the back of the house from where he had first came out, and kept going past the house to where there was a clearing behind the house's known as "the dust bowl". It was a dusty cleared flat top where all the neighborhood kids played full court basketball with two cut open milk crates facing opposite of each other. No one was out at the time, so it was the perfect place to go and hideout while he figured out how to die down the heat that was on him.

It had been at least a few years since he felt the wrath of mom's belt, and he knew he'd be reminded of the sting today. Lil Man found a spot off to the side of the clearing where there were a few crates where bystanders of the basketball game's sat. He sat there and just watched the back of his own house through some bushes until he noticed some activity at the back door. "Boy!! Get ya lil ass in here now!!" It was his mom, and she was still strapped with the purple belt! He decided not to prolong it any further and stood up to go and face the music, even though he knew the tune would be devastating to his ears as the strap put in its work.

When he reached the back door, his mom was in it holding the metal screen portion of it open for him. Surprisingly she didn't even touch him as he walked by, but the flames he felt on him from her eyes were drama enough. "Get upstairs in that room of yours and don't come out until I tell you to!!" He was glad to oblige and she didn't have to say it twice. Not knowing what his punishment was going to be kept Lil Man up in his room feeling more than nervous. But he had secretly still looked forward to getting with his cousin's and the girls they had promised for him the next day.

Taking the car was crossing the line, and deep down Lil Man knew it. Being up in his room felt lonelier and colder than ever. His lonely thoughts were soon interrupted by heavy footsteps getting closer and closer to his room. It had to be grandpa, coming to deliver the punishment he thought. "This is it!" he said to himself. "Time to pay the piper." He sat back on his bed and waited as the footsteps pounded louder and louder, thumping to the rhythm of his heart it seemed. His bedroom door then swung open in what seemed to be slow motion, as grandpa came in and turned to face Rahim.

Lil Man was shocked at what he had noticed, no belt! No type of strap. Not even a broken off "switch" from the bushes out behind the house, which would have normally been routine. He thought that this was either about to be a royal rumble wrestling match, or just straight boxing. Lil Man couldn't believe grandpa had come in unarmed after how mad he had looked outside. And even more shocking, what he had heard next hit him like a ton of bricks! "You're not going to school tomorrow, so be sure and get plenty of rest. I'm taking you to get your driver's license. Here!" Grandpa had tossed a Pennsylvania driver's manual on his bed for him to study and walked out.

Rahim couldn't believe what he had just heard. He had just stolen his grandmother's car, and joyrode in it to lord knows where. And on top of that hadn't been the best of boy scouts in school. He even brought the car back hours later after taking it, and smashed it in front of his entire immediate family! "There had to be some catch to what grandpa had just said", he thought out loud to himself. All that and he was invited to be rewarded with a license. But there really wasn't a catch at all. Even though he had been well disciplined, Lil Man was also a bit on the spoiled side of things. And it was situations like this one that actually made it harder for him to mature on his own. He still couldn't believe what his grandpa had told him, especially after all the sweating and heart pounding. But oh well, he sure was relieved. Rahim's inner thoughts and feelings had switched from nervous to calm, relaxed and then a little excited. He started imagining what it would be like to venture out into the world on his own two feet, or even better his own four wheels!! He just laid there almost in a daze, thinking how his social life could possibly change. He also couldn't get the girls off his mind. Lil Man wanted to relax with his thoughts, but he really didn't know how far from that he actually was.

He sat up to turn his stereo on low, and began studying his driver's manual quietly. After a few hours he was knocked out fast asleep. His rest was so good that he dreamt about driving his grandma's car again. Playing music and meeting girl's felt so good and real to him in that dream, that Lil Man woke himself up out of it with a hard-on like he never had before! It was right then that he realized he was still

0-0 on the "scoring" card with the ladies. This definitely needed to change a.s.a.p.! It really wasn't in his plans to "get any" either. He just didn't have any prior experience or approach technique. Oh well, he just had his driving test on his mind now. He decided that this priority would be a major breakthrough into his social life.

The next day, Lil Man woke up focused on acing his driving test. He had only read through the book for a couple hours the night before, and skimmed over it some more after breakfast. It was all pretty easy actually. And just like that, his grandpa took him to the DMV and he aced the test with no problem. He had obtained his learners permit and the actual license would be on the way soon. Even though he hadn't had his own car, Rahim felt like he had gained his first piece of life's American pie.

Once they had gotten back home and shared the great news with mom and grandma, Lil Man waited around to catch grandpa alone. Grandpa was upstairs sitting at the foot of the bed taking off his shoes, about to get adjusted after the driving mission was accomplished. "I really appreciate you taking me to get my license Pop Pop, I thought you were going to be mad." "Hey man, it's alright! I had a feeling you'd be running off with that car sooner or later. I gotta get some rest for work, but you should be getting a letter from the DMV about your test soon. What are they cooking downstairs?" This was one of Lil Man's moments to exhale a deep breath.

Lil Man was shocked and a bit confused. He hadn't gotten scorned at all from grandpa about the auto theft prank like he thought he would be. Instead, he almost seemed to have received praise and the subject had been changed in a matter of a few quick sentences. The realness of it all was that grandpa was actually proud of how well

Rahim could drive on his own. He was always secretly curious of the matter, and Rahim's stunt did none other than show and prove. He had gained a lot of points with grandpa, and he was impressed.

"Smells like spaghetti! I hope Grain made some garlic bread to go with it!" Lil Man jumped on the opportunity to change the subject with grandpa, and just like that it was a done deal. He had gotten away with taking the car, and even managed to pull off getting his license out of the deal. What a day!

Later that afternoon, Lil Man took the stroll a few neighborhoods over to go see his cousins. Immediately that familiar smell had hit him in the nose again. He had caught the whiff before he had even arrived on the block fully. He wasn't too sure of where it was coming from, but it was definitely the chronic again!! He just kept strolling, pretending to ignore the scent. "Wassup cuz!!??" They had a circle of about seven heads formed on the corner of Lil Man's aunts' block. "Aint nothin man, just chillin you know?" Lil Man was trying to be as cool as possible. Truth was though, the scent was so strong in the crowd that he became dizzy and wanted to sit down somewhere. The clouds of smoked stunned and dazed him, but he just couldn't let it show. In fact, he seized the opportunity and decided to take the initiative.

"Stoop! I know you didn't just skip me! Man pass that over here!" Lil Man knew he had no idea how to smoke. In fact, in the back of his mind, all he could think about was that bathroom situation back in school that had lead him to trouble once before. But he just couldn't be an oddball now, not with his older cousins and their buddies observing. "Sure thing little cousin, here!" Before he could even blink or get another word out, Rahim was holding a perfectly rolled Phillies Blunt, stuffed with some of North Philadelphia's finest weed. At this point, all he could do was improvise and act as natural as possible.

All in one smooth motion he handed the Blunt to his own other hand and raised it to his lips, taking a deep toke of the nicely rolled bat. He had studied his cousin's facial expressions from when they smoked before, and decided it was best to imitate one. There he stood with his cheeks both puffed up full of herbal smoke. Now that he had the smoke in his face, only one problem remained. Lil Man had no idea how to inhale! This is where he discovered he had some of the city's best acting skills. Lil Man licked his lips with the smoke still in his face, and let it slowly seep out the corner of his mouth, all while looking at the others to see who was really watching him. Great! Nobody noticed his phony puff, so he even conjured up a slight little cough and a line to make it official . . .

"That's the good stuff man!" He turned to the bushes and spit out a habitual spit. Secretly, he badly wanted the taste to go away. "The best little cuz! We don't smoke no bullshit around here man! The ladies just won't allow it ya dig?"

"Oh yeah! Speaking of the ladies, where they at cuz?" Stoop had rang a bell when he mentioned the girls. This was all Lil Man was really waiting for. "They're already in the lab waitin for us man. They don't smoke, so we came out here to do our thing while they get comfy." Anyone could see that Stoop had done this all the time. He was a natural at luring female company for the gang. Whenever the rest of his brothers and buddies wanted to take a break from their busy schedules of doing dirt or whatever it was they did, he was the 'go-to guy' when it came time to get the team laid. Stoop was a true kitty connoisseur.

Lil Man always took thorough mental notes on things Stoop Head did and said. Even though he wasn't exactly a role model for anybody, it wasn't very hard to tell he knew what he was doing in the streets. "C'mon cuz, I bet the one I got waiting on you is starting to get chilly. She's probably gonna want a hug once we get we get back down into the lab". The "lab" was just another name for the basement, a decked out spot where the guys hung out and watched games and boxing on tv. It was mostly decorated with empty crushed beer cans and ashtrays, and paper wrappings with half eaten food. A teen guy's paradise.

The guys unconsciously moved their crowd toward the house and down into the lab where the girls were half dressed and giggling. Nothing had filled the air but their snickering and cigarette smoke. "Damn! Cut that fan on, y'all ladies tryna kill us down here or what?" Rocky had lead the line down into the dimly lit room where the girls were waiting and Lil Man brought up the rear. Lil Man always fell back behind the crowd and just mostly listened, one his many learning techniques. Even though he was secretly excited about finally getting to meet these girls and possibly 'getting some', Lil Man was hardly prepared for what he saw next.

The room was warm and cozy, and Stoop Head had a black light up in the ceiling. The effects of the light made lightly colored clothing and anything white glow in the dark. It was a very cool effect, especially for the eyes of a horny teenaged boy. The guys poured into the room where the three girls were waiting, and among the chicks sitting there topless and high as a kite was who else? None other than Vernie, breast naked sitting there fancy free cuddling and French kissing Monie, the girl next to her.

Across from them was their other girlfriend Tasha, topless as well and rolling up some more of the green bud.

"I could've sworn I told y'all not to smoke when I'm not down here with y'all!! Now what would you have done if someone came in besides us and smelled that shit?" The girls were certainly as loose as the guys had wanted them to be, but Stoop Head felt the need to remind them who was still in charge. When Vernie and Lil Man had finally made eye contact, it was awkward and a relief all at the same time for him. Back when they went to school together, he had always imagined what it would be like to see her naked. He wanted to do things with her he had no idea he even wanted to do, and at this particular moment there was absolutely no way for her to hide what kind of girl she really was.

"Boy, shut up and come bring that thing over here! You may be the boss out there, but you know who really runs the show when these tittie's are out!" Everybody in the room burst out laughing all at once. Lil Man's ice was completely broken and his comfort level was at an all-time high. He went over and sat right in between Vernie and her kissing buddy. He put his arms up, and around both the girls sitting beside him. Across from them, their girlfriend was already busy working on cousin Rocky, banging her forehead into his stomach in a smooth yet frantic motion. It was as if she had been waiting on him to feed her all day!

Deep down, Lil Man really couldn't believe the settings he was in, but he had no choice but to play it cool. Stoop had turned on some music and just stood there drinking another can of beer. He raised the beer up and grinned at Lil Man, giving him his nod of approval as Lil Man made out with Vernie while her girlfriend copied Rocky and

Tasha's performance on him. Yup, this was definitely going to be a party to remember for Lil Man. Monie lifted her head up from Lil Man's lap with her face shining from her own drool. "Why in the hell do they call you Lil Man!? We're gonna have to get you a new name after this shit!!"

Everybody had laughed again and the laughter soon died down into erotic moans as all the girls got busy. Maze came over and pulled Monie up out of Lil Mans lap. "Don't you think them two need some time alone?" he said as he grinned at her palming and squeezing her plump rump. Maze walked Monie over into another corner of the lab as they disappeared into the darkness. "That was perfect! It's just me and you now Lil Man! I had been waiting for this forever!" Vernie's beautiful face lit up with excitement as she swung her leg around to straddle Lil Man. She was obviously lying, and anyone in their right mind could see that Vernie did this type of thing all the time. And this fact definitely prompted Lil Man, "Yo cuz! Toss me one of those hats over here!"

As Vernie grinded on Lil Man getting hotter and wetter than ever, he definitely wasn't about to lose his cool head and signaled for his cousin to toss him a condom. These parties had actually taken place so often that Stoop Head had a large Tupperware bowl of variety condoms already set aside. The bowl was plastic and white, so it had glowed brightly under the room's black light effect. He had named it the 'The Magic Bowl'. Stoop had randomly picked a rubber out of the bowl and tossed it on the couch next to Lil Man and Vernie. It was a "Tuxedo", a black condom from the Lifestyle brand. In less than twenty seconds, Lil Man had ripped open the rubber, squeezed its tip and rolled it down over his stiff rod.

Vernie's face had showed how happy she was to have the nice size she felt under her that Lil Man had for her to work with. Once the rubber was on securely, they went at it immediately! All the girls had worn pleated skirts that day. And since they had frolicked around before the guys had come in, none of them had on panties. The girls' underwear was randomly tossed to the floor, making it convenient for the guys to have their way once they came back in. Stoop Head and Mazes buddies were just on a separate couch rolling up more weed. They had done this type of party so often that it was normal for them to just chill and wait for one of the finished girls to come over and start serving them.

The entire situation lasted for maybe another two hours. In that period of time, the three girls had been rotated among the seven guys about four full times. It had definitely made for a beautiful workout! Towards the end, Maze had opened all the 'labs' windows. He then turned on the oscillating fan, pointing it outward in the main window. The girls were all sweaty and worn out. "Girlllll I got's to go!" Tasha jumped up as if she were in a big hurry. "Y'all know I have a boyfriend!" Everybody bust out in laughter again. "Yeah girl, we know. We know." Vernie and Monie just looked at each other smiling and shaking their heads as they fixed their hair in Stoop Heads oversized mirror.

"Ok beauty queens, give us a call." He hadn't really meant for them to call, but Rocky saying 'give us a call' was the girls cue to leave. He wasn't being rude at all, they just never let any girls that ever came over develop the habit of sitting around after the session was done. The most they stayed after finishing up was maybe about ten minutes, and that time was strictly for cleaning up behind themselves and walking out looking almost as presentable as they did coming in. Stoop Head, Maze and Rocky had rules to their game. And Lil Man picked up on just about every one of them.

SCHOOL IS IN

After the girls left, Rocky and Maze put the finishing touches on cleaning up the 'lab' while Lil Man and Stoop Head went outside to finish up chatting. "We got them outta here just in time man, my mom will be home from work any minute." Stoop Head always tried to come off as some sort of tough guy, like a mobster, but whenever he and Lil Man were alone he spoke with the words of a scared little boy. He was a boy who was afraid of his mom's strap just like any other boy who had real respect for his mom. "It looked like you and Vernie were getting a little personal back there, like you two knew each other." Stoop had noticed how much close and personal attention Vernie had given Lil Man during the 'session'. "Oh yeah? What makes you think that Stoop?" Lil Man was trying to change the subject. It seemed like his big cousin may have had some personal feelings towards Vernie.

"Oh, nothing really man. But I do have eyes you know? I aint no fool either, she was slobbering on you like y'all had been married for years or something man! I aint never seen that girl do it like that, and she been around here a few time's man." Lil Man decided to just be honest. It was obvious his big cousin knew what he was talking about, so there was no need to try and hide it. "Vernie used to be in my class at my old school man. Everybody around my way wanted a piece of her. Not to mention she was partly responsible for some drama I went through in school. I think she performed on me so well, calling herself trying to make amends."

After Lil Man gave his cousin the scoop on how and where he knew Veronica from, he immediately noticed a wild look in Stoop Head's eyes. Stoop's attitude had changed as well, going from cool and calm, to hyper and vigilant. "You mean to tell me that all this time, that broad was the cause of your troubles? My mom told me you had chick problems a while ago, but I had no idea it was corny ass Vernie! Just say the word cuz, and we can get her dealt with right now! I know everything about that chick."

In Lil Man's mind, Vernie had just put on the show of a lifetime as far as he was concerned. So revenge was the last thing on his mind when it came to her. Not to mention he had just watched her get pounded and punished by six guys besides himself. He was satisfied just knowing she had no inner dignity, which explains why she played around setting guys up the way she used to in school. Her current behaviors weren't too much further up the moral ladder. "Naw man, it's cool. Just let the hoe be a hoe." Stoop Head burst out laughing when Lil Man said that. "Class dismissed lil cousin! I taught you well." Stoop was impressed with Lil Man's attitude towards the situation. And now that Lil Man had all Stoop Heads hard to get approval and respect, there was no telling how far it would take him.

"So what are you doing for cash? A dude like you needs to have some paper in his pockets man. I know you ain't got a job! So it's only right I look-out for my lil cousin you know?" Lil Man had been thinking about working, especially since he had his license on the way. But he really had no idea where to begin looking for work. So Stoop's proposal had come right on time. "I'm not working right now, I just been going to school and going home. I'd love to get a gig though cuz! What do you have in mind?"

Stoop Head took a cigarette out from his inside jacket pocket. He lit it in a cool pose with his collar flipped straight up, the way the Fonze would have lit a cigarette if he had smoked and this was 'Happy Days'. He shouted at some strangers walking by out of nowhere. "God I love this dude!" The couple he shouted to just looked at each other a hurried on about their business, as if frightened. "Listen Lil Man, I have the perfect gig for you. Just come by after school this Friday, I'll fill you in on all the details then alright?" Finally! Lil Man had something to look forward to on the weekend, and it even involved making some money. After just doing three girls in one day with a job coming up, he felt pretty damn good about himself. "Sure thing Stoop, I'll be here! I gotta get going though, see ya Friday man!"

Stoop Head just puffed his cigarette while smirking at his younger cousin. "Alright cuz, and keep it quiet to! We don't need any surprises getting spoiled ya dig?" "Aight Stoop, later man!"

TIME 2 GET PAID

It was just Wednesday when Lil Man had spoken to his cousins last. He was a bit eager to see what his popular older cousin Stoop Head had lined up for him. He had never really gave it too much thought before until now, but his older cousins used to dress a bit flashy for some guys who didn't have regular everyday jobs. They were always loaded with cash. Their most notable trademark of fashion was probably their jewelry. Stoop Head was known for being one of the few guys in his neighborhood to wear diamond earrings in both of his ears. His two brothers Rocky and Maze were both known for wearing two-fingered rings, designed with their names in cursive writing, all 14 karat solid gold. The three brothers also wore matching herring bone gold chains. The trio also dressed alike most of the time, either in Fila velour sweat-suits or Sergio Techini. And all of their footwear never looked over a day old. Lil Man thought about how they dressed and attracted woman, and decided he couldn't wait to work with his cousins. He was so worked up that it didn't even matter what they did, Lil Man was all for it.

The two days went by in a breeze, as Lil Man just normally went to school and came home to do his homework and eat dinner. He concentrated on trying not to think too hard about his new upcoming gig. It was already Friday morning, and Lil Man was at the kitchen table killing a huge bowl of Cap'n Crunch, his all-time favorite cereal. "I need you to come straight home after school and cut the grass. Then after the grass all of the windows need cleaning. I'll have everything you need put together by the time you get home." Grandma's voice was like a loud screeching cat, murdering the beautiful harmony of the cereal being crunched. When she shouted that list of after school chores at him, Lil Mans entire mood went sour. "Grandma, if you don't mind I had plans after school today. Will it be ok if I cut the grass tomorrow?" He could tell by the way she stopped and turned towards him that she wasn't having that. "What's so important that you can't come straight home and do as I asked?" Lil Man sat his empty bowl in the sink, grabbed his book bag and headed for the door as his grandma continued to fuss. But he didn't have time to plead his case. He was already running late for school. "Ok Grandma, see you later after school!"

Lil Man walked to school wondering how he was going to pull off not going straight home. "Oh well" he thought to himself. He couldn't worry too much about it. Making money with his older cousins wasn't an opportunity that came along every day, and those windows and grass just weren't going anywhere. This was in the back of his mind throughout that entire school day. He couldn't stand Stoop Head up, not after all the cool points he had just earned with him. Grandma's chores couldn't have come at a worse time. "Wow, what a jam!" he thought to himself. He made up his mind, he had to go check Stoop out and just face the music with grandma afterwards.

While sitting in his last period algebra class, Lil Man found himself daydreaming and staring up at the clock waiting for the final bell to ring. Once it did, he gathered his things and rushed out of class. He headed toward the exit of the building, and once outside reality had hit him. He was a little over twenty city blocks from where his cousins had lived. And he was about to walk there as if he had no idea grandma was at home expecting him. He just started walking and figured he'd get the journey out of the way as quickly as possible.

Lil Man's long legs were carrying him at a steady pace. "I'll be there in no time" he kept telling himself. But as his luck would have it, he was only about six blocks into the long walk before he was interrupted. Lil Man had heard a cars horn beeping at him from behind as the car was pulling up closer to him. It was a silver BMW, and its windows were tinted entirely too dark to see inside of it. The car was too nice to belong to anyone he knew he thought, so he ignored it and kept walking. But the driver of the car was obviously persistent, and blew the horn more rapidly as it drew even closer to Lil Man. He became nervous, and when he reached the corner decided he couldn't take the suspicion from the mysterious 'Beamer' any longer. He stopped at the corner and removed his back-pack, slamming it to the ground in an angry gesture. He then turned to face the shiny car and began yelling at it with his fists and face balled up tightly. The car that had also been cruising to match Lil Man's pace stopped with him at the corner.

"What the hell do you want huh!? Do you know who you're messing with!?" Lil Man figured that if he showed he wasn't scared, the car would drive away. His grandfather always taught him to face his fears, but he wondered if this was the wrong moment to be following that advice. The two passenger side windows where Lil man stood came down simultaneously. He noticed that the inside of the car was just as dark as its windows, and he still couldn't make out who was inside. But the next two things he did see made him more nervous than ever.

First, thick clouds of smoke poured from the windows of the car. It was like the thick fog in a zombie movie. Then, from amidst that fog came pointing a steel grey double barreled shotgun, aimed straight at Lil Man's chest. He knew there was no way on earth he could outrun the blast from that gun. And even if he did dodge around the corner fast enough, there was no way he could outrun a BMW on foot. For some silly reason, Lil Man felt he had no choice but to try the macho approach again.

"You hear me!? What you punks want? I ain't got nothing man!!" The gun retracted back into the smoky interior, and the windows both went back up. Just then, the drivers' door flew open and Lil Man heard laughter that he thought he recognized. "Take it easy lil cannon, I mean cousin!" Out of the car with the widest grin on his face came the driver, it was Rocky! And inside the car was none other than Maze and Stoop Head. Lil Man was so relieved to see that it was his cousins he didn't know what to do! He could've just ran up and kissed and hugged them all he had been so scared. That's what he wanted to do. But he was quickly reminded of who they were by all the flashy things and had to control himself. He just strolled towards the car in a cool manor, grinning back at Rocky. "Man, you fools were all about to get hurt out here!" All the men inside of the car continued laughing even harder. "Hop in lil cousin, it's time to go and start your new job with ya lil cool ass!!" Lil Man got in behind Rocky and shook everybody's hand. The car screeched away and headed toward the 'lab'.

For it to be only in the late ninety's, the interior of the car was very futuristic. Aside from the leather seats and the custom velour trimming and ceiling job Rocky had done, there were also six ten inch monitors installed. Two were in the front sun visors, another two were in the headrest, one was imbedded in the dashboard in between the ashtray and the stereo and one hung directly from the middle of the ceiling. There was a DVD player installed between the two front seats, and an eight disc CD changer was in the trunk along with a long list of various speakers and amplifiers. It was also necessary for this vehicle to sit atop four of the shiniest twenty two inch chrome wheels imaginable. The car was built for auto-shows and fashion, but this was Rocky's everyday ride. And his two brothers had similar vehicles. Lil Man didn't know exactly what his cousin's had done for a living, he was just sure that this wasn't fast-food money they were dealing with. But he would soon have the entire inside scoop on their operation.

They were all almost on the street where they lived, when Stoop Head reached into his inside jacket pocket and pulled out a clear sandwich sized zip-lock bag almost completely stuffed with a glowing white powdery substance. "Lil Man, say hello to our money maker! We call it white girl." Then Stoop Head pulled down the armrest that was imbedded into the seat between them, and pulled out another sandwich bag. But this bag was almost twice the size of the first one, and instead of the powdery residue this one was filled with chunks of light green grass with orange hairs. "And this baby right here will be your money maker! Say hello, we call this one Incredible Hulk."

Rocky pulled the car into the driveway and parked in the back of his mom's house. The driveway and back-door lead straight to the 'lab', where they could go in un-noticed by neighbors. And if they were really quiet enough, they could usually come and go without their mom detecting them either. It was a hustler's paradise, as long as the wrong person didn't know what they were into. They got out of the car all at once, and without hesitation walked straight for the backdoor and into the 'lab'.

It was Stoop Heads idea to bring Lil Man into their 'game' and he was also pretty much the brain of the outfit, so once the guys settled down he naturally spoke first. "So, now you know lil cousin. All I need now is for you to decide what you want to do. If you want to work for me, you have the choice between pitching that herb, or being our look-out. But there's a couple thing's you have to get through your head first." Stoop Head had a serious tone and look in his eye, and Lil Man was just as serious following along and paying attention while his older cousin broke it all down for him.

"If you decide to take the look-out position, you would have to go on a few runs with us so you can see the customers and know what they look like. But a look-out won't make as much money as the herb man. If you take the herb, it's all yours. And you can knock it off whenever you want, in school and all. I only have two rules and advise you to follow them wisely." Stoop then stood up and walked over to a table that had an over-sized beach towel for a table cloth. The towel hung to the floor, hiding a safe beneath the table. Stoop Head knelt down and lifted the towel up. He then started on the combination as he continued speaking to Lil Man. "The first rule is that you speak of the things you saw today to no one ever, unless it's just us!" Stoop opened the safe, and pulled out a black

'Dessert Eagle' handgun. "The second rule is that you enjoy yourself while making money!"

Stoop Head held the gun up limply, pointed it at the ceiling while he stared it down with lust in his eyes. Lil Man looked over at the open safe and noticed stacks upon stacks of money, stacked up squarely and wrapped tightly with thick tan rubber bands. "That's it Stoop!? Don't say nothing and have fun!? Man that's easy, I'm in!" Even though they spoke lightly of the situation, the presence of the huge 'Dessert Eagle' really put a serious emphasis on what Stoop Head was saying. "Two of the guys that were here the other day worked for me, but now they don't. They fucked up by bringing that third guy, no matter who he was supposed to be! They broke a rule. So they're not with us anymore."

Lil Man nodded and agreed with Stoop. "I feel you cousin! Break a rule and get kicked out! That's simple enough!" Maze chuckled. "Naw Lil Man, it wasn't simple at all! Those dudes are not here with us no more, as in their souls floated to the sky, feel me!?" Lil Mans facial expression changed to a concerned one. He looked down at the drugs on the coffee table. He then glanced at the money in the safe, then back up to Stoop Head with the gun. "Damn, so it's like that? My cousins are threatening me now?" (click clack) Stoop Head cocked the 'Eagle' back and sat it on the table. (ch' chick chick) Then Rocky pumped the shotgun. "Hell no we not threatening you cousin! We're just safe that's all. Cautious. And we're all family and got real love for each other. So we're gonna work without the mistakes of them outside dudes, feel me?"

Lil Man was in now, and even though he still had a few things to learn about his newly acquired staff, he felt ready for anything. "So when do I start y'all?" Lil Man was a bit eager to see what his schedule was going to be like. Even though he was all for the operation at hand, he still wanted to get home and handle grandma's chores. She was sensitive about her windows. "First of all, don't be addressing everybody all at once! You're reporting to me now. And after me, it's ya cousin Rocky, got it?" Was Stoop serious? He had to be with all these drugs and guns out lying around right now. "I'm just messing with you cuz! We don't roll like that. But as long as you're holding that work and you're done something, or if there's anything you need just come and give me a holler. Cool?" Stoop Head really wanted his younger cousin to be as comfortable as possible. He had planned on keeping him around for a while.

"You can start tonight if you want to. There are no set hours. Just get rid of what you can, but carefully. We don't do the jail thing ok?" Lil Man picked up the zip-lock bag of herb off of the coffee table, which was a half of a pound and put it in his book bag. "I got you cuz, I aint got time for that jail thing either. I still have to wash windows and dishes at home!" They all broke out laughing. The best thing about working with Stoop Lil Man decided is that he always liked to have fun. Even though he was obviously very serious about his money, he always made sure the environment was comfortable and relaxed. That's probably why they're so 'hood rich.' There was no drama, and any silliness was handled by Stoop personally and quietly. Lil Man thought of him as sort of a drug dealing ninja.

"Cool then, I'm gonna catch y'all tomorrow. I gotta make sure everything cool in the house before I start putting this work in." Lil Man was being sure to keep the lines of communication very clear, about everything! The last thing he really wanted to happen was his soul floating up to the sky. "Yeah, which reminds me cuz, be sure you put your stuff where nobody can smell or find it. That's your work, so it's your trouble and your trouble alone. Plus you can't afford to lose any money you know?" Stoop let Lil Man know that he was now 'put on', and not to let anything come back to the 'lab'.

"And one more thing before you leave Lil Man, Rocky, toss him a stack." Before Lil Man could get out the door Stoop Head stopped him again. And when he turned around, Rocky was tossing one of the wrapped stacks of money at him. "Don't count it now Lil Man, but that's all for you. Welcome to the 'Lab Rats!" Rahim had no idea his cousins had called themselves the 'lab rats', but it made perfect sense. And now that he was working with them, he would be learning a lot more about them. He put the money away and started out the door.

DECISIONS, DECISIONS

Lil Man walked home from his cousin's house, and not to his surprise grandma was fussing. "Boy! I know I told you to get your butt straight home after school! I needed them chores done and you come waltzing back in here all late and what not! Go and get ya butt up in that room and don't come out!" Lil Man was relieved his grandma had sent him straight to his room. He got a clean chance to hide his weed and count his money in peace. He thought to himself, if Rocky had dropped him off he'd be home a lot sooner. But he also knew that his cousin's didn't want anyone to know they had a new member on their team, so it sort of all worked itself out. Lil Man was getting sick of getting sent to his room every day. He definitely had plans to fix and put a stop to that.

Lil Man had a loose floor board under his bed that he could easily lift. It had just enough room to hide what he had. He tucked his herb away in it and put the loose board back in place. Then he took out the stack of money he had and began counting it. "5, 10, 15, 20, 25, 30, 35, 40 . . ." Lil Man had never counted this much money on his own before. The most he ever had to his name was maybe about three or four hundred dollars and that came from going house to house and shoveling snow in his neighborhood. In his stack of money, there were five's, ten's and twenties. Lil Man was surprised to see he had counted all the five's and was up to seven hundred dollars. He still had the ten's and twenties to count. Once he was finished, he counted out thirty five hundred dollars.

"Stoop must be feeling extra generous!" he said out loud to himself. Once he realized one of his cousins had just given him three and a half thousand dollars, he just sat and imagined how much they had all together. After a few minutes, he couldn't think about it anymore. He just wrapped the stack back up and put it with the rest of his stash under the bed. Lil Man lied there on his bed faced with major decisions to make. He had to figure out how he would have all this money without his family catching on to him. And the last thing he wanted to do was draw any heat back to his cousins. And without any close friends or anybody to trust, he would definitely be working alone.

The next morning, Lil Man woke up to the scent of his mom's cooking. He looked under his bed to scope out his stash, giving himself a reality check on the goodies he came up on the day before. They were safe, so Lil Man went downstairs to have breakfast before he went out with his newfound work. "Good morning everybody! How's my baby brother doing this morning?" Everyone in the kitchen was smiling back at Lil Man, as he came in sounding overly cheerful. "He's just fine Rahim, and how about yourself? What are you so happy about?" He was wondering what he said or had done out of the ordinary to make his mom ask such a suspicious question. "Oh nothing mom, I just had some great sleep that's all. And it's Saturday, you gotta feel good on a Saturday!"

He hoped his reply was normal enough as to not draw any further suspicion. "I think I may ride my bike or take a walk after breakfast, I gotta check out these new surroundings of ours. I wonder if there are any arcades are nearby." Lil Man was doing his best to try and sound like an innocent and harmless teenager. Whether they bought it or not, he wasn't too sure. What he was sure about was taking his goodies out and building up some clientele.

After breakfast, Lil Man went back up to his room to see what he'd be taking out with him. He had a few loose sandwich bags, about six of them and put twenty dollars' worth of his green into each one. He then counted out two hundred dollars to keep in his pocket, in case he didn't sell anything. His plan was to find the nearest hang out area and shop his weed. After putting everything together he went down to the basement, and took his mountain bike out the back door. He wasn't expecting to see his grandpa out there working under the hood of the Mercury. "Where you off to?" Lil Man thought it would be best to shoot back a quick line at grandpa and act like he was in a rush. "I'm just running to the store real quick, I'll be right back."

He got away from grandpa, luckily without being asked to bring anything back. He rode off down the drive-way and around the corner, headed toward the main boulevard. He remembered seeing a small shopping plaza not too far away. "Maybe there's some pot-heads there" he thought to himself. He rode down the boulevard for about five or six blocks until the mini plaza came into sight. It wasn't a very busy place, just big enough to shop his weed comfortably. The place wasn't big enough to be considered a mall either. With just a few stores, a pizza shop and a laundry mat Lil Man was sure to find his comfort zone somewhere here in the plaza. He rode his bike around the parking lot for about five minutes, so he could get a better look at all the stores and see where he'd 'post up' at.

"Perfect! They have an arcade, and there's a bar and a Burger King. I'm gonna love this spot!" Lil Man had gotten so thrilled about seeing stores he liked, that he burst out talking to himself. A little embarrassed, he glanced around quickly to make sure no one had caught his 'crazy' moment of self-conversation. He parked his bike outside of the arcade and walked inside. It was almost love at first sight. There were plenty of guys and girls his age, and a few others filled in the older crowd. And out of the older ones, he could tell they smoked chronic. But to be sure, he kept to himself for a while.

The place was smoky from peoples' cigarettes, and there was a constant buzz of conversation in the air along with an occasional girl giggling out loud. Lil Man went to the change machine to get some quarters so that he could blend in playing some video games. He decided to play one of the driving games, since it had a seat. He figured he'd get a better feel of the crowd if he sat and played something comfortable. He was right. Without paying too much attention to his own game, he noticed a group over in the corner eating pizza. They were all young and could not stop laughing. It was obvious they were as high as giraffe asses. One of the girls in the group made eye contact with Lil Man, and he grinned at her and pretended to focus back on his game.

His plan worked. In less than five minutes the girl was standing behind Lil Man, watching him drive the "Pole Position" racing game. Before she could say anything, Lil Man saw her reflection in the games screen. He still pretended not to know she was there, even though she reeked of 'Mary Jane'. Lil Man played it so coolly, that the girl couldn't take going unnoticed any more. She started smacking and popping her bubble gum ferociously! Lil

Man raised one eye brow and slowly turned to the girl as if she were interrupting an important meeting. "How you doing cutie?" Lil Man had already known the girl was buzzed off of weed, but their up close encounter confirmed it further. Besides the aroma, her eyes were extra squinted and blood-shot red.

"I'm doing good, just hanging out that's all. What's your name?" Lil Man hadn't known it, but the girl saw him in their school and already liked him. He was different from most of the guys that went to their school, and she could tell he wasn't from the neighborhood. "My names' Katousha, and yours?" The way she was talking lowly over the noise in the room and leaning over Lil Mans shoulder, even Ray Charles could see she was throwing herself at him. But Lil Man was still secretly focused on trying to get rid of his herb. "My names' Rahim, but everyone calls me Lil Man." The girl started giggling again. "Lil Man? I hope that doesn't mean you can't put your pole in position." As soon as she said that, Lil Man crashed on the game and it was over. Katousha didn't waste any time trying to blow his mind with seduction and succeeded in getting his attention from off of the game.

Although a little distracted, Lil Man decided to capitalize on the opportunity. "Well, that's it for that game. Do you know where there's any good herb around?" Katousha's eyes lit up as much as her high would allow them to when she heard the word herb. "Yeah, my girls and I usually get it from some guy after school. We usually get enough to hold us over the weekend because he's so far away and take a while to get here. Nobody even knows where he's from. We think he may be from Jersey." Lil Man grinned at her. "Is that right? Well I have a surprise you might like Kat. I can call you Kat can't I?" Lil Man was now returning her flirts. "Boy, you just keep looking like that and you can call me whatever you want!"

And just like that, a few quarters in a video game and a couple of slices of pizza and Lil Man became the new weed connect for the entire area. Katousha wasn't lying when she said the regular guy was far. As it turned out, everybody was getting their chronic from the same guy and was sick and tired of waiting on him whenever they called him. Lil Man made it a point to let his new customers know that they wouldn't have that problem with him. He didn't live far at all, and the chronic he had from Stoop Head was at least three times better than what the people were used to. An hour after talking to Katousha, and he had gotten rid of everything he had on him.

"Give me a sec Kat, I need to go and check on my bike real quick." Lil Man walked outside and saw that his bike was cool. He also saw a pager store next door to the laundry mat a couple stores over. He went to the entrance of the arcade and waved for Katousha to join him. "Uh oh, Katousha got a new boyfriend! That girl never goes to anybody off of one single wave!" Her girlfriends teased her as she seemed to break her neck to join Lil Man outside.

"Wassup Lil Man?" Katousha seemed extra excited to be called by Lil Man as she skipped towards him in a childish manner. She was sixteen, and over-developed for a girl her age with the face to match. But Lil Man really liked her smile. It made him feel like there are still some good girls left. But after the crush he had on Vernie and the way she laid the whole crew, he would definitely remain skeptical about females from then on. "I just wanted you to walk me in the pager store and maybe help me pick one out. I'm really gonna need it with these 'trees' I have! Plus you can be the first with the number, and pass it on to your friends so they can let me know when they need something."

Lil Man and Katousha were really getting along after that day. She would page him all the time during the week for weed, and they sort of became an item in school. And the way her friends smoked, Lil Man's business was doing very well. He was seeing about six hundred dollars a week for three months straight, without ever touching the money he had gotten from Stoop Head. The entire time Lil Man was 'hustling', his family at home never suspected a thing. He was able to maintain an innocent image of just going to hang out with some new friends at the plaza, playing video games and eating pizza. He stayed careful about spending, and never went beyond paying a thirty dollar a month pager bill. His pager was his 'Bat Signal' for customers who wanted weed. He would accumulate customers by the bunches and have them all meet him at the arcade in the plaza. People showed him a lot of love, and Lil Man's operation ran quite smoothly for an amateur teen. And his appearance kept suspicions from the law off of him, he had never dressed too flashy. The situation was great, at the time.

SUMMER TIME

School was finally out, and by now Lil Man had become well known for his chronic. In fact, he had gotten so large that Stoop, Rocky and Maze often came around to see him in action. And Stoop continuously kept offering him protection. "Remember lil cuz, whenever you need anything just let me know. You're making some nice paper now, so you may want to invest in some heat. You know our boys have the finest of toys!" Stoop Head, Maze and Rocky were known for having the latest guns. Cherry wood grain handled revolvers, rubber grips on the pumps of shot-guns, infra-red lasers. They had it all. Rocky even had a custom made glow in the dark bullet proof vest he had shipped in from Singapore. They were smart, but sometimes overly flashy.

"I don't think I'm going to need that type of heat right now cuz, I'll keep it in mind though." Lil Man didn't really want a gun, even though all the 'Lab Rats' were well aware of the possibility of being robbed. He just gathered as much cash as he could at one time, and put it up whenever he got up to about one hundred fifty dollars. Lil Man's cash was adding up fast, but he was determined not to let it show. And Stoop head admired his lil cousin's humble pie. That's why he didn't mind helping him and introducing him to their business in the first place.

What Rahim really had his heart set on was getting a car. But he knew he couldn't get one by himself without blowing his cover with his family. So he had to be patient, especially if he wanted anything like the cars his cousins drove. He didn't have any intentions on shining as bright as they did, but he was determined to become independent on the road. He had a clean driving record, so it seemed the world was at his feet by the pedals.

Grandpa had a getaway day planned for the family the following weekend. Lil Man had saved up a lot of cash, but still had no way to really spend it yet. Once the family went out to Hershey Amusement Park, it finally hit him. "What in the world does he have that big grin on his face for? You must've told him he could drive back home huh?" Grandma always asked questions about Rahim when he wasn't around. She was either trying to stay hip and in tune with the younger generation, or she was bored. Maybe she was really genuinely concerned about her grandson at times, either way she always made it a point to constantly question his actions whether he was happy or sad. She just didn't know what was on the boy's mind. But Lil Man certainly spoke it once he got back to their picnic table out in the park.

"Guess what!!?? You guys will never guess what just happened to me!!" Lil Man came running up with some exciting news. "Uh oh! He must've run into one of those old ugly girls again." His moms guess was wrong. "Nope, I bet he found himself a way to land a job out here!" Grandpa's hopes were high, but he was also incorrect. "Uh uh! You guys can guess all day and I bet you'd never get it!" Lil Mans crafty grin showed he was scheming. He saw the look in everyone's eyes and how badly they wanted to hear the news he had for them. He didn't want them to raise up too much of a fuss out in public, so he just decided to go ahead and let it out.

"You see that great big sign over there? That yellow one with the flashing lights?? I won, I mean I really won! It was easy!" Lil Man was all excited, and pointed to a flashy sign across the amusement park that read "WIN BIG! $10,000!!" There was a vendor's stand out in the park where the players had to throw darts through a series of small rings, and hit a bull's eye as the target moved. The game was virtually impossible to win, a common gimmick. Everyone tried but nobody ever won. Lil Man had his picture taken at another booth and paid the dart vendor to display his picture as the recent winner. It was the perfect plan to front to his family so he didn't have to hide his money anymore. He paid the guy at the vendor a hundred bucks to go along with the story. And for Lil Man, it was worth it. His hustle back home was doing great and he could no longer keep hiding and worrying about the element of surprise.

His acting did so well, that everyone gave the darts a try! His pop, who was even lucky to be there along for the trip in the first place after all the arguing he had done with mom, blew about thirty dollars trying to win at the game himself. The lucky son of a bitch almost came close once to, missing the bull's eye by a couple of inches. They were really convinced Lil Man had gotten lucky and he was off the hook with his self-conscience a little. He could now go and get a good vehicle of choice and do a little clothes shopping once they got back home and didn't have to hide his money in the floor boards anymore. He even opened an account, depositing about three grand every other week. It all came from weed, and luckily his family never caught on. There was no way Lil Man could see breaking his mom's and grand mom's hearts. Grandpa was a little easier to talk to, but Lil Man couldn't let him in on anything either. He was under the oath of the 'Lab Rats', and he was enjoying all of the money he had made.

Once they had gotten back to Philadelphia, Lil Man asked his grandpa what would be a good car to get for starters. He knew that grandpa knew a lot about cars, and since he wasn't going to blow too much on a brand new one, decided they had better just get a clean good running vehicle from a used car lot or maybe an auction. Lil Man's first car was a 1986 Mercury Topaz. It was clean inside and out. And even though it was nothing near what his older cousins had driven, Lil Man felt pride in his new ride. What he wasn't too proud about was living the lie and facade of having weed money with no job and having to front to his family. 'Oh well' he thought. 'What's the worst that could happen?'

Lil Man had been dealing with the pressure of his family trying to pry into his business. They had always made suggestions, and formed their own opinions about him, saying things and not really getting to know him. Growing up like this was very frustrating. Especially while hustling and trying to stay out of jail. Lil Man didn't want to sell weed. But opportunities were limited in the job market, and selling drugs became easy. Lil Man didn't want to become greedy, but after a while he became the 'go-to' guy for weed and people started asking him about other drugs. Pills, powder and crack cocaine were soon added to his menu. He didn't keep too much of the hard stuff around, but whenever the order needed to be filled Stoop Head or Rocky was only a phone call away. Maze moved down south to Virginia with a few of his friends to expand their business there.

Lil Man was seventeen now, and he started looking more and more like his cousins every month. Jewelry, sneakers and clothes became a fetish, on the weekends anyway. During the week he tried to dress as normal as possible, and he didn't do anything fancy to his car. He wanted to keep attention and jealousy to a minimum. Every once in a while, the 'Lab Rats' called meetings in neutral areas of the city, just to settle up on any loose ends and to make sure everything was running smoothly. It soon became obvious that Lil Man and Stoop Head were thinking alike, level headedly, while Rocky and Maze were wild and always ready to bar-hop and run amuck. Maze came back from being out of town and decided that he couldn't live in the country. He would be too bored after being accustomed to the city life. Then one night while the four of them were out for drinks, Maze was approached and arrested by two detectives. Lil Man found out later that he had shot someone after one of his many bar fights he had while down south in Virginia. The detectives never mentioned anything about drugs. That Fall Rocky began serving a life sentence for first degree murder. Staying drunk all of the time while you're hustling doesn't mix.

After Maze had gotten locked up, Lil Man started being more careful about the life-style he was into. He still hustled, but he became more conscience of the hours he had done it and of his whereabouts. Instead of posting up at the arcade, he moved his work to a near-by abandoned recreational center. It hadn't opened for years. A lot of guys from the neighborhood had still used its basketball courts though, so it wouldn't be Lil Man out there all alone. The Rec center still looked fairly busy from the basketball activity. Lil Man would just hang around on the benches watching the games with Katousha, while he served customers who had paged him one at a time. He and Katousha was becoming an item. After a long day of hustling, she had walked Lil Man halfway home one evening and they stopped and started kissing along the way. The area where they had stopped was beautiful, the garden of a small mansion owned by a Philadelphia Eagle's player. The spot was secluded, and the grass was so soft that Katousha aggressively tackled Lil Man in it right there on the spot and they got it on, rolling around back and forth inside a colorful bed of flowers going at each other like animals in heat. Katousha had been hooked ever since that night.

They both had one more semester of school left, and Lil Man had a feeling having Katousha for a girlfriend in school would be a bad idea. No matter how good things seemed, he would never completely shake the thoughts of Vernie and what he had went through with her. He fought over her and ran a train on her and her friends with his cousins. In Lil Mans mind, Vernie had given mostly all females a bad reputation. And even though Katousha was cool and acted nothing like Vernie, Lil Man knew he would never fully let his guard down. But as it turned out, when school started back up Katousha was right there by Lil Mans side. She had even started making deliveries for him throughout the building.

Once again business was booming for Lil Man, but he was making so much money from drugs that it gave him a sort of an awkward feeling. He developed an inner feeling of 'it was too good to be true'. It made him nervous. "I'm not going to be doing this too much longer" he told Katousha. "I'm getting older, and I want to do something legit, something clean, a career!" Katousha understood exactly where Lil Man was coming from, and even found herself turned on by his positive way of thinking and speaking. But as fate would have it, he couldn't even finish out the school year and go through with his positive plans . . .

LAW AND ORDER

There were only a few weeks of school left, and all Lil Mans hustling had finally caught up with him. School security had always done random sweeps of the hallways and searches of lockers and back packs of rowdy and suspicious students. But one afternoon, Lil Man found himself personally targeted by one of the security guards in the hallway, even though he wasn't rowdy or suspicious. "Hey you!! Get over here!" Lil Man had given chase, but the guard called one of his partners to cut Lil Man off as he tried to cut through the auditorium. Lil Man thought he would ultimately be fine, being as though he never kept any drugs on him. But this one time he had to run, as least to try and buy enough time to get rid of the two ounces of weed he had stuffed in his underwear. Lil Man never carried that much on him until now. It was supposed to be for some college kids coming to meet him during his lunch period. Then it finally dawned on him, he had been set up.

Somebody snitched on Lil Man, and at that point it could have been anybody. He didn't trust anybody. He was even feeling iffy about Katousha who had been by his side since he started his grind at the arcade a few months back. He only knew the people he sold to on a regular basis, and most of them were way too high all the time to even try to hold a conversation with. The guards cornered and tackled Lil Man in the auditorium and held him for Police. "Dammit! Let go of me dammit!" Lil Man knew there would be no negotiating. His hustling run was over, and now his family would find out what he was doing in school. The only two things he could think about were who ratted on him and the money he had saved up. Lil Man had taken the thirty five hundred dollars Stoop Head had given him and turned it into a few hundred dollars short of sixty thousand in just a few months. And depending on what he was going to be charged with, he knew some of that would probably be going to a lawyer.

The police arrested him, and Lil Man was charged with possession of a controlled substance with intent to deliver along with some other narcotic related offenses for being on school property. The judge sentenced him to eighteen months at Vision Quest, a juvenile placement where the young offenders were stripped of all modern technologies and subjected to live a life of natural hard living. In the courtroom in front of everyone including the judge, his lawyer and family and even Katousha who came for support, Lil Man cried. Not a whimpering cry, but a tear of pain trickled down his cheek as he heard the sentence with his family. The pain had come out. Lil Man had been arrested and let out before for fighting, but had never been sentenced. He had never been away from his family nor had his freedom taken away for so long before. Eighteen months. It wasn't too bad. He decided to just grin and bear it.

In the courtroom, the judge had allowed Lil Man fifteen minutes to talk with his family and Katousha since this was his first real offense and he was still a juvenile. Katousha had already began crying and was prepared to do the bid with Lil Man. They never had made it official, but Katousha felt like she was Lil Man's girl. They were close throughout the entire summer, and for the school year up until Lil Man had gotten busted and shared secrets with each other no one else knew. Lil Man had known about Katousha being molested by her step-father when she was only seven years old, and she knew about him wetting himself in front of the entire first, second and third grades on stage during a spelling bee when he was just six. Lil Man remembered being terrified in front of all those students up on stage. As soon as it was his turn and the teacher called upon him, his light colored tan khaki pants turned to the dark color of cardboard as he began whizzing on himself from being nervous.

"Why Rahim, we raised you better than this." In the courtroom, Lil Man was getting all kinds of speeches and lectures from his mom and grandparents. It was kind of embarrassing with Katousha there. He really wanted his family to step outside and be alone to talk to his girl privately. He thought about telling her where his stash was so she could continue getting money while he was away. But he got rid of that thought fast. She would have to 're-up', or get more supply from Stoop Head or Maze, and there was no way he was sending her to them after what happened to Vernie. He decided to just let it go and forget about hustling. He didn't need Katousha getting into trouble over some dirty money. His money was safe in the bank and would be gaining interest, and his remaining stash was safe in the floorboard at home.

"Promise me you'll write me back!" Katousha saying things that sounded serious, letting Lil Man know how she really felt about him. "Ok Toosh, I'm gonna write you back." They were both being sincere, and it turned out that they would be extreme pen-pals for Lil Mans entire 'vacation'. They hugged and kissed, and then Lil Man initiated a group hug before being cuffed again and taken back to his cell to wait until being transported to the Juvenile placement the judge had ordered.

After all their goodbyes were said and done, Lil Man's family along with Katousha had left the courtroom in tears. Lil Man had a blank stare on his face, still not believing he was going away for a year and a half. Reality really kicked in when they added shackles to his ankles, normal procedure to avoid prisoners from trying to run. They put Lil Man in the Sheriffs van and began the ten hour ride up-state to the mountains where the camp was stationed.

BUFFALO SOLDIERS

Upon arriving at the Juvenile placement site, Lil Man immediately noticed something strange about the place. It was extremely dark, and there were no paved streets or sidewalks, just dusty paths of gravel and dirt roads with very little light. And off in the distance, there were five gigantic tipis arranged in a circle form, just like there were Indians living in them. In the center of the camp site there was a huge camp fire going, and the flames were tall as trees as if they were licking the clouds with fire. There was amber from the fire flying around everywhere. As Lil Mans van came to a slow stop, he heard a very deep voice shout out: "Everybody circle up!!" It was the camp leader, a six foot five, three hundred pound Indian chief who went by the name of 'Running Bear'. He was in charge of all the staff on the site, while the staff was in charge of all the juveniles.

As the van parked, Lil Man took in as much as he could before getting out and becoming part of the camp. The Sheriff had them exit the van, about ten of them, and lined them up in front of the camp. Lil Man found out that 'circle up' meant for the juveniles to come out of their tipi's and each tents occupants were to form a circle in their group, all joined by locking their arms from shoulder to shoulder. It looked funny to Lil Man at first, but he would soon be a part of one of these circles. All the kids in the circles were in uniform, grey sweats with matching shirts and a pair of white cheaply made Converse hi-tops, not Chuck Taylors which are popular in a lot of places til this very day.

There were around seventy kids circled up in front of Lil Mans line of ten people who rode together on the hellish uncomfortable ten hour ride in the barely breathable Sheriff van. Six tipis made up the camp, five for gents and one for ladies. There were about ten to twelve occupants per tipi. Lil Man just stood in silence while 'Running Bear' gave the camp instructions, more like orders. He always spoke in an echoing thunderous voice. "Standing here before us we have ten of the most disgusting maggots you can find on the face of this planet!" 'Wow' Lil Man thought, 'is this guy serious? He doesn't even know our names, how can he figure we're disgusting maggots?' Later, Lil Man found out that this was the routine speech for any new comer's just stepping foot off of the van, each speech more degrading than the last one.

After addressing the camp and introducing Lil Mans group as the scum of the earth, 'Running Bear' then turned to the new line-up and began yelling to the new faces. "Understand this! None of us give a good hot damn why you're here! We don't care about you, we don't care about you're momma's! While you're here all you will care about is team-work and getting the job done! Is that understood??" There was an eerie silence from Lil Mans group after the camp leader spoke. He was obviously looking for some type of response, but of course none of the newbie's knew what that was. "Algonquin! What do I need to here once I've finished speaking??" All at once one of the groups 'Running Bear' had just called out to all responded in a roaring "sir, yes sir!!" 'Okay' Lil

Man thought to himself. 'This place is all about discipline huh?'

One of the new kids in Lil Mans group saw fit to burst out laughing. Bad move, as the staff would be sure to make an example out of him very quickly! "You find something amusing maggot??" 'Running Bear' zeroed all of his attention in on the laughing kid while two staff members simultaneously tackled him down in the dirt. Later, Lil Man found out that this was known as a 'duff', when staff members had to tackle and get physical with a kid who got out of line. By the time he got up, the kid who was laughing was bleeding from the mouth and both elbows, all scraped up from the gravel and getting 'duffed'.

"Anybody else find the situation amusing??" "Sir, no sir!!" the entire camp roared in response. "Great! Let's move on then! Over here we have Wilson, Robins, Johnson, Bowman, Stevens, Rodriguez, Hammond, Jones, Silverman and Watson!! They are new to South Mountain, and we will be showing them the ropes, literally!!" The scene was so entirely surreal that Lil Man wasn't even going to stress about what 'Running Bear' meant by that. All he could do was go with the flow. After about thirty minutes, the newbies off of the van were in the same uniform as the rest of the camp. Everyone had been issued hygiene products along with a net knit case to keep them in, and a sleeping bag. Yes, luxury sleeping with mattresses, sheets and pillows were now a thing of the past. Nothing but sleeping bags and tipi's from here on out.

Lil Man was exhausted from his ride, so he knew as soon as his body reached a laying position he'd be out for the count. Lil Man made sure he had gotten a good look at all the faces of his peers. There was no one from his neighborhood that he recognized, and even if there were, he was in a non-social mood. As far as he was concerned, he didn't know anybody and nobody had known him. It was best to keep it that way, most of these guys looked like they didn't have much to lose and would probably be comfortable extending their stays. Lil Mans plan was to do his time and to make it as short as possible. He wanted to get back to his money and family. Hugging up with Katousha wasn't sounding like such a bad idea either.

Three of the staff members marched Lil Mans group over to the 'chow hall', a large auditorium like setting with wooden picnic tables. Lil Man grew fond of the 'chow hall' lights after a while. It turned out to be the only electricity in the entire camp. Everything else was naturally powered, meaning if there was a heavy load, you'd be using horses and a wagon to move it. The camp felt like a re-enactment to Lil Man, cowboys and Indians to be exact. The tipi groups were even named after real Native-American tribes. This would be an eighteen month stretch Lil Man wouldn't easily forget.

He had an appointment with the program director, to see when and where he would split up his time. Ms. Colleen the program director explained that Vision Quest had camps all across the United States. She suggested doing three months at each camp, and being on your best behavior. That would be the best way to make use of the time, traveling and reaping the rewards of self-control. Ms. Colleen understood that all the kids in the camp were frustrated, and she tried to offer the best advice she could to make it easier on the new comers. She was also an easy way to get extra time if you weren't careful. Ms. Colleen always urged the kids to "just call her Collie", while she strutted around the camp in tight skirts and always leaned over when she spoke in an even tighter half buttoned blouse, revealing her gorgeous double D cleavage. There were stories about Ms. Colleen getting a couple guys some extra time when they first came in. Supposedly she flirted with them in her trailer and the guys went on a touching frenzy. That added sexual harassment and attempted rape to their list of charges.

Only staff had known what Lil Man was there for, and he wanted to keep it that way. Most of the guys incarcerated, whether juvenile or adult, always killed time by telling stories of their life on the outside world. Most of the guys exaggerated, or just blatantly lied to make themselves look or sound better. Some even did it just to feel better. But Lil Man always kept his story to himself, always observing his juvenile peers and listening. He often thought to himself how most of the stories he had heard sounded so ridiculous. It wasn't hard to see that Rahim Bowman was definitely more mature than a lot of the other 'inmates'.

The first camps routine was mostly consisted of eating and a lot of downtime. If you enjoyed reading, you would definitely have the time to knock some heavy books out. And if you were into horses, you'd definitely get a kick out of the nearby stable, literally if you weren't careful. Lil Man decided to take in all he could about the horses. By the time his first three months were up, Lil Man knew how to saddle, groom and shoe a horse. The most important thing about being around a horse was to always let the horse be aware of your presence, by keeping one hand on it at all times, especially when walking around it from one side to another. If you didn't do that, consider yourself kicked. And horses kick with the strength of twenty men put together!

Another important lesson Lil Man took in about horses was to be careful as to not spook them. Horses have a weird peripheral vision where they cannot see straight ahead or behind them, only to the sides. So if you spook a horse and it doesn't see you, there's a very good chance you may find yourself trampled. Lil Man was learning about horses and learned something about himself that he never knew . . . He loved horses!

The next three months of Lil Mans 'tour' would consist of going from upstate Pennsylvania, all the way to Uvalde Texas. It was a tour bus ride that lasted almost a day, and then it would be horse back once the Texas border was reached. What? Horse back? In the previous camp Lil Man had learned everything about horses except riding. The way he carried himself rubbed off on a few other guys in the camp, the guys who really wanted to do the right thing and get back home. But of course there's always that one, one person who doesn't understand what relax means. There's a bad apple in every bunch, and in Lil Mans new Texas bunch the apple's name was Council Calhoune.

Council was from San Antonio, and had been locked up for grand theft auto. When he was free, he used to take keys off the walls in dealerships and come back and drive the cars away after the lot closed. He wasn't making any money off the cars either, just a teenaged joy rider. But he was tall, just like Lil Man was, and had all the lime light and attention of the staff until Trooper Bowman showed up. The program had taken a turn for the boot camp side of things, so everyone was called by their rank and then last name. All the kids were Troopers, while the staff members were Lieutenants, Sergeants, Captains and

Majors. There were also rumors of a General who was the program director in Texas, but Lil Man never met him.

Lil Man knew he may end up fighting one day, but he was doing so well with his own program that he didn't see any imminent threats or reasons to risk getting time tacked on. The rule of the program was that if any fight was reported and you were involved, you get an extra three months depending on the severity of the brawl. Some guys even got sent to other placements over their rumbles. It had to be over one hundred degrees when Lil Man's name was called to come and get mail. Yes! It was another love letter from Katousha. Letters from Katousha always made Lil Man's time a bit easier, although they were a bit of torture at the same time. She would always mention how she was going to "do it" when she saw Lil Man, and what she would wear. Some of Katousha's letters were nothing short of a porno film on paper.

Lil Man grabbed his letter from mail call and headed back to his Tipi when he was approached by Council Calhoune. "Ya thank yar purdy impawtant huhh boy??" Council spoke with a deep southern accent that was so deep, Lil Man almost didn't understand him at first. But from the body language and the jealous tone, Trooper Bowman put it together fast. 'This dude is a hater' he thought to himself. "Look man, you don't know me and I don't you. How bout we keep it that way and go about our business." Lil Man turned his back after speaking and tried walking away when he felt Trooper Calhoune grab his shoulder. Huge mistake. All Lil Man wanted to do was go and read his letter. He was already tense and still adjusting to being away from home. Without even thinking he turned in one swift motion back towards Council and swinging a wild haymaker that landed in Calhoune's mouth! Council fell to the ground and before another move could be made other troopers were drawing attention to the scene yelling "fight! They're fighting!!"

Lil Man wanted to leave it at just the one punch, but he saw a relentless look in Counsil's face that said he wasn't giving up. He wanted more. So Lil Man had to let him have it. Not only were other troopers looking on, but he also knew that if he didn't show Calhoune who was boss in this situation, he'd just make matters worse later. Two more lefts and a powerful right to Council's jaw put him to sleep while Lil Man straddled over top of him. Before he could swing another punch he felt himself being tackled like he was in the NFL! Two Sergeants had 'duffed' Lil Man and restrained him for about ten minutes, while another Sergeant was dragging Council and trying to revive him. The fight was over before it started as far as Lil Man was concerned. He didn't look for drama, but when it came he put it to rest. The frustration of being away from home had made for a ticking time bomb.

The counselor of the Texas camp had to routinely interview both boys and get their stories about what happened. Lil Man decided to just tell the truth and keep it short. "He grabbed me, so I hit him. He looked like he wanted to hurt me so I kept hitting him. I have nothing against the guy, we don't even know each other." The counselor recorded Lil Mans statement about the fight for the files. The staff hadn't gotten Calhoune's side of the story for another twenty minutes. He was still knocked out cold. But the truth must have set Lil Man free. A Lieutenant came to Lil Mans Tipi and informed him that he wouldn't have to face any new consequences for the fight. As it turned out, Council Calhoune had been starting fights ever since he was sent to Vision Quest. The incident was recorded and he had to see another Judge to be sent to another placement. But Lil Man still had over a year left, and he wouldn't have to worry about that type of silliness for the rest of his stay. The word spread quickly how he put Calhoune the bully on his back pockets.

It was back to love letters and horseback riding. And just in time for Lil Man's birthday. He turned eighteen while in the Texas camp. For his birthday he got an hour on the phone! Standard time was only ten minutes, Happy Birthday! Of course he split up the call between mom and Katousha. The staff had issued everyone a used pair of jeans to wear whenever it was time to ride. You have to wear jeans when riding a horse for comfort on you and the horse. Sweat pants didn't have enough grip and could give the rider a serious rash. Among learning to ride horses, the guys also was learning the basics of military and boot camp procedures. Instead of the usual circling up, the camp now gathered in 'formation', a military term used when soldiers gather and awaited further instructions. Everything began with the 'formation'. It was arranged in size order from tallest to shortest, and every command was given from the 'formation'. Marching was the only way a platoon could travel, unless a drill instructor called 'at ease', meaning the platoon could take a short break and relax temporarily until further instructions. Hearing the words 'at ease' felt like a vacation!

The best part of being tall in a platoon was that the tallest people on the ends of the 'formation' were considered squad leaders. It carried some extra responsibilities, but Lil Man didn't mind at all. He did as many extra activities as he could to help him keep busy and kill time. Being a squad leader and being tall also got you a tall horse. Lil Man rode 'Short Stop', a beautiful thorough bred who stood almost seven feet tall. It took a while to achieve perfection, but after a few weeks Lil Man and 'Short Stop' had formed a bond. And by the time formations had to be done with horses, Lil Man had 'Short Stop' under control and looking great. 'Short Stop' was one of the Majors horses, and for the kids was a bit wild and hard to control. But the staff took a liking to the maturity and discipline Lil Man carried himself with, and decided 'Short Stop' would be the perfect challenge for him. They were right, and it almost crushed Lil Man's heart to pieces when it was time to move to another camp.

The next camp was in Douglas, Arizona. And every day felt like two hundred degrees! It was probably the most laid back and relaxed camp out of all the Vision Quest camps. Even the food was better, and Lil Mans time was getting shorter. He had less than twelve months left when he reached the Arizona camp. He had spoken to the director about finishing his time on an 'Ocean Quest', but found out that a kid had drowned while on a boat trying to escape and the 'Ocean Quest' had been shut down as a result. All the guy's conversations now were mostly about how they wanted to finish up their 'Quests'. Lil Man's heart was mainly set on the 'Ocean Quest' mainly because he heard it was stationed near Hawaii. It would've been the perfect spot to take pictures, he thought.

But every camp had their own uniqueness and specialty. For the first time in months, Lil Man was assigned a bunk as opposed to a spot on the Tipi floor with a sleeping bag. The bunks weren't the Hilton or Four Seasons, but were still one hundred times better than the floor with a thin sleeping bag. Out in Arizona, Lil Man saw a lot of new wild life for the first time. All the staff here seemed extra cool, and most of them looked like they were drunk or high. But that didn't stop them from hiking and mountain climbing all the time. In one weeks' time during mountain climbing, Lil Man saw scorpions, javelinas, armadillo's and even bob cats. They were amongst the wild for real, but had been taught how to remain calm and deal with an animal if approached or attacked. It was hard to imagine, but the staff always reiterated . . . "If you see bears, remain calm and do not run!!" Lil Man was glad they never encountered any bears, because he sure as hell wasn't just going to stand there if they did. His plan would be more like 'ok, you guys stand here with the bear. I'll go and get help for y'all!!'

Even though Arizona was blazing hot most of the time, he enjoyed the camp he was in. Not only was the staff cool, but for the first time in months he began interacting with other juveniles and saw that some of them were ok to. One kid named Epifonio, or Epi for short loved to play chess and a card game called Casino. Lil Man didn't know how to play either game but surely became a pro once Epi taught him. Chess became a major past time towards the end of Lil Mans stay. It was the perfect time killer while exercising the mind. Sometimes the guys would wager snacks, to make the games more interesting. In Arizona, Lil Man got a package that made him want to go home more than ever! It was from his mom and Katousha. Mom had written a letter saying everyone was fine and that the new baby was walking and talking. Wow! Already! Katousha's letter was more detailed and explicit . . . It had read something like:

"Dear Rahim, I have been missing you more than words could explain. When you get home, I just want to wrap my arms around you! And my lips want to wrap other things about you, keep in mind that I have four lips here, all juicy and waiting for you! People from school have been asking about you. I just tell them you have a job out of state. I told my mother about us, she's excited and wants to meet you when you get out of there. How's the food baby? I can't wait to cook for you, so when I see you make sure you're hungry! I have many things to feed you, wink wink. (smiling and licking my lips) Enclosed is something I think you'll enjoy, just to remind you what kind of sweetness you have waiting for you. Be good, and hold your head baby. We all can't wait til you get home! Much love x's and o's, Katousha. P.S . . . I love you!!"

Wow! After Rahim read Katousha's letter, he just lay there on his bunk staring up at the ceiling. 'This girl must really love me!' he thought. He dug into the box that his package was sent in. Besides the underwear and hygiene stuff his mom bought him, there were also a pair of black thongs with pink lacing. There was a sticky note attached to them . . . "Smell me" Lil Man cupped the thongs with both hands, smothered them into his face, and inhaled deeply through his nose. It was Katousha's scent, and it was wonderful! She was being extra freaky in her letters, each one freakier than the last. And even though it would've been torture to the average, Lil Man was just glad he had a 'cookie jar' to go home to. He hid her panties with his personal things so she could wear them for him when he finally got home. He had built a lot of fantasies around that pair of underwear!

The drill instructors at the Arizona camp began teaching all the guys 'Buff Steps', a form of drill team style dancing which looked magnificent when performed properly. The only downfall to practicing 'Buff Steps' were the uniforms. Tight jeans, wool shirts with suede elbow patches, blue wool and leather beret and large yellow leather cowhide gloves made up the uniform along with well-worn cowboy boots. Without some will power, anyone would be ready to pass out dressed as a Buffalo Soldier. But the experience was worth the heat, Lil Man thought. The squad looked great practicing, and couldn't wait to perform. His mature side was making the best of his time.

The program director had told Lil Man they would be performing soon, tour style. The best platoon had been chosen to perform 'Buff Steps' at grade schools and colleges and during public events. You guessed it, Lil Man's platoon was the best! The tour would take them through Phoenix Arizona and they would wind up in Gardena California, performing in major surrounding cities like L.A. and San Francisco. Lil Man looked up at the map on the wall in the office of the program director. He couldn't believe they were going to visit all of those places on the map. The program director explained that our platoon was being rewarded by doing the tour and besides all the fun of performing, the last few remaining months would fly by in a flash. And it did. By the time Lil Man's squad had performed in L.A, he had only two and a half months left before he'd began getting home passes.

The residential part of the program was all the guys favorite. Not only were you close to going home, but your curfew had been lifted, there was a squad bay with free arcade games, the food was much better, and everyone got to go home a couple times before being released for good. A lot of eyes would be on guys when they came back from a home pass to see how they were dressed. For over a year and a half, everybody was used to seeing everybody in nothing but grey sweats, and the same pair of worn out Converse. So many guys talked trash about the things they were into and how much money they were getting, that it was really sad to see them come back almost looking worse than when they left when they had on their own clothes. Lil Man remained humble for a reason. He knew he'd be clean, so there was no reason to brag. He left it up to the dreamers to have their fun.

On Lil Mans second home pass visit, he was allowed to stay home for good, and go to court to be discharged.

BACK ON THE BLOCK

The first thing Lil Man wanted to do when he got home, besides eat a Philly cheesesteak and see his family and girl, was check on the stash up in his room. Yes! It was still all there and untouched. He hadn't done any inventory, but he had a nice amount of all the goodies, weed, some powder, and some crack. Lil Man also checked his bank account. Since being locked up and not touching his account, he had accumulated around six thousand dollars in interest. Wow, freedom was feeling better than ever!

He spent the first couple of days in a hotel suite in downtown Philadelphia with Katousha. For those two days, they ate at restaurants and held hands walking around downtown. Going to the movies and shopping was always a relaxing thing to do, as long as you had money, and Lil Mans pockets were ok. He found himself in a romantic mood after the way Katousha worked her magic on him in the hotel room. She had done all the things she said she would do in her letters, and more! If Lil Man didn't still have a dark cloud in his conscience about Vernie, Katousha probably could have gotten a ring! Nahh, 'it's still early and we're still too young' he thought.

"Baby, I need to get back to work. You know the paper will run low if I don't keep working." Lil Mans code name for hustling was 'working' and Katousha was trying to play a major wife roll. "Yes, I know you have to do what you got to do. But maybe you should explore some new options Rahim. It's getting crazy out here and I don't want to hear about some punks getting jealous trying to rob you, or you getting hurt in any kind of way. Please think about it." Katousha's tone was very pleasant and soothing to Lil Mans ears. And she had called him by his real name, indicating that she was sincere and serious. The look in her pretty face showed concern, it was a look that took some of the hardness out of Lil Man for a second and made him respond "Ok, I'll definitely think about it."

Lil Man wasn't about to get soft or fully let his guard down for his girl, but he thought 'maybe she is right.' He wasn't planning on getting robbed or shot, and he damn sure wasn't trying to do any more years anywhere, especially since he'd be charged as an adult now. He was really starting to think about giving drugs up for good.

Stoop Head had written Lil Man twice while he was away, stating the game hasn't changed, only some of the players. Lil Man wanted to talk to Stoop in person about what he meant by that. Stoop also mentioned that Lil Man didn't owe him anything, in fact if he needed something Lil Man was to tell Stoop and he'd take care of it. Stoop Head and Rocky was only getting richer and richer from their dealings and still living down in the 'Lab' where it was almost rent free as long as their momma had everything she needed. Lil Man decided to pay Stoop a visit.

"Just keep in mind baby, before you went away you were thinking about a career. If you get with your cousins, try not to get in any deeper ok?" Lil Man convinced Katousha that he'd stay out of trouble, dropped her off at home and then proceeded to check out what was left of the 'Lab Rats', Stoop Head and Rocky.

Lil Man pulled up, parked in front on his aunt's house and then walked around the back to the entrance of the 'Lab'. The door flew open fast before he even had a chance to knock. "Welcome home baby!!" It was Rocky, excited to see his cousin home from being locked up. "How was it man? I know you got some war stories for us!" Rocky was hoping to hear some drama or about some negative situation, but Lil Man cut all that out quick and kept the visit on an adult level. "Nope, no drama for you cuz, I was in there chillin. I mean one dude got out of pocket one day but you know he got put in his place. Put him to sleep a lil bit, nothing major. Where's Stoop at?"

Rocky had almost looked disappointed not to have heard more, he was expecting to hear about weapons, blood and all out violence. But it just wasn't like that. "Stoop upstairs ordering our food, you want something?" Lil Man jumped on the order fast! He knew Stoop knew where to get the best Philly cheese-steaks from, and he knew just how to order them. "Yeah man, tell'em to order me a cheese-steak and a Sunkist soda!" While Lil Man was away, he had dreams about the most mouthwatering Philly cheese-steak and how he would devour one as soon as he got home. He started to get one while he was with Katousha, but their time together turned out to consist of 'proper' romance and sophisticated down-town restaurants. It was time to get down and dirty with a good grub from 'the hood' as far as Lil Man was concerned. "Aight, I'm going to tell'em cuz. Have a seat."

Lil Man took a seat right where Vernie had first given him fellatio. The 'Lab' hadn't changed a bit except for some studio equipment and a large sixty inch plasma screen t.v Stoop Head had bought for whenever there was down time. Rocky and Stoop Head came back downstairs. "What's up baby!!??" Stoop Head had a large smile and seemed just as excited to see his cousin as Rocky did. "You put on a lot of weight killer! What the hell they had you eating, horses?" They all burst out laughing. "You just don't know cuz, I been smelling horses asses for the past year and a half man!" But Stoop Head did know. "Cuz, you were up at 'the Quest' right? I did a year there when I was fifteen. That was around the time we first had started out. I guess they want our whole family to have spent some time there huh?"

Stoop was joking about the family all going to the placement, but he and Lil Man both wondered how much of a coincidence it really was. "Anyway, the food is on its way fella's. Y'all feel like playing some John Madden while we wait?" Rocky, always bored unless the conversation was about blood had gotten excited when he heard the name Madden. "Yeah! Put on Madden, I'm going to crush both of you!" Football on PlayStation was like America's favorite past-time next to the real game.

"So where y'all cars at? I haven't seen one BMW on the entire block." Lil Man always looked for the signature foreign cars with chrome wheels whenever he came around, it was a sure sign that his cousins were home. "We had to upgrade cuz, I have a truck now, a Suburban with twenty sixes. And I bought this ungrateful bastard a Mercedes, CLK model." Stoop Head had called his brother a name, teasing him whenever the cars were mentioned. They always shopped together but claimed Rocky never said 'thank you' for the car. "I saw that truck out there, wow! That thing is pretty Stoop!" Lil Man was glad to hear his cousins were still doing well.

"So how about you cousin? You ready for your upgrade?" The room was filled with temptation among some of the most successful hustlers in Philadelphia. And Lil Mans next words would either put him back into the game, getting him in deeper, or put him on another path towards job seeking and depleting his saved up funds. Lil Man had dreamed of having a nice vehicle, and he was ready to move out of the house with his family and becoming independent. "I think it is time I upgrade Stoop!" Lil Man had sealed his fate with those words, and he knew his cousins didn't play too many games besides John Madden football on PlayStation. There was no turning back now.

"Cool, we can go to the dealer this weekend. And you know I still have a position for you cousin. We have some friends in Connecticut that I have some work for, but one of us has to go and take it to them. If that person is to be you, you'll get five thousand a trip cuz. And you'll be making the trip about every other week, cool?" Lil Man thought about it and new Stoop wanted an answer immediately, and hesitation would have been considered 'half-stepping' or 'pump-faking'. "I'm with it cousin. Just hook it up and I got you. Oh yeah, I got some work still left over from before I got booked, what you think I should do with that?"

Stoop Head and Rocky started laughing. "The same thing we do with everything else Lil Man, sell it!" And just like that, Lil Man was back in the game and would be put onto set amounts of paper making runs to Connecticut. All he had to do now was find a place to stay so he could keep his business away from his family. He also had the problem of either keeping it from, or breaking the news to Katousha. They were becoming serious. He never wanted to mix his dealings with her and get her involved, but Katousha was already hip to the game. She had brothers and cousins who hustled to. In fact, one of her cousins had been robbed and killed during a transaction, and that was her main reason for trying to get Lil Man to find another means of livelihood. Lil Man finished his sandwich and went home.

ON THE ROAD AGAIN

That weekend as promised the 'Lab Rats' met up, and the entire mission was about what kind of vehicle Lil Man wanted. Stoop Head told him to name the dealership and they'd be on their way. "Acura, I want the new Legend coupe." Lil Man was saying it as if they were just telling jokes, like they were still all children talking about their dream cars that they wanted when they had gotten old enough. But this wasn't a dream or a joke. Stoop Head jumped onto the expressway, headed towards the Acura dealership. The two brothers in the front seat of the Tahoe had lit blunts, and Rocky even had a glass of ice filling it with Bacardi Limon for the ride.

"Lil Man, the secret to picking out your dream car and making it look 'fly' is getting it while you're high. Being buzzed or high while you put your ride together does wonders for the imagination you know?" Lil Man took the blunt from Rocky while nodding his head in agreement. "I hear you cuz, but I kind of know what I want already. Lil Man was getting "on" of off the weed and found himself checking out the interior of Stoop's truck for ideas. Stoop had seven inch screens everywhere as usual, and had a sound system that could wake the dead up and make them come out of their graves dancing. The seats were cream colored leather with Ralph Lauren horses on the headrests. Even the floor mats were Polo.

Lil Man sat there wondering, "how rich is my cousin? He's buying me any car I want like its Christmas and he's Donald Trump!"

They pulled into the Acura dealer parking lot and all the cars had been lined up perfectly in rows by name. There were 'RL's and TL's, Integra's, MDX S.U.V's, NSX's and Lil Man's favorite, the Legends. It was a clear and sunny day, and the beauty of the vehicles could have made them all aroused. The cars looked like lonely and gorgeous woman, waiting to be driven home. But unfortunately, only one of the ladies would be getting lucky today. "There she goes! I want her, that bitch is bad!!" Lil Man was referring to a navy blue Legend coupe. The car was beautiful, with a moon roof and matching navy blue soft leather seats or 'butters' as guys would call them in the 'hood'.

"You sure that's her cuz? She might be a little tight for them big girls you probably gonna be picking up!" Stoop Head always had jokes. "Yes sir, that's my new chick right there!" After some conversation about how Lil Man would hook the car up and have it looking, he and Stoop went into the office to do the paperwork and purchase the car, while Rocky stayed in the truck and rolled some more weed up for the ride back. Lil Mans license had barely been driven on, so there was no red tape to put it all in his name, especially since he had his own money to keep up with the insurance. About a half an hour went by and the keys to the new Acura were in Lil Mans hands. He drove off of the lot following Stoops truck, smiling all the way. Stoop pulled over to fill up at a gas station and Lil Man parked at the pump on the opposite side. They got out of their cars to chat some more when Lil Man noticed how everyone's eyes were glued to Stoop Heads truck. That's when it hit him, 'it's the wheels. I gotta get some of those'.

Rims are hardly necessary for a car, but it adds a lot of beauty if you get the right style and size. Having nice wheels on your car also make's getting a girls phone number a hell of a lot easier, especially if your pockets could back up the car you drove. "It's still early Stoop, take me where you got your wheels from." Lil Man was serious about having a ride that looked as good as the team he was on now. He thought 'forget about hiding it anymore, we only live once and can't take our money to the grave when it's time to go.' He followed Stoop Head to the rim and tire shop. "I can't stay cousin, but get with us when you're done here ok?" The brothers shook hands with Lil Man and were on their way.

Lil Man didn't know too much about what kind of wheels to get or stay away from. He wasn't too aware of the prices either. He decided to just talk to the guy running the shop. "How are you buddy? That's great! Listen, what do you have in chrome to fit on a 2001 Acura Legend?" The young guy running the shop pulled out and put a wheel guide on the counter between the two of them. "Pages seventeen to twenty one all fit your car. We have them all in stock, but when you decide what you want, let me know. Depending on what size you want we may have to order your tires." "Okay, thanks" Lil Man replied and began browsing through the booklet. After about fifteen minutes, he finally decided on a design he thought would fit the shape of his Legend.

"How much for these?" he asked. The guy informed him that the set of wheels would be sixteen hundred dollars, and the tires for those wheels would be about one hundred forty a piece plus mounting, balancing and installation. Lil Man was about to kick out twenty two hundred dollars to put glass slippers on his new ride. After about an hour at the tire shop, Lil Man finally pulled off with his new wheels, looking and feeling great. He headed back to the 'Lab' so he could figure out what he would do with two cars now. "Stoop, let me use your phone." He called Katousha and told her he had a surprise for her. She sounded excited over the phone, but Lil Man had only decided to leave one of the cars parked in her driveway since nobody at her house drove at the time.

"Lil Man! Is this what you had me all excited about? A parking space? You had me thinking I was about to get a car!" Lil Man wasn't into arguing with Katousha, but whenever she got pouty, he egged her on just a little, only because they both knew it would lead to intense sex. "Did you ever think that maybe you COULD get a car if you didn't scream all of the damn time? Come here girl!" Lil Man put an arm behind the small of Katousha's back and pulled her in closely. They began kissing passionately, ferociously, until they wound up on Katousha's mother's couch, half naked and sweaty. Lil Man had stroked her for about an hour and twenty minutes straight before opening up all his plans to her. He wanted to make sure he left her kitty throbbing in case there was something she didn't agree with.

Once they finished, Lil Man told Katousha to meet him in her driveway after she got out of the shower. She hadn't seen the Acura yet and Lil Man knew he was about to put a smile on his cuties face. He was also about to let her know about the first Connecticut trip, so he had to play it smoothly. He wasn't exactly sure how she would react. Lil Man went and sat in the car listening to music while he waited for Katousha to come out of the back door. A half an hour went by and Katousha finally was coming out, her face lighting up with surprise and confusion all at the same time. Lil Man hit the button for his power window to automatically roll the window down for him. "You like this babe?" He was showing off, but had to keep her in positive spirits for when he laid the news on her. "Boy! Whose car is this? I can't be hiding no stolen cars here Lil Man! These neighbors are newsy as hell, and be snitching on everything! You know my mom gonna ask if she sees this!"

'Wow, the Acura looks too good to be mine huh?' he thought to himself. "Get in momma, I want to show you something." Katousha walked around to the passenger side slowly, keeping her eyes locked on Lil Man as if to say 'what the hell are you up to?' She got in, and Lil Man was playing her favorite slow jam, trying to set the mood. 'Between the Sheets' by the Isley Brothers could get almost anyone in the mood, especially a girl who was in love with you already. Lil Man decided to use Ron Isley's voice to help put his lady in a trance. "Look at the registration in the glove box." She reached in, and Katousha pulled out the paperwork for the car containing Lil Man's name and address on it. It was all legit.

"So you're just blowing all of your cash? Are you sure that's a good idea, I mean I was there to see what it took for you to make that money Lil Man. I know you're gonna start acting crazy once you're cash gets low and you have no income, I'm just concerned for you that's all." Ron Isley wasn't quite doing the trick. Katousha worked her way around her favorite song, only to still find a way to take on a motherly roll. She was still satisfied from the sex, she was throbbing. Lil Man could tell her stuff was aching from the way she walked and sat once she got in the car.

But the great sex and favorite song turned out to backfire, she was deeper in love. And there was no way Katousha was letting Lil Man start slipping, nor would she stand for him getting locked up again.

He did his best to try and understand where she was coming from. "I know you care about me Toosh, but you know I gotta make moves. I have a trip to take, and I wasn't sure if you were down to ride with me or not. But it's out in Connecticut where I have to go, and I would appreciate the company." She sat and looked blank for a few seconds, then Katousha shot a sharp and stern look at Lil Man. "Are you crazy!? Do you think I'm stupid? I know what you're going out there for, my brother even used to drive out there. Lil Man, look at me and tell me you're not back into that already!" Damn, Lil Man couldn't get a thing passed Katousha. They both had really gotten to know each other, and at that moment together in the car they both realized how in love they were. Anything over eight months with somebody and having a good time with them will grow on anybody, even the coldest person. Lil Man was caught up in Katousha's heat, and she caught chills from some of his cold ways. But there temperatures blended together well, making for a comfortable feeling.

CHANGE 'GON COME

After Lil Man took his lady out to a romantic dinner, he finally convinced her that he only had to drive out to Connecticut a few times at the most. Sometimes Lil Mans smooth talk worked on Katousha, and sometimes it didn't. They both had minds of their own and were young, and put a lot of effort into trying to understand one another's opinion. This tactic was definitely making their relationship stronger, and before long they were almost reading each other's vibes, completing sentences for each other and all. "So when is the first trip?" She was now anxious and ready to hit the road for the one hundred twenty mile ride. "As soon as I decide the best time to leave, I will call and let you know."

Lil Man was really waiting on Stoop Head to see when he'd be leaving, but he didn't want to sound like he couldn't make moves on his own. Deep down, Lil Man had secretly been having inner issues about his cousins. He knew what Stoop and Rocky did, and why they had so much money. But he still wasn't clear on why they were so generous to him, 'I'm just the baby cousin' he thought. Lil Man finally received the call from Stoop to come and meet up with him. They never discussed serious business over the phone. Stoop gave Lil Man all of the ins and outs of their connection in Connecticut.

"I really appreciate you riding with me babe, I don't know the guys were going to go meet, but if anything looks shaky just look in the glove box and try to improvise. Katousha looked inside of the glove compartment. In it were two .380 caliber handguns, one was chrome and the other black. "I finally let my cousin talk me into taking some protection from him. We going to be making a lot of cash over the next couple of months and there's no telling what type of weirdo's or haters we'll come across. It's best we be safe than sorry ok?" Katousha closed the glove box back and crossed her arms with her eyebrows arched extra hard. Lil Man thought she was just pouting again, but she was really upset.

On the highway, Lil Man had decided to let Katousha play whatever songs she wanted to. Giving her a sense of control kept her quiet whenever she became pouty. Lil Man just had one small request, then he'd let Katousha get back to playing DJ. "Put on 'On The Run' by Kool G. Rap." It was Lil Man's favorite song. The video reminded him of a mafia movie, and he knew the lyrics by heart. Listening to the song, he wondered if his cousins 'had him like a flunky' as he drove to do pickups and deliveries. He didn't want to think too hard about that, Stoop Head and Rocky were showing Lil Man a lot of love, and so was Maze before he went to jail for life. 'It's like I'm in a mob' he thought. But the difference was he was working for his cousins.

Lil Man and Katousha finally reached Connecticut, and only had another thirty minutes to drive before they were to meet their contact, a guy named Shy would be meeting them in a Wal-Mart parking lot in the middle of a small town right outside of Stamford. Once they got into town, Lil Man pulled into a gas station to refill the tank and get some beverages. He decided to let Katousha drive since they were in the Acura, the car was a bit flashy and he figured if she drove while he lay low, they would be less likely to be stopped for anything as long as she didn't speed. He was wrong. They had gotten pulled over coming out of the gas station. "If they ask, we're just here visiting family. They'll probably ask since we have Pennsylvania tags. Just be cool babe, and we'll be on our way."

The officer was behind them for about three minutes before he finally got out and walked up to Katousha's window. "How you folks doing this afternoon? License, insurance and registration please?" He had asked for credentials before he allowed Katousha a chance to reply to the 'how you doing?' part and Lil Man swore she would catch an attitude. She handed over the papers along with her license while smiling. "We're just fine officer, how about you?" The officer ignored her question and continued with his 'investigation'. "Is that young man beside you Rahim Bowman?" Lil Man sat up straight and immediately handed the officer his i.d, being as cooperative as possible and keeping attention away from all the heat in the glove box. "Yes sir! Rahim Bowman right here, may we ask what the problem is sir?" Lil Man knew that Police enjoyed being called sir or ma'am as a sign of respect, he learned that while in boot camp at Vision Quest. "There's no problem. This is a mighty fancy vehicle and when the tags came back as a male owner and I saw her driving, I had to check it out. Especially since I couldn't see you lying down over there. You ought to be proud that we'd keep an eye out for you if this ever wound up stolen. You folks take care now." The officer handed their papers and I.D's back and walked back to his car.

"See babe? We're legit." Lil Man knew that that was a close call, and he was glad to still have his Mercury back home. He'd never drive the Legend to do this ever again. They pulled into the Wal-Mart parking lot and spotted their contact. Lil Man handed Shy two small plastic shopping bags that were in the trunk, and Shy handed Lil Man a paper bag. They both got back into their cars. Lil Man counted the money in the paper bag, it was fifteen thousand dollars and he'd be keeping five. Lil Man sat there for a second thinking if the ride was worth it. He was up another five grand and hadn't done any hard work. He told Katousha to pick a place to eat so that they could rest before driving right back to Philadelphia.

The couple stopped at a Cracker Barrel restaurant, and sat down to order. "I loved the way you handled that cop Toosh, putting your sexy voice on and all that. You were cooler than I'd thought you'd be." Katousha loved whenever Lil Man gave her praise, especially if she wasn't sure about her actions. She often sought his approval on certain things, as if he was the boss. Lil Man had a lot more street experience than his girl, but at the end of the day she was really the boss. Lil Man wore the pants, but she had on the panties, and if he wanted to get out of his pants and into those panties she had to feel like a boss.

"So what do you think? That was easy enough right?" Lil Man found himself seeking Katousha's approval now. Even though the transaction went smooth, they were both still consciously aware of the high risks involved in that type of ride. Katousha was trying to keep cool, she didn't want to seem like she was complaining too much. "It was ok I guess, I just hope it doesn't become a major habit. They ate their food while Lil Man changed the subject to more positive things. "You wanna get an apartment together Toosh? We can definitely afford a nice one to." The question put the brightest smile on Katousha's face. They were young, both were barely twenty years old, and were making the type of decisions they always let their parents talk about. "I would love to Rahim! Yes!" Uh oh, the first name again. She was really excited.

"Toosh, a lot of guys my age would probably kill to see this type of paper. We really should keep a low profile and draw less attention from haters." Katousha couldn't wait until Lil Man had started talking about a more positive subject again. "You mean low profile like those tires outside? Ever since we were in school I knew this type of change would come. Your focused Rahim and can do whatever you put your mind to."

Wow, a double whammy. She used the first name and hit Lil Man with some words of wisdom. The more Katousha spoke, the more Lil Man saw what type of girl she was. Caring, wise, sincere and had a sense of humor. He was starting to look past her pretty face, thick thighs, large booty and breast. Katousha was really aiming for a ring in the long run but for the moment, Lil Man thought that maybe some nice shoes and a good handbag would do for now. They finished their meals with ice-cream and left the restaurant to head back home to Philly.

But it would actually be awhile before they went apartment hunting. Stoop Head was so glad about how smoothly Lil Mans run had went that he decided to just split each run fifty fifty with him. Seventy five hundred dollars for a drive to Connecticut and back. It was real good money for a young guy without a real job. But Lil Man always kept up the hope that he would not be involved with drugs too much longer, even though he had wound up making the Connecticut runs with Katousha for a few more months, until around the time it started getting cold outside.

Lil Man had saved up a lot of cash from his runs, barely spending any except to keep gas in his cars, and once in a while he and Katousha would go out. But when the snow really started sticking to the ground and things got a bit slow, Lil Man asked his grandpa to take him to get a snowmobile. The streets of Philly were nasty and deserted whenever it snowed, and a snowmobile would be the perfect antidote to a boring wintertime curse. Lil Man got grandpa to drive him over the bridge to New Jersey in his pickup truck which had been geared up for winter conditions. A 4x4 with snow tires, the truck was perfect to pick up Lil Mans snowmobile from the Suzuki shop.

Lil Man picked out a neon orange and black snowmobile with dual skis in the front. He also bought himself and Katousha helmets and pads to match the vehicle. 'She's gonna love this stuff' he thought, and decided to take the machine to the park and practice for a while before he shared the news with his girl. After about two hours, he was ready to pick up Katousha and take her for a ride. "Babe, while things are a little slow right now I think I'm going to put some time towards music. Katousha had looked lost at first, but of course Lil Man would explain. "My cousins invested into some great studio equipment, you know the kind where you can make your own tunes and beats." Katousha understood a bit better now, but then just thought Lil Man was making up excuses to gallivant with his cousins.

"What made you want to do that all of a sudden Rahim?" He didn't know why, but it seemed like the more Katousha thought about Lil Man doing music and spending more time with his cousins, the more she was against it. "I really think it may be a positive outlet away from hustling. There are a lot of guys who has no problem doing both, but I simply don't want drugs around us anymore. I'm going to do something that will keep us from having to peddle drugs anymore Toosh." Lil Man sounded sincere, and in his heart and mind he really was, but Katousha still had a hard time being fully supportive, even with his anti-drug dealing incentives. They rode around on the snowmobile for the rest of that day until it began getting dark outside.

"I'm here for you no matter what you decide to do Lil Man, you are your own person. But I noticed that every time you get around your cousins you come back with a new adventure, one involving drugs or new guns. I want you around boy, do you hear me!?" Katousha had become emotional again. Thinking about the risks of robbery and jail time was upsetting to her. She knew that she would be lonely without Lil Man around. "Maybe I should get back to work to, that way I won't have to think about you so much" Katousha said. "No girl of mine has to work, as long as I have some, you can get some. Besides, I like the way you think about me all the time. Knowing you care makes me want to keep going girl! It makes me want to keep getting better and better." Lil Man returned some emotional words back to Katousha, even though the 'L' word never actually came out. But she had plans to change that.

BEAT-MAKERS

Throughout most of the rest of that winter, Lil Man was spending a lot of time in the 'Lab' with his cousins. The three were all rotating and taking turns operating and learning the different music equipment. Lil Man never mentioned it to his cousins or anybody, but he had planned to move away with his girlfriend and start a family of his own. "Lil Man, how does this sound?" Rocky was playing around with a guitar attached to an amplifier, playing different patterns of notes. "Cool cousin, sounding pretty good!" Lil Man was on the computer looking at different types of sound effects, and learning how to change their pitches. Stoop Head was rapping and writing, and lighting blunts to pass around.

The three would stay in the 'Lab' for hours at a time, usually until they either came up with something that sounded good or until they passed out one by one from either being too high or sleepy. Lil Mans new cell phone had rung a lot. It was either Katousha or somebody wanting some weed or coke, but it was mostly Katousha. "Baby girl, we'll never get anything done if you keep me tied up on the phone. You know I'm doing this for us. I'm not even hanging out. I'm working on a career as we speak." Katousha never believed him. She was too busy focusing on the chatter and laughter in Lil Mans background. As long as it sounded like he was having a good time while being away, her insecurities arose.

Lil Man was determined not to let Katousha distract him. He knew that in order to get out of the drug game, he'd have to make a hit song that would be sure to get him paid. "Rocky, check this out." Lil Man found a combination of sound effects that blended well together. Rocky and Stoop Head got excited and hyper when they heard the beat. Stoop Head starting rapping to it immediately . . . "I ain't Jay Z and don't pretend to be. I just get my grown man on playin Bantumi. Put your beans in my pot baby you can trust me. I'm trying to see if its love or you just lust me. I've seen better attitudes on chicks that are ugly. Do woman want to make love or just hump me? I'm getting twisted, rolling blunts up in the ducky. And got a big ass tool in case they try to pluck me. Plus I got a full deck, go ahead take a card, pluck me. But I hope you're feeling lucky. Wind up in the trunk B!"

Stoop was going on and on before Lil Man finally cut him off. "Hold up cuz, those are some hot lines. But what the hell is a Bantumi?" No matter how much fun they were having in the 'Lab', Lil Man wasn't going to be a part of any raps that didn't make sense. Lil Man added technicalities to the fun, just to make sure their songs could get put out. "Bantumi is a game cousin, it's just like Mancala. It was named Bantu or Bantumi by African tribes who got their hands on the game once upon a time. The name also means large group of African languages. You wanna play?" Stoop Head was exposing his knowledgeable side. He was more street smart than anything, but when it came to vocabulary all three of the cousins were experts really. "Ok, let me finish up this track. I think we may have a hit on our hands."

Another two hours went by, and Lil Man had perfected the beat he was working on. "Dammit! We may have to sign a deal with Diddy Combs or Wu-Tang Clan. You're beat is tough cuz!" They were all excited about the finished beat Lil Man had made, and once Stoop started rhyming over it, it just sounded better and better. The trio was now faced with the task of how to put their song on the market. "I know a chick who works for the radio station. Maybe she can get our song played on the air. In the meantime, we have to make more music. I think we can put out an album if we keep going at this rate. One song is gonna wear out fast, and people will want more. Hey, this hustle is just like selling crack." The three of them laughed at Stoop Head's pun, but the truth was that Lil Man was glad the attention was going away from drugs and into music. It was a positive change for the better.

Stoop Head got in touch with the girl he knew named Katrina that worked at Power 99 fm radio station in Philadelphia. She worked as a studio engineer and rubbed shoulders with all the DJ's at the station, and it helped that Stoop was on good terms with her. They were sleeping together and Stoop had spoiled her rotten before pretending to move so he could date a new chick. Katrina was thrilled that he called and told Stoop to bring her the demo of their single right away. Katrina was even more thrilled when she heard the song. "Wow! This is hot Stoop Head, the DJ's are gonna love this!" She was right, the DJ's loved the song so much that they made copies to send to DJ's in other major cities that they knew. They even made personal copies to play the song in their cars. Within a couple of weeks, the 'Lab Rats' had a hit single being played on the radio all over the country.

Lil Man shared the news with his family and Katousha. They were all happy to see him happy, especially Katousha, who knew Lil Mans real mission behind making music. He finally decided to start apartment hunting with her. That weekend Stoop Head received a call from Katrina saying that a producer from New York wanted to meet with them. They were to meet him at the radio station at two o'clock that Saturday. "Let's go shopping, we may have to take pictures and I'm trying to be looking fresh." The three went out early Friday morning for haircuts and to buy new sneakers, jeans, shirts and jackets. Lil Man developed a habit of always matching a cap with his outfits and sneakers. A lot of fashion sense in the streets came from music videos, but Lil Man had his own style. His favorite rapper, Prodigy of Mobb Deep, had always worn whatever he wanted. Whether it matched or not, he'd just make it look good in a video. Lil Man had picked up Prodigy's sense of not caring what anybody thought about what you had on. He felt like, if you feel it then wear it. "Don't be a follower."

After shopping, the three went to get their cars washed. It was still a bit chilly out, but the weather was breaking and Spring would be rolling around soon. Bright colors would be worn on sunny days, and dark colors were for cooler days. But the 'Lab Rats' had decided to wear brights when going to the radio station whether if it was cold or not. They each spent almost three thousand dollars, and only had maybe three outfits each. Lil Man was just glad he had his own cash. Katousha would have had something to say about his spending, as if it was her cash or she put work in for it. Stoop and Rocky had bought shades to wear with their outfits. "Cousin, you should have grabbed some of these Gucci frames. They were only four hundred, on sale!" Four hundred dollars for some sun glasses? Lil Man didn't care if they were Gucci, or if they actually gave you some coochie, he was not paying four hundred to impress some hoochie. "I'll pass cuz, one of us has to show their eyes, to let them know we're serious. Who knows what we're about to get into."

For the first time in a while, it had seemed as if Lil Man was the elder of the trio. He was thinking level headedly and maturely, being serious about leaving drugs alone and pursuing a music career. Neither Lil Man nor his cousins knew much about the music business, but they were all eager about this first meeting and their ears would all be wide open. After they had gotten their wardrobes together, the three went out for lunch and then decided to take it easy for the rest of the day. "No partying tonight fella's. Even though it's Friday, we want to make sure we're on point for tomorrow. So no drinking and plenty of rest are on the menu for tonight. Chill out with one of your ladies or something." Lil Man didn't know if his cousins would listen, but he was showing where his head was with his responsible suggestions. He gave his cousins pounds and hugs, a pound being a handshake like gesture, and left to go and relax with Katousha for the rest of the day. He took her to a hotel suite.

"I know you might be a little nervous about your first music meeting tomorrow, everyone's nervous their first time doing something. Aren't you glad it isn't our first time doing this?" Katousha was getting freaky, unbuckling Lil Mans jeans while putting her tongue down his throat. She was being aggressive, making one move after another and not giving him any time to speak or respond. This was one of the things he liked about her so much, never having to say too much for sex. Most of the time she was horny and more ready than he was, and Lil Man satisfied her completely. They went at it for about a steady hour before Katousha passed out sweaty and worn out. Lil Man showered, and stayed up trying on different clothes and checking himself out in the full length mirror. He was getting ready for the meeting, feeling like a kid on the first day of school.

The next morning, everybody got up and moving around ten a.m. Lil Man took Katousha home and left to go meet up with his cousins. "Here, take the keys to the Mercury just in case you or your mom needs to go anywhere. Just don't let anyone else drive, I only trust you. We shouldn't be that long, and I'll call you once we're done ok?" Katousha had a pouty look on her face, hand on her hip and her lip poked out. With her head held low, Lil Man could tell she wanted to go with him. They reached a point where they wanted to be a part of each other's accomplishments and high lights, but Lil Man knew this was strictly a business situation. Not to mention having her there watching would probably only make him more nervous. Lil Man still had a certain shyness that hadn't been completely broken yet when it came to Katousha.

The 'Lab Rat's' met up at a diner on Roosevelt Boulevard in North East Philly for breakfast before going to the radio station. "So! Did everyone have enough pussy last night?" Stoop Head was feeling good about things obviously, and cracked jokes to spread the positivity on to Rocky and Lil Man. Rocky responded first. "Yes sir! I was poking and stroking until the booty started smoking!" The three started cracking up loud, attracting attention from nearly everyone in the diner. But they didn't care. All three of them were a bit nervous still, but was feeling really good. "Are you sure Rocky? I came downstairs to get me and my shorty something to drink and I could've sworn your ass was in the 'Lab' playing 'Madden'." They were all laughing, but Lil Man was quiet. He was thinking about where they were going, and how their lives could possibly change. Deep down he just had his fingers crossed for the best. They finished up their breakfast and got in their cars for the ride to the radio station.

On the way to the station, Lil Man tuned his radio to Power 99 FM, just to hear what was happening on the air and what was being played. Lil Man noticed the end of an announcement about a 'special guest' this afternoon. Lil Man was more excited than before, and while driving he wondered if Rocky and Stoop were listening up in the car ahead. Twenty minutes of driving and they were there, in the parking lot of the radio station. They were about a half an hour early, so Lil Man, Stoop Head and Rocky had one final time to adjust themselves before going in. "Suite 419 on the fourth floor fella's." They smoked cigarettes to kill time while checking themselves out in the reflections of their cars. Lil Man popped in some chewing gum and it was Showtime. They went in.

The radio station wasn't a very busy building, it was actually very quiet. "We have a two o'clock executive appointment." Stoop Head was speaking professionally, but the receptionist was so gorgeous that there were so many other things that he really wanted to say to her. He just smiled and left it at that. "Yes gentlemen, they are waiting for you upstairs in suite 419. Just make a left down that hall and the elevators are across from where you'll see the plants." "Thank you very much" Stoop head replied smiling. Once they had gotten upstairs, the entire floor had reminded them of a dental office. Carpet, plants, leather love seats and coffee tables with magazines about music were everywhere. The three sat down outside of suite 419 and waited. Lil Man chewed his gum nonchalantly while flipping through a magazine calmly, looking relaxed with one leg crossed in an 'L' shape over his knee. He looked natural, like he had done this all of the time.

Through the frosted glass door they could see a figure approaching, coming to let them in for their interview. Once the door opened, a tall and slender woman appeared. She resembled a young librarian, with a long skirt, ruffled blouse and rectangular shaped frames with the chain attached. She was holding a stack of folders in one arm while she held the door open with the other. "Right this way gentleman. My name is Diane Vander'perch. Have a seat and Mr. Combs will be in to see you shortly. In the meantime did you happen to bring any additional material to submit into your file?" As the receptionist spoke, the three were still in shock over hearing that a 'Mr. Combs' would be coming to meet with them. But Lil Man snapped out of it sharply. "No we didn't Diane, right now we just have what's playing on the radio but we're currently working on new hits." Lil Mans response was right on time, Sean Combs had overheard him speaking as he entered the meeting.

When Diddy walked in, the 'Lab Rats' suspicions were over and it was official. Their meeting had been called by the C.E.O of Bad Boy records. But Mr. Combs immediately displayed a no non-sense attitude as he sat at the head of the table where the interview was taking place. Once Diane left and shut the door he began as the three stood to greet Mr. Combs with handshakes. "Alright, you guys definitely have a hit on your hands, but I do not understand why there are three of you. I'm only interested in doing business with two of you at the most, the man responsible for the beat and the man behinds the lyrics, that's it! So if you're a group, know that I'll only be signing two of you. The other thing is you have to come up with a better name. Bad Boy only deals with the best, and there's no way in hell I'm signing cats to my label calling themselves rats. I don't care what it means or how you came up with it. Take care of those two underlying factors and we can do business. This is my card. It has myself and Mrs. Vander'perche's numbers on it. Call her when you're ready, and not a moment before. Do not call me! She will explain all the details of the deal to you once you're ready. I'm looking to hear from you within seventy two hours. Thank you gentlemen, and enjoy the rest of your day."

Diddy stood up extending his hand for a final shake, indicating that the meeting was over. One by one the three shook his hand and exited the room, and next the building without getting more than a word or two in with Puffy. Of course, there were dozens of things running through all their minds, but Lil Man felt the best about the meeting. Diddy said that he liked his beat. But the problem would be playing the elimination game. The three had gotten back downstairs and outside to their cars before anyone openly spoke about what just happened. "That didn't go so well" Rocky spoke first. Rocky knew he really hadn't contributed much to the song. He wasn't really into music that much, and didn't really have an ear for making beats or rhymes. "Well, I think it went extremely well" Lil Man spoke next. "Once we come up with a new name, we basically have a new record deal coming our way, and we heard that from Bad Boy himself. The rest is easy. Whoever is not signed will do security, so no matter what happens, we can work and stick together!"

What Lil Man said put both of his cousins at ease, especially Stoop Head. Stoop thought he'd have to be the bearer of breaking some bad news to somebody. But Lil Mans quick thinking solution was perfect. Lil Man was good at keeping the peace. There was no way Stoop wasn't going to be signed, he had written his own raps on top of buying the equipment. And Lil Man did the majority of the work on the beats. "You both know one of us has to keep holding the block down anyway right?" Rocky was still seeing the big picture as him not being in the group, but the truth was, he had rather sell drugs anyway. It was what he was good at, what he was used to. And the way things were going Rocky saw no need for a change, his maturity kicked in by encouraging his brother and cousin to come up with a great name for their group and to do music.

They got into their cars and headed back towards home. Lil Man was glad he had some good news to share with his girl.

WHAT A WOMAN WANTS

Lil Man and his cousins had pretty much decided who was going to do music, and who would keep the 'Candy' shop running. All they had to do now was come up with a new name for the group and report back to Diddy's receptionist. Lil Man rode by Katousha's house to share the news, but his other car wasn't there. He figured she was just out shopping with her mom, so he decided to just surprise her later and drove home. When Lil Man had gotten home, his house was empty to. He decided to call Katousha's cell phone. "Hey babe, I'm done with the interview. It went great!" He could tell Katousha was driving so he didn't want to keep her on the phone. "I'm glad to hear that babe! Guess who I'm with? Your mom and grand mom, we went food and shoe shopping. We're on our way to your house now." "Cool, see you when you get here babe." Lil Man had two things on his mind now, the record deal and how the hell his girl wound up shopping with his mother and grandmother?

'Oh well' he thought. Maybe it was a good thing. Lil Man didn't bring Katousha around his family too much, even though they were going on two years of being together. She had come with them when they visited him while being locked up, and there was no telling what type of bond or alliance they formed without him around. Lil Man's main reason for keeping his girl away from people is because he felt Katousha could be too naïve sometimes, believing almost anything she heard. He felt she wasn't properly tamed or 'schooled' enough to roam free around his people yet. Not without knowing some of the bullshit they were into, mainly gossip and bogus stories about him from when he was smaller, plus their drinking. Katousha's family weren't drinkers, so he felt she would never relate to his family.

Lil Man had no idea how wrong he was. When Katousha returned with his family, he saw that they had a real good time. She was full of positive energy, laughter and smiles. Lil Man wondered if she'd been drinking with his mom, or if she had snuck a little of grandpa's special extra strength cough syrup. Whatever it was, she was in a great mood. "Baby, I found the most awesome shoes and boots! You're mom took me to Germantown, and there were woman's shoe store's I never knew existed. Why haven't we been going there? Do you hide me from your old neighborhood for a reason?" Ok, things were back to normal. Katousha had confirmed why Lil Man never left her alone with his family. She'd see and hear new things that she didn't understand, and he was always left to deal with her suspicions and the burden of explaining.

"I never thought you would feel like riding all the way up there babe. It's not like Germantown Avenue is around the corner. That's almost a forty minute ride for some shoes babe. But as long as you're happy it's fine with me. By the way, I have some news you can all discuss for your girl talks. I met Puff Daddy today, and he wants to sign me and Stoop Head to Bad Boy Records!" Everyone in the room became quiet and stopped and looked at Lil Man when he made that announcement. They were mostly checking to see how serious he was. When they saw that he never gestured that he was joking, they began congratulating him. "That's wonderful baby! I knew you could do it!" Katousha was the most excited, while Lil Man's family was still in disbelief. "Seeing is believing" his mother shouted over to them.

Lil Man never received much support or encouragement from his family. They were always too wrapped up into their own problems, to the point where they didn't have any real positive or guiding advice to give him. He was basically on his own out in the world, like a lion's cub that went astray from the pack and had to survive and eat. "Baby, let's get out of here. I want to celebrate and I'm not letting anybody steal my joy." Katousha said goodbye to everyone and gathered her bags, heading towards Lil Man's car. Lil Man sort of just stormed out saying nothing, even slamming the door shut behind him.

"It's really time to get our own place babe, I'm not sure how much more of their shit my ears can take." Lil Man using the word shit was equivalent to Katousha using his whole first name. Not only did he sound serious, but he really was. Lil Man always had trouble communicating with his family. No matter what he brought to their attention, they always made room for doubt and disbelief. It became overwhelming on top of frustrating. "Let's just go and get something to eat, or do you want to go to the movies? Better yet, let's just do both. I don't even care anymore. Let's just enjoy each other." Sometimes Katousha was the only person Lil Man enjoyed talking to, she listened to him, and she always knew what to say to put him back at ease. He enjoyed talking to his cousin Stoop to. Stoop Head could relate to Lil Man's situation at home, his mother was the same way. And why wouldn't she be? His mother and Lil Man's mother were sisters.

"We have until Tuesday to come up with a name for our group, then we have to call Puff's receptionist to go over the details and finalize the deal. If things sound right and go well, I'll be going into music full-time." Katousha was just happy that Lil Man had found something to do that he enjoyed, and that he was finally closer to getting away from the world of narcotics. "So do you have any ideas for new tracks?" "I have a few, but I actually have to get them started before I can see where they're going or how they'll turn out." Lil Man and Katousha loved talking about music together. It made them both sense that they really had something in common. Katousha was the type to listen to all kinds of music. She even had some country favorites by artists like Dolly Parton and Reba Mcentire. If you walked in and surprised Katousha, you could catch her singing "I'm A Survivor" by Reba.

"FO-Kissed! That's it! I've got the new name of the group!"While driving the idea came to Lil Man out of the clear blue sky and he shouted and startled his girl. "We'll name it focused, like the word and with the same meaning' only spelled differently with a kiss." Katousha became intrigued whenever she saw Lil Man brainstorming. The way he thought kept her turned on. Whenever they were alone, she'd be in her panties most of the time . . . or they'd be on the floor somewhere. "That sounds great babe! How would you spell it?" Lil Man didn't mind sharing his ideas with Katousha, she always had honest and positive feedback for him. "F O, K I S S E D. AAhhhh, I know you like that momma!" Lil Man was smiling brightly and was proud of himself for coming up with the name. "I'll call Stoop after we eat and see if he likes it. Whatever name we came up with, he said he'd get tee shirts and sweat shirts printed with the names emblem on them."

After Lil Man and Katousha left Red Lobster where they had dinner, Lil Man called Stoop Head from the parking lot while smoking a cigarette. "Yo! I got the name for the group cuz! 'Fokissed'! Me and my girl headed to the movies, and afterwards I'll come by and break it down for you." Lil Man was excited to tell Stoop the new name, and by the tone of his voice over the phone Stoop sounded like he loved it to. Lil Man knew he'd love it even more once he saw how it would be spelled. "Give me some ideas babe, I want you to be involved as much as possible. You know, be the woman behind the 'great man'." Katousha was smiling and laughing, she felt good about Lil Man accepting and respecting her opinions about something that was so important to him. Lil Man figured that that was what a woman mostly wants, attention and respect. As long as a woman felt respected and paid attention to, she'd be happy. Lil Man was an ace at convincing people. The only ones he had trouble with were the ones in his house, and he was determined to change that very soon.

"So, since you're the queen behind the operation, have you had any ideas about where you want to reside? Wherever it is, we'll have his and her thrones in our castle!" Lil Man referring to Katousha as his queen made her feel special, and referring to his and her bathrooms as 'thrones' made her giggle. He had a sharp sense of humor, and kept his lady feeling good with a smile on her face. The two oversized 'Bahama Mamas' from Red Lobster helped out a great deal as well. "I was thinking maybe Mt. Airy, or maybe the North East. Somewhere nice that's not too far. I don't think I'm ready to move out of Philly just yet." Lil Man was just happy that he had her on board with him, Katousha was an understanding partner.

Lil Man and Katousha went in to see "Bruce Almighty." Jim Carey had been one of Lil Mans favorite comedians and actors, and knew seeing a new movie from him would put Katousha in high spirits. He was secretly setting up the cherry on top for the evening. When the movie was over, crowds of people had come out of the theatre buzzing, laughing and talking about scenes from the movie. Katousha couldn't stop giggling, especially since Lil Man had snuck a bottle of Banana Red 20/20 into the movie. The bottle was sort of flat and was perfect for back pockets or purses. Katousha had been drinking throughout the entire film with a cup of ice. Lil Man decided not to go over to see Stoop and Rocky after all, since the movie theatre was only about five blocks away from the Radisson hotel. They went there instead. Lil Man pulled in front of the hotel's lobby, and went in to book his suite. He came back and gave Katousha the key and room number and sent her upstairs alone. He wanted to smoke some weed while she had showered and got ready for him.

"Ok baby, I'll wait upstairs . . . Love you!!" Katousha was inebriated! But she was so sexy with it, hair and nails flawless. And the dress she had worn to match Lil Mans colors fit her like a tight leather glove, with black leather thigh-high boots to go with it. She didn't normally dress like that, but with all the good news Lil Man hit her with, she felt sexy and wanted to surprise him at the end of the night anyway, so his decision to go to the hotel instead of the 'Lab' turned out to be a perfect one. Lil Man smoked the joint he rolled and then went upstairs to meet his lady. When he walked into the room, she was sitting in a lazy boy chair with her legs crossed. She was still sprinkled wet from her shower and had put her boots back on for a sexy touch. All she had on were a towel, the boots and some lip gloss. Her panties were on the bed in plain view, indicating to Lil Man to 'come and get it'.

They went at it all night! Katousha was so sexy and her body was so beautiful, that Lil Man's soldier stood at constant attention. Not only that, but he took it slow on Katousha, exploring her body in different areas and discovering new pleasures. His aim was making love, as opposed to just stroking and poking. He had started slowly at her neck, kissing and gently pecking, working his way down to her belly button and beyond. Katousha was squealing uncontrollably. She could hardly catch her breath from the sensations and tingles that shot through her body. Their sex was so incredible that they both had yelled out their own names! By the time they were done, Katousha and Lil Man were almost virtually inseparable. In spirit anyway, of course they still had their own lives to live. But they were both sure that they wanted to spend their lives with each other. They had reached a higher level of intimacy.

The next morning, Lil Man was up just an hour before check out time. Katousha was still out cold, grinning and smiling in her sleep when the sun ran across her face, as if to be having dreams and flashbacks of the night before. Lil Man showered quickly, and decided to wake his lady up once he had gotten out of the shower and dressed. "Good morning babe, it's time to go. Where would you like to go for breakfast?" Katousha woke up smiling. She felt worn out from the night before, but it was a pleasant soreness caused by the guy she loved. "You pick the place baby, I'm having whatever you decide." Lil Man had to spring it on her while the mood was still a good one. "I have to meet up with my cousin's babe. I was supposed to last night, but decided to roll with my baby instead. But once I'm done with them I'm all yours ok?" Katousha didn't mind at all, she was in a state of pure bliss. "That's fine boo, just call me or stop by. It's your choice. She showered and they both finished getting dressed and left for checkout. After breakfast at I.H.O.P, Lil Man drove Katousha to his other car and gave her the keys. "Mwah! See you later baby! Call me!" They kissed and departed for the time being.

Lil Man sat there in his car for a moment, watching Katousha closely as she pulled off in the Mercury. He had hundreds of things running through his mind about everything that was going on. 'Does she really love me the way she says she does?' he wondered. 'Damn! We just had a meeting with Puff Daddy!' he reminded his self. 'I have enough to get my own apartment and keep up with the rent, or I just may be able to afford a nice house.' Lil Man sat and assessed the situation. Reality kicked in, and suddenly he realized that he had a pretty good life, on top of a pretty and good girl who loved him. It was time to be independent. Lil Mans assessment proved that if you really wanted to, you could give a woman what she wants, without even spending a lot. Respect, attention and understanding were all the things a woman wanted.

HITCHED

Lil Man went to meet with Stoop Head and Rocky and leaving Katousha. "So what do you think about the name 'Fokissed' cousin?" Lil Man wanted to check Stoop's face for an honest opinion. He was prepared to hear the worst, but expected the best. But they all new the name was creative and fit the struggle perfectly. "It's perfect cuz! Now show me what you meant about how it's spelled." "It's easy man, F, O, kissed." Stoop Head's face lit up bright. "Wow! That's hot! Like a kiss to the Fo head!" Lil Man wrote down the unique spelling of the name. "I'm gonna get started on the marketing right away! We need tees, sweats and maybe some hats. We're definitely going to need some posters and flyers featuring the single for promotion. When are we gonna call Mrs. Google search?" Stoop Head was so excited that he forgot Diddy's receptionist's name. "Her name is Vander 'perch, and I'm going to call her right away."

Lil Man contacted the receptionist and informed her that they had settled who was going to be in the group. He also gave her the details of the group's name. Mrs. Vander 'perch sounded pleased on the other end of the phone and told Lil Man that she would be forwarding the information to Mr. Combs. She told Lil Man to expect a call back before the end of the week. After Lil Man hung up the phone, Rocky turned his music back up. He was playing

Jay Z's 'Dead Presidents' parts one and two. After that he then played 'Streets is Watching'. Lil Man was tuned in to the beats of the song. "I wonder how much Jay Z pays for his beats." The three looked at each other shrugging their shoulders and shaking their heads. "Who knows? But when he raps on a track it sounds good, and he gets paid! Instead of worrying about him, we need to be doing just that! It's time for another hit!" Stoop Head and Lil Man were on the same page, and Lil Man spent a couple hours working on a new track.

Rocky was sitting on the couch flipping through tracks on the stereo and playing the Play Station. "I'm playing 'Siphon Filter'. I should get a lot of shooting practice since I'm gonna be security for you guys." His comment sounded a bit frustrated, but Rocky really couldn't complain. He was still hustling and making money, while Stoop Head and Lil Man had been working on music and hadn't made any money yet. They were still in the dark about how musicians get paid from record labels. "Man, cut that shit out! Don't start whining like a damn baby!" Stoop Head was putting his younger brother in check. "We have to think like business men. There's no room for pouting, crying and certainly not jealousy. We're still a team! This is team Fokissed, right Lil Man?" Lil Man hadn't heard a word, he was at the computer and track board, sampling different sounds with head phones on.

While Lil Man worked on the beat, the two brothers argued back and forth. "What the hell do we need him for anyway? We were doing just fine by ourselves Stoop! Damn, you always gotta change things man! Next thing you know we'll be locked up somewhere!!" Rocky was finally speaking his mind about how he really felt about Lil Man being around. He was jealous. And the more he spoke, the louder he became. "What's wrong with you man? That's family you're talking about! Not some damn stranger from the street. Don't let me hear you talking like that again about OUR little cousin!" Rocky was mad as hell, but he knew he had to calm down. He couldn't beat his brother fighting, and there was no way he would pick up a gun to him. Rocky really had to just let it go, and think about the situation. He needed to evaluate why he was so upset with Lil Man.

Lil Man took off his headset to ask the guy's how his beat sounded so far, but when he turned around he saw nothing but red faces and wrinkled brows with arched and squinted eyes. He sensed that he just missed something. There was tension in the 'Lab'. "What's wrong y'all?" After searching their facial expressions, Lil Man knew that his cousins were both upset. He just didn't know what it was about. "It's nothing man, we good. I need some fresh air though. I'm going for a drive. You can take the laptop home with you and finish up the beat ok cousin?" Lil Man saved his work, shut the program down and wrapped the computer up to take it home. He gave the cousins 'pounds and hugs' and left for home. "Take it easy fella's. And be sure to listen out for Vander 'perches phone call. She has all of our numbers."

It was only around three in the afternoon, a little late to be apartment hunting and too early to go in and lounge around. Lil Man just stopped and bought a newspaper and 'The Apartment Hunter', a magazine featuring local apartments for rent with prices and availability. He decided to get back with Katousha and see if she felt like going through the apartments together. He called her cellphone. "Hey babe, I'm done over at my cousins. I was trying to see if you wanted to look at some apartments." "Sure, ok.

Where are you? You're not too far I hope, I'm missing you!" "Not far at all babes, I'll be right there." Lil Man had only wanted to stop by Katousha's house so that they could look through the apartment material together. But Katousha had something bigger, much bigger in mind for him.

When he pulled into her driveway behind the house, Lil Man noticed Katousha watching him from the kitchen window, smiling. She went down to the basement to let him in. "Hey, that was quick. You must've been right around the corner." Lil Man had arrived at Katousha's house just fifteen minutes after hanging up with her. "Well, you know how it is, when it comes to my baby I'm there in a flash." The two sat down on the love seat and Lil Man opened up the newspaper to the classified section to see if there were any apartments for rent. Katousha started flipping through the 'apartment hunter'.

"Oh my God Rahim!! Look at these apartments! They're gorgeous! They even have a heart shaped pool." Katousha was referring to a new 'gated community' just built in Audubon, Pennsylvania. The apartments were designed for engaged couples who were either rich or just had really great jobs and could afford the fourteen hundred dollar a month rent. Lil Man was impressed, but wasn't sure if he'd be willing to pay that much, especially if they would be almost an hour away from Philadelphia. "Ok, that's one we can definitely consider. But let's look at some more." Lil Man had put his eye on a Korman Suites Community. The apartments there were lavishly designed as well as affordable. There weren't any swimming facilities, but there was an indoor gym and the landscaping was beautiful. He showed it to Katousha.

"How about these babe?" After Katousha read the profile on 'Korman Suites', Lil Man pulled them up on the internet so that they could see some better pictures of the place. They had two main areas in Philadelphia, one in South West Philly, and the other near Cheltenham Avenue near West Oak Lane. Katousha looked at the pictures on-line. "Yeah! I like these! But do you think they'll be enough room for ALL of us?" Lil Man had sensed right away that Katousha was hinting toward something, but before making any assumptions he'd thought it would be better to just ask. "What do you mean ALL of us babe? It's just me and you." Katousha jumped up and headed back towards the kitchen. "Would you like something cold to drink?" She took out two glasses and prepared them with ice.

"No, I don't want a drink Toosh. I want you to tell me what you meant." She poured fruit punch into the two glasses and came back and sat next to Lil Man. "Baby, I'm a little confused and worried right now. I mean, I'm sure that I love you. But I'm not sure how you'd feel about any new additions to our club." She didn't have to say another word. It had struck Lil Man immediately. Katousha was pregnant, and she had felt guilty because she had known for over two months and hadn't said a peep to anyone about it. "Babe, you could have told me. We had options to explore and decisions to make together. You cannot keep things like this from me." "I'm sorry Rahim, I was scared. I didn't know how you'd feel. We were having so much fun with it being just us. I didn't want you to think of it as a burden. I'm sorry."

Lil Man was silent for a couple of moments, taking deep breaths and letting reality set in. He turned back to Katousha, holding both her hands as he looked directly into her eyes. "Katousha, you don't have to be scared. I love you to! And I'm happy about this. I know we'll have a beautiful baby. But for something this important, you have to promise not to hide things. Ok? Now, are you absolutely sure you're pregnant?" Katousha was teary eyed, trying to keep from whimpering and nodded her head 'yes'. "Ok, so all we have to do is take care of our baby." Lil Man said that while smiling, and it made Katousha feel a lot better.

"It's just my parents though Rahim. They are stuck in their beliefs. They will never accept me having a child unless we are married." Wow! This was all a bit much, but Lil Man always kept a cool head. In fact, there was no way he'd get upset with Katousha. She had become his best and perhaps his only friend in the world. Even though his cousins had shown him love, he still didn't quite trust them fully. He still hadn't figured out why Stoop was being so generous with his money, and helping Lil Man get to the level he was on. "It's ok. We can get married! But this isn't my formal proposal ok?" Lil Man and Katousha hugged and squeezed each other tightly right there on the couch. They were having a baby, and talked for the first time about marriage.

Just as Lil Man and Katousha were releasing from their hug, her parents had walked in. All they saw was him backing off from her and her face wet full of tears. Not a good look. "What the hell is going on in here!?" her father barked. "Good afternoon sir, ma'am. Katousha and I were just having a deep discussion that's all. She had become a little emotional during our talk." Without giving too many details, Lil Man had told the truth, but Katousha's parents naturally had to make sure. "What's going on Toosha!?" her father growled again. "It's just like he said dad, we were talking about something sensitive to me that's all." Lil Man had taken Katousha by the hand, "Maybe I should be going babe, but I'll be keeping those two places in mind. Ok?" Katousha walked Lil Man out to his car. "They don't believe us, they always think the worst. My dad is very overprotective of me." Lil Man started up the car and rolled the window down. "I understand, just try not to give anything away until we decide what we're going to do. I love you baby, and I'll be calling you tonight."

Lil Mans plate was quite full. Working on music for Bad Boy, selecting an apartment to move to and his girl was having a baby. He definitely needed some rest and a little time to sort everything out. But the best way to clear his head he decided was by working on the music and making more beats for Stoop Head to rap to. He sat up in his room at his desk on the lap top for hours, going over sound effects and playing around with different concepts for the next hit. After a while, he took a break and tried calling Katousha, but she didn't answer. This was highly strange he thought, especially since it was eleven at night and Katousha always answered her phone for Lil Man.

He started to worry, and had called her another five times before he stopped and just went to sleep. Lil Man tossed and turned wondering what was wrong. He tried not to think of her out with another guy, but naturally those thoughts haunt guys about the woman they love. He kicked that thought to the curb. There had to be some other reasonable explanation. The next morning when Lil Man woke up, he tried calling her again. No answer. 'What the hell is going on with that girl" he thought out loud. He did everything he could to keep from jumping to conclusions. But after he ate some breakfast, he couldn't help but to go and see what the problem was.

Lil Man drove to Katousha's house. He parked around the corner so his obvious Acura wouldn't have given him away. With his car out of sight, he walked around to the back of the house where Katousha's room was. He called up to her window, "Babe! It's me, Lil Man!" He noticed the curtains scrambling in a hurry and finally they opened, along with the window and she stuck her head out explaining immediately. "Rahim! My dad took my phone and said we can't see each other anymore! I gotta get out of here, I was waiting for you!" She threw two packed bags out of the window. "I'll be down in five minutes!" Lil Man was relieved that his woman had still been faithful, but was very disturbed that her parents were working against them now. With two families that weren't supportive now, Lil Man and Katousha moved into the already newly furnished Korman Suite apartment in South West Philadelphia. They weren't too far from the expressway, but no one knew where they were living and Lil Man intended to keep it that way.

After settling into the apartment and breaking it in for about a week, Lil Man suggested that they take a trip to Las Vegas and get married. Vegas had an abundance of wedding chapels that were open twenty four hours a day. They chose a chapel near the McCarran International Airport called 'The Little Church of The West' that had one hundred dollar marriage license specials. After checking out the chapel, Lil Man and Katousha went shopping for her wedding gown and his Tuxedo. They decided to hire a photographer who made a sharp video of their wedding and took awesome professional pictures. They broke the news to their families by sending the video copies and picture's back home in the mail. "I know you wanted things to be much different babe, but we just didn't have anyone's support. Sometimes when you want something bad enough in this world, you have to go out and take it!" And that's exactly what they did, taking each other by the hand in marriage.

The day before their wedding, Lil man had gotten a call from Stoop Head. Stoop said that they had to go to Manhattan, New York to sign their contract at Bad Boy records and to receive their first advance checks for their first single. He mentioned that the contract consisted of producing at least ten more hit songs for distribution in a two month time span. "You think we can swing that cousin? Diddy ain't playing any games, and the songs have to be hot!" Lil Man was confident that they could meet that dead line with no problem. "Yea! We got this Stoop! How much is our advance?" Lil Man was curious to know just how much his music was worth to a major label with his cousin rapping over the beat. "We're getting fifteen thousand a piece, but once we sign and receive payment, the song no longer belongs to us. Bad Boy will own its rights."That was fine with Lil Man, fifteen thousand dollars for smoking blunts and mixing sounds on a computer? They can have the constitution and the rights!

Lil man had his wife, wow! He was still getting used to the fact that he was married. He had money, and would soon be having a child. He was happy, and life was feeling good. In the video's and pictures Katousha sent back home, she also wrote her mother a letter to share with her father. She told the truth about being pregnant, and decided that her parents just had to swallow it all and trust that she would be a responsible woman. Besides, what could they say? She and Lil Man were now twenty one and legally married. And he was certainly in a position to take care of her and their new child.

LIFE IS GOOD

Lil Man and Katousha had flown back to Pennsylvania so that he could get ready for the trip to New York. "You know if money ever gets tight, which it probably will, we can always grind a little bit. Maybe take a couple rides out to Connecticut. We are getting used to being on the road now." Lil Man knew he didn't ever want to hustle again, but he was just reassuring Katousha that they would be ok. "I know you don't mean that Rahim, you are finally away from that lifestyle, and I'm happier than ever now that we're married. I just want to have our baby so we can start raising him." Katousha instinctively said 'him', hinting towards her wanting the baby to be a boy.

"Did you just say 'him'? Did you take one of those Pepsi smears or a mammoth graham to find out what we're having?" Katousha laughed so hard that she caught a bad case of cramps in the side of her belly. "It's called a pap-smear and a mammogram, and neither tells us what we're having Lil Man. You're thinking of an ultra sound silly." Lil Man loved making his girl laugh, but didn't mean to cause her any pain. He tried to keep his jokes to a minimum. "Why I gotta be all that?" The main reason Katousha wanted to have a boy, is so that the child would bear the traits of his father. She knew that Lil Man was intelligent and handsome. She daydreamed all of the time about what the child would look like. She could not wait to give birth.

Lil Man had made three more tracks that were album worthy, and he was eager to let Stoop Head hear them so that he could begin writing and rhyming to the new beats. "Wow cousin! I think you just made us rich with this one!" The first beat Lil Man let Stoop hear had a classical melody, sort of like Frank Sinatra meeting Run DMC. The beat was awesome! And Stoop Head had started rhyming to it immediately. "Uh, ya boy just wrote another song. I have no time to write every wrong. I just have time to get ya chick out her thongs. Watch me blow weed smoke from the bong, their gonna play this one from here to Hong Kong. She suki on the pipe cause it's long." Stoop Head's lyrics had gotten explicit at times, but most Hip Hop and Rock and Roll music was. Lil Man just made sure to do his job, and that was to make awesome and catchy beats that the world never heard before.

The three had discussed going to New York. They were to come to the Bad Boy office in Manhattan to sign and finalize their contract, and also submit any new material they had finished toward their upcoming album. Lil Man and Stoop Head had completed three additional songs that sounded great. They released one of the new songs to the radio stations, generating and building a buzz for the upcoming album. Lil Man and Stoop Head were having the time of their lives. Rocky said that he would stay back and hold the block down while his brother and Lil Man went to Manhattan. After meeting with the staff there and receiving their checks, Stoop and Lil Man chose to stay in New York for an extra day to see what type of clothing stores they had.

"They have some of the best shopping in the world here cuz, they even have a 'Wu-Wear' store. 'Wu-Wear' was a song and a clothing label originated and created by Wu-Tang Clan's 'RZA'. "I always wanted some 'Wu-Wear' stuff cousin, we have to find that store!" They bought all sorts of jeans, sweat suits, sweat shirts, sneakers, boots, fitted caps and any other clothing good enough to be worn in a music video or out in a club. They were sure to get Rocky some gear to, his brother knew all his sizes. Stoop Head was feeling good, and showed it on i-95 heading back to Philadelphia. "We're going out cuz!! The clubs are gonna love us tonight baby!" Stoop called his brother and told him to get ready, that the three would be club hopping tonight. Stoop had made one more stop to a jewelry store.

"You see anything you like Lil Man?" Stoop had given Lil Man the generous vibe again, stating that anything he had chosen would be on him. Lil Man wanted to cease the moment right away, but this time he would have some questions. "They have some really nice pieces in here cousin, but why? Why are you doing this for me?" Stoop Head had made a remark similar to the one he had made when purchasing Lil Man's Acura. "We got it, so we have to spend it. Tomorrow isn't promised, and we cannot take this money to our graves with us cuz. Just enjoy it while we can." Stoop Head had spoken as if he expected the world to end soon. His generosity, even along with his explanation had made Lil Man suspicious again. Even though they were family and Lil Man had put in some work, Lil Man still had doubts that anyone would be this generous with this much money. Lil Man even had thoughts that Stoop was sleeping with Katousha, but then he realized that they had never even met before. 'Why is he spending so much bread on me!?' he thought.

"This thing right here is beautiful!" Lil Man was referring to a twenty six inch platinum Cuban link chain, with a platinum medallion attached. The medallion was circular shaped and was molded to form and depict 'The Last Supper', a scene from the Bible where Jesus had prepared a final meal for He and his twelve apostles. The chain was gorgeous, and without even looking at the price or asking Stoop Head simply said "wrap that up please." The short Italian woman who ran the family jewelry store carefully polished and wrapped up Lil Mans chain for him. Stoop Head also purchased a new watch for himself, a black Movado with a huge rock in it at twelve o'clock. Even though Stoop had acted like it didn't matter, Lil Man was paying close attention to the final total of the sale. The two items came up to fifty seven hundred forty dollars.

Lil man kept trying to remind himself that his cousin was rich, but just couldn't help thinking that there was another motive behind all the spending and frivolous splurging. Stoop always had positives quotes that he would blurt out like "If you look good, you'll feel good." And "Money doesn't bring happiness, but happiness can bring money." While Lil Man tried to understand his older cousin's logic, he had his own life to focus on. But he still showed a lot of appreciation towards his cousin for the acts of kindness and kept working hard on music together with him. They were now in a legally binding contract with Bad Boy Records.

Lil Man had arrived back to his apartment. He had planned to consult Katousha about going out for drinks to celebrate the contract signing, but there were no signs of her when he first walked in. He then noticed gurgling sounds coming from the bathroom. Katousha was on the bathroom floor, hugging the toilet seat and throwing up. Ever since he had learned that Katousha was pregnant, Lil Man had been looking up information to find out how to deal with nausea, and stomach cramping. He ran to their kitchen and got Katousha some salt free crackers and some cold ginger ale. He sat the crackers and ginger ale down on the coffee table and proceeded to join Katousha on the bathroom floor, gently rubbing her back and trying to comfort her. "I got you some crackers and ginger ale waiting babe, come and try it and see if it helps." Lil Man learned from experience that the term 'morning sickness' was a figure of speech. A pregnant woman could become nauseated any time of day, and anything could trigger it from images on TV to smells and odors or scents in the air.

Lil Man knew that he wouldn't be going out to celebrate now. Seeing Katousha in this condition wouldn't allow it. He wouldn't have been able to enjoy himself knowing she could be at home curled up on the bathroom floor hugging the toilet. He called Stoop Head to cancel the evening, and heard something he didn't expect on the other end of the line. "Its cool cousin, I was about to call you anyway. I'm heading to the emergency room, I'm not feeling well at all. I'll give you a call back later and let you know what's going on." That was a little strange but convenient to Lil Man all at the same time. But he had noticed something very wrong in Stoops voice. Stoop had sounded short of breath, and he was coughing and hacking over the phone. He really sounded terrible all of a sudden when he was just fine riding back from New York.

Katousha had calmed down from her throwing up spell and began eating the crackers and drinking the ginger ale. Within a few moments, she was all the way back to normal. "I never knew it would feel like this, but I'm still happy to be carrying your baby Rahim." He was glad she had said that, because Lil Man felt like Katousha would start blaming him for getting her pregnant and begin lashing out at him because she felt so badly. "Just take it easy babe, I was going out to celebrate the deal we just signed, but I changed my mind. We can just chill here. Better yet, you can help me with some beats." Lil Man was getting Katousha involved so he wouldn't be just sitting at the computer tuning her out.

After Katousha saw how a beat was made, she wanted to try and make one on her own. She played with the beat for about an hour. When she was done, her beat sounded great! It sounded just as good as Lil Man's, if not better. "Damn girl! That's hot! My baby has talent! Our baby gonna come out of you dancing!" Katousha's beat had sampled Minnie Ripperton's "Loving you" song and had cuts that Katousha threw in from the Super Mario Bros. 3 video game. Her first beat sounded like she had been a producer for years.

"Damn babe! You got me ready to write rhymes to your beat, just like Stoop be writing to mines." And that's exactly what Lil Man did. He wrote a song to Katousha's track, helped her to sharpen it up and in an hour the song was done. "This has to get put out, we're with Bad Boy now and I know people gonna love this one!!" Katousha found a new way to conquer 'morning sickness'. She became a self-made producer. Lil Man was practicing his rhyme to his girls track. "I just came to rep my city, and I pity the fool who not tryna rep it with me. I'm not Mr. T, I'm Mr. Mackabitch one half of Fokissed. We'll show you how to come snatch a bitch. We stash cash underneath mattresses, but the weak things you do only fly if your actresses. Before you practice this analyze how whack you is." Lil Man had actually over wrote to the beat and had to leave out some great lines. They would just go to another song.

Fifteen thousand dollars for a hot track was equivalent to about one hundred seventy five thousand per album. With that much money being paid out, Lil Man decided he and Stoop could afford some bonus tracks to add to the album. "Making music is fun babe, but it's your thing. I'm still going to find a regular job. Maybe I could go to school and study law. Have you ever slept with your lawyer?" Lil Man couldn't believe it. This is the same girl who was just praying to the toilet and she's already horny again!? Wow! Life is good. Lil Man had read that when woman are pregnant, they can be easily aroused. Katousha was already aggressive sexually as it was, so now she was a triple threat. Lil Man's new favorite position had become 'doggy-style', to keep pressure off of his woman's belly and to avoid crushing his unborn seed.

He also started stroking her with the notion that if he kept her open, her actual labor would be easier. The GYN had said a woman would be ready if she dilated around three centimeters, and that it was ok to have sex to keep from tightening up. It was music to both Lil Man's and Katousha's ears. After hearing that news from the GYN, they had done it more and more often. Katousha was having so many orgasms, that sometimes she couldn't tell if it was her water breaking or not during sex. They tried to moderate, slowing down and being more careful in case it did actually break.

"We should start thinking of a name for the baby Rahim." Katousha was more and more excited about being a mother every day. She had already been shopping for baby furniture, bottles, pacifiers and anything minor enough that either a boy or girl could use. She wanted to get as much shopping out of the way as possible, so that her girlfriends would be forced to be original getting gifts for the baby shower. On top of that, Katousha had already begun decorating the baby's room. Within two weeks it had started looking like Pee Wee's Playhouse in there! Lil Man was just glad to see her happy. He was happy to, but in the back of his mind it seemed like Katousha may have been jumping the gun a little bit.

The next day, Lil Man had called Stoop Heads cell phone and Rocky had picked up. "Yo, wassup cousin? Yea, we still up here in this crazy ass hospital. Shit is crazy though, so I'm gonna leave it up to Stoop to tell you wassup." The way Rocky sounded over the phone, Lil Man could tell something was seriously wrong but he had no idea what it was. He decided to go and see him. When Lil Man got into the hospital and told the front desk his cousin's name, they had given him a visitor pass to get into the quarantined unit. 'That unit is usually for special patients who are staying' he thought. Staying meaning Stoop wouldn't be coming home any time soon. He took the elevator to the seventh floor, and made his way through the corridors to find Stoops room.

After turning down two long hallways, Lil Man finally saw Rocky standing outside of Stoops Heads room, leaning against the wall talking on his phone. They greeted each other with a pound and a hug. "What's up with Stoop Head cousin? Give me some type of heads up. I can't do the surprises right now." Rocky had lifted his head from talking on the phone to give Lil Man a response. Looking into his eyes, which were halfway hidden under Rocky's oversized fitted cap, he looked like he had just been crying only moments before. "I really don't want to say" he whispered to Lil Man in a low hospital voice. "It's best you hear it from him." Lil Man was starting to feel nervous. Rocky, as tough as nails as he was had been crying about something. About his brother. And now it was time for Lil Man to find out what was going on.

He went over to the water fountain and got a drink, trying to gather himself and prepare for whatever he was about to find out. He walked into Stoop Heads room and saw him. Lil Man was startled. Stoop didn't even look the same from the day before when they had driven back from New York. "Wassup cousin? What's good with you?" Stoop Head could hardly speak, but his face looked almost blank mixed with embarrassed features. "Hey Lil Man, you sure didn't waste any time. That's why you're my man! You are always reliable. I can always count on you." Stoop Head looked extra sickly, and it was scary to Lil Man seeing this overnight transformation. He didn't want to do anything but be straight forward, and find out why Stoop Head was in the hospital. "What's going on Stoop? Why are you here?" Stoop head sat up in his bed and adjusted himself the best he could. Watching him, Lil Man thought that even sitting up in bed had looked painful for Stoop Head. "My ride is over Lil Man, the doctor gave me six months to be on God's green earth. And I have to remain here just to make it that long. I fucked up, bad!" Stoop Head ended his sentences with a series of coughs. He tried to explain it to Lil Man without coming right out and just telling him. "I was on medication for a while, but I had gotten sick of taking that shit! (cough, cough) Real gangsta's don't need any damn medicine!"

Lil Man knew that he was sick, but still hadn't pin pointed exactly what was wrong with his oldest cousin Stoop Head. "About two years ago, I was diagnosed with HIV. The doctors prescribed me medication to suppress it. But what can I say? It finally beat me. That shit blew straight up to full blown AIDS! I'm outta here cuz." Lil Man could not believe his ears. Everything Stoop Head just told him sounded surreal, like a bad dream. Lil Man was waiting for Aston Kutcher to come out and tell him he'd gotten 'Punk'd'! But it wasn't a dream, or a reality show. It was all one hundred percent real.

"Damn cousin, I really don't know what to say! How long? I mean who? What were you . . . ?" Lil Man had begun to stutter. He couldn't figure out the right words to say to a man who was on his death bed. Someone he was close to. Someone he had worked with. Lil Man decided to just listen and let Stoop Head do the talking. He was pretty sure he had some requests, and he'd carry them out for him. "I gave Rocky and my mom mostly all my money, almost four million to split. I want you to keep the rest. It's a cool million and some change left over, but more importantly I want you to take the studio equipment. I already told my mom you were coming to the 'Lab' to get everything. She's also going to give you the keys to my Suburban. It's yours now cuz. Take care of it all, and more importantly take care of your body. All those girls, and not one condom. There's no telling how many chicks are heading to where I am right now."

Now Lil Man understood why Rocky had been crying. Hearing a loved one's dying wishes could drive you to tears. Just the very thought of not having that person around anymore was hurtful. The pain that humans fear the most was sitting right next to Lil Man, death. Lil Man wanted to pick his cousin up off of that bed and laugh it off. Like "come on man, stop playing!" But he couldn't. All he could do is just let Stoop know how he felt. "Is this why you were being so nice to me Stoop? Why you spent all that bread?" Lil Man figured it was time to get all the answers out now. "Of course lil cousin. I knew these days were coming, and as you can see I won't be taking anything to the grave with me. I just want y'all to make sure I look good in my box. Listen, there's probably going to be a lot of females at my funeral for me. All bad bitches! I hit all of them raw dog. So if you find one irresistible, make sure you wrap it up ok cousin?"

At that moment Lil Man had realized that he had been so secretive about getting married and moving with Katousha, that he never even told Stoop Head and Rocky. "I'm married Stoop, and my wife is going on three months pregnant." Stoop Head cracked a smile, trying to hold in his laugh because it would hurt. "I know cousin, my mom told us. She said you sent video's and pictures from Vegas. That was some smooth shit. Wow, I always wanted to be like my little cousin." When Stoop Head had said that, Lil Man felt himself about to break down. But he just kept talking to avoid the tears. "See? That's exactly why I had to get out of there! They talk too much. They think they have my best interest in mind, when actually they just be right on the verge of getting my ass locked the hell up! Moving out of my people's house was the best move I ever made man!"

"Yea, there's nothing like true independence. And living in America, we're in the best country for independence and true freedom . . . as long as we can stay out of jail! This really is the land of opportunity. You just have to be ambitious enough to take advantage." Lil Man and Stoop were having one of their deep and intellectual conversations. That was another reason Stoop liked having Lil Man around, they were relating on higher levels. Whenever Stoop Head tried talking to his brothers like this, he only got hot air for feedback. They weren't willing to let their minds elevate. It was easier to sell drugs and have sex than to actually think. "Now that I think about it Lil Man, you're the brother I never had, but don't let Rocky hear that shit. I'm not sure if he'll ever change. I just want you to live your life to the fullest. Stick to the music thing, and when you get a chance you can explain things on my behalf to the people at Bad Boy. And whatever you get your hands on, always remember it's not going to your grave with you."

Stoop Head was dropping jewel after jewel, words of wisdom in layman's terms. And Lil Man was surely taking it all in. He felt glad that he had worn a condom a few years back with Vernie and her girlfriends. That situation turned out to be more treacherous than he thought. But either way he loved Stoop Head. He was truly the big brother he never had. Seeing Stoop Head sickened on that bed when he had just been talking about clubbing made Lil Man realize how short life really could be. They wrapped up their conversation, and departed with a pound and a hug. Lil Man hugged Rocky in the hallway and told him to be strong before leaving the hospital.

Stoop Heads funeral was four months later, and not six. He actually managed to cut his time shorter by smoking and drinking whatever his brother could get into the hospital to him. He also refused a lot of his medication. It made him feel soft, weak, like he wasn't capable of surviving on his own. Stoop Heads attitude wouldn't allow him to feel dependent. He was after all a self-made millionaire. Lil Man looked at the situation in the strongest way he could . . . Life was good, but it could also be very bitter sweet. Lil Man placed his Platinum chain and medallion on Stoop Heads chest at the viewing, and kept an eye on his casket until it closed and was lowered into the ground. "Some things you can take with you cousin."

PICKING UP THE PIECES

Lil Man had waited until after the funeral to get back into music. For a while it hadn't even felt right to him, making beats that Stoop Head would usually be rhyming to. He couldn't get the images out of his mind from the days when Stoop had first brought him into the 'Lab'. Even though the drugs weren't the most positive thing to be involved in, Stoop Head had done his part in showing love and sharing his good fortune.

Lil Man called his aunt to see when it would be a good time to come and get the studio equipment. She had told him anytime was fine. When he had gotten over there, he went up on the porch and rung the bell instead of just going straight to the 'Lab'. It was just another circumstance reminding him that his cousin was gone. "Rahim, do you mind trying to talk some sense into Rocky? He's not handling things too well. He's been doing nothing but drinking bottle after bottle like he's trying to give himself alcohol poisoning. He comes in late at night, cussing and fussing. I'm an old woman now. I can't deal with that kind of thing anymore." Lil Man listened to his aunt, and ensured her that he would talk to Rocky.

Lil Man walked back into the kitchen to go through the door leading down to the 'Lab'. Walking down the steps, he had called out to his remaining cousin. "Rockayyyy! Yo Rock, you down here man?" There was no answer.

Lil Man called back up to his Aunt after checking out the room. "Rocky isn't here Aunt Betty!" "Alright Rahim don't worry about it." Lil Man had started disconnecting the wiring to the track board, amplifiers and speakers. (Click Clack) Lil Man had heard a gun cocking, and as he tried turning around he wound up placing his temple against the ice cold barrel of Rocky's Dessert Eagle handgun. "Man, just who in the fuck do you think you are!? Coming down here, taking my brothers shit. Going on trips that I was supposed to take. Riding around in your little pretty ass ride, that WE bought you! You got a lot of fucking nerve lil Man! You've got real balls of steel coming here after shedding those crocodile tears at the funeral."

Rocky was obviously drunk, and he was even a little delirious for having a gun to his cousin's head. Lil Man had to talk him down calmly. Rocky was talking like he was about to murder his own cousin. "What are you talking about Rock? Listen, I know what you're going through. The same two brothers you lost were my cousins. What you're doing right now is not part of the plan. You probably have Stoop flipping in his grave already." Lil Man turned and faced Rocky with the gun still in his face. He was making fierce eye contact with him now. "Think about what you're doing cousin, and put that gun away. Our family doesn't need any more pain, and we damn sure don't need any mistakes!"

Lil Man had touched a nerve, and Rocky slowly began lowering the gun. As soon as the opportunity was clear, Lil Man pushed the hand with the gun towards the wall and hit Rocky with a sharp right hand to his jaw, causing him to drop the gun. The gun fell to the couch and bounced to the floor, discharging a loud shot. Lil Man then stood over

Rocky, pulling him halfway up off of the ground by his collar. He then held him there in position delivering two more swift blows to his nose and mouth. Rocky fell back to the ground, slowly nodding off to sleep in a drunken daze. Leaving him lying there, Lil Man grabbed as much of the equipment as he could with two arms and proceeded upstairs to leave. His Aunt had left Stoop Heads truck keys on the table for him to take. Miraculously, she never heard any of the commotion. She had been in her upstairs bedroom with the door shut and the air conditioner on. Thank God for menopause and heat flashes. Lil Man put the things in the trunk and pulled away.

He drove to his apartment and unloaded the music equipment. Once he was done, he had asked Katousha if she felt like driving. She agreed, and drove Lil Man back to his Aunt's house to get the Suburban. When they followed each other leaving Lil Man's Aunt's house, they noticed Police coming in a hurry. They drove the cars home and went inside. "Damn they were slow! They were just responding to that shot I bet." Lil Man hadn't told Katousha what had happened yet. "Shot? What shot!? What the hell happened Rahim!? And what's with the blood all over your jeans and sneakers??" Lil Man had no idea he had blood on his clothes, but explained that he and Rocky had got into a scuffle after Rocky put a gun to his head. He told her the gun fell and went off when it hit the ground. "Rocky must've gotten hit when it went off, so he basically shot his self." When Lil Man explained what happened, Katousha had given him a weird eye as to say 'I don't fully believe you. Did you shoot your cousin?'

Lil Man had actually been the only one besides Stoop Head interested in building the team stronger. The situation between him and Rocky was one hundred percent self-defense. There was no way he'd even have a gun on him walking into his Aunt's house, but he realized now that that was a mistake. Lil Man still had his chrome and black three eighty hand guns. He urged Katousha to obtain her license to carry once she had their baby. The license was in the best interest of their family's safety. He had misdemeanors on his record, so he would be able to apply for his as well. You had to be safe living in Philadelphia.

Lil Man was doing all he could do to maintain steadily and pick up the pieces in his life. He and Katousha began visiting their families frequently, and tried to live as normal as possible behind all of the drama. That summer, Katousha had given birth to a baby boy. She and Lil Man had named him Mekhi, after her favorite actor Mekhi Phifer. Lil Man had gotten his mother to babysit, while he and Katousha caught a train to Manhattan to have another meeting at the record company. The meeting was initially scheduled to discuss the absence of Stoop Head, and to renegotiate a new deal concerning Lil Man's music.

The train ride from Philadelphia to New York was only about two and a half hours. Lil Man and Katousha thought it would be fun to ride in coach class. There would be more people and buzzing going on, and that made for a less boring ride. Their decision turned out to be a good one, because something funny definitely happened on the train. Right behind Lil Man and Katousha sat a very elderly couple. They were riding from Florida to New York and had to be in their seventies or eighties! The elderly woman was having a problem with her seat. When an attendant walked by, she reached for his attention. "Excuse me sir. Is there any way we can exchange seats? I seem to keep sliding out of my chair." Before the attendant could answer, the woman's husband interrupted. "Don't pay her any mind. She just has a very slippery butt!" Lil Man and Katousha were chuckling for the rest of the ride after hearing that one.

They shortly arrived in Times Square and caught a taxi to the record label's office. Katousha stayed in the offices' lavish lobby area and drank coffee, while Lil Man went into his meeting. "Hello Mr. Bowman, I'm Diane. We met before in Philadelphia. I wasn't sure if you'd remember, it was a little bit ago." The consultant had been talking like she hadn't seen Lil Man in years. It had only been a few months. "Yes Diane, I remember you very well!" She got right into it. "Ok great! Tell me, what's going on with your group 'Fokissed'? We hadn't heard from you in quite some time." Lil Man broke it down for her. He explained how he had been mourning a death, and that the death was of his partner in the group, Stoop Head. He explained how it was just him now, and that he'd been continuing to make music but that it was taking a little longer because now he was working alone.

"Ok, I see. Well I will notify Mr. Combs of the circumstances and let him know that you are continuing to work, just alone. You are under contract so you can just simply submit your new materials by uploading them via the company's web address ok? And Mr. Combs left this for you because he was feeling you guys' music so much." Diane had slid a yellow envelope to Lil Man. "Thank you very much Diane, I will be in touch very soon." Lil Man exited the meeting and got back on the elevator to go downstairs and meet Katousha. "Wow! That was fast! Is everything ok?" Katousha was prepared to sit for hours, but the meeting only lasted about twenty minutes at the most. "Yea, everything is fine. I just explained that the group is now a solo mission. She understood and gave me this. I'm still under contract with the label."

Now Katousha was being nosey. "So what's that in the envelope?" "I'm not even sure babe. It could be a letter bearing bad news for all I know. Let's find a place to sit down and eat, and we'll find out there ok?" "Whatever you say daddy" Katousha said smiling. She was horny again, and it showed whenever she made obvious verbal sexual advances towards Lil Man. Her horny code all boiled down to one message: "You better put it on me good tonight!" Lil Man was focused on music, and was glad he still had his job.

They caught another taxi cab, and asked the driver to take them to a good restaurant to eat. "Have you ever been to 'Justins' sir? 'Justins' is very good!" Lil Man had heard about Justins on the radio and read about it in magazines. It was a restaurant owned by Sean Combs himself, and was named after one of his son's. "That sounds great! Take us there!" Lil Man and Katousha went inside the restaurant.

They were both immediately impressed by the atmosphere of the establishment. They were even more impressed by the soft music that played, perfectly timed and was soothing for that point in the afternoon. They decided to sit at the bar and have a few drinks before being seated at a table. Katousha was star struck inside the restaurant. She had been panning from left to right, spotting random celebrities before Lil Man cut her off and brought it to her attention. "Baby, this is Diddy's restaurant. Stars eat here all the time. We have to act natural, like we belong here you know?" She understood exactly what Lil Man had meant, but still couldn't help herself from scanning the tables and spotting people she had only seen on TV or had read about. To keep things simple, Lil Man just ordered them both Filet Mignon with red wine. He didn't specify the year.

A few moments later, a waiter came to their table holding a bottle of wine. "Good afternoon sir! I present you with a bottle of 1972 Domaine Leroy Musigny, compliments of the house! Your meals will be up right away, and enjoy the wine sir!" The waiter had come out of nowhere with the wine. "1972? This shit is expensive! This bottle cost over a thousand dollars girl!! Did you order this before we got in here or something??" Lil Man was excited about the wine they received, but he did his best to whisper to Katousha and not cause a scene. There was a small note tied to the top of the bottle: 'Heard your new music, keep up the good work . . . Welcome to Bad Boy!! S.P.D.C.'

"Katousha, look. Read this note, Diddy sent this to us. It's a thank you and welcome to the team type of bottle!" The bottle was just one of the smaller perks of joining the record label. "Open your envelope Lil Man, I'm curious now!" Lil Man had to admit, he was curious about the contents of the envelope to. He opened it slowly and with suspense, to arouse Katousha. Once he pulled the contents of the envelope out, he saw that it was a check for forty thousand dollars. He pushed the check across the table in front of Katousha for her to see. "This must have been meant for me and Stoop to split. What do you think I should do with his half?" Katousha batted her eye lashes and looked away. "You and him had that discussion in the hospital Rahim. He told you to live your life to the fullest. So that's what you had better do. Your cousin showed us damn near overnight that tomorrow is never promised! But do what your heart tells you to do."

Talking with Katousha was just like talking to Stoop Head sometimes. She knew how to get deep and intellectual, just like Stoop Head used to do. The only difference was her squeaky babyish voice, and the fact that she was a female meant she added more sugar and spice to the jewels she dropped. Lil Man wondered if he was supposed to be generous to someone the way his cousin was generous to him. He hadn't received an expiration date, but he wanted to carry on Stoops legacy somehow. Even if it were only subliminal. But at the end of the day he had his own family now, a wife and a son. And Lil Man would be happy as long as they were happy.

Lil Man and Katousha finished up their dinner, paid and tipped the waiter and then hailed a taxi outside. With all the pretty and fancy cars they had seen parked outside of Justin's, Lil Man had kind of wished he had driven one of his own toys. They took the taxi back to grand central station, and caught another train to Philadelphia. "I wouldn't mind living in New York for a while, a few years maybe." Katousha was striking up conversation on the train since the ride back had been quieter than before. "Why only for just a little while babe?" Lil Man asked. "Because I know it would wind up being one of those places I'd get tired of, like Philly. Don't get me wrong, I love where we're from. But when you visit other places, the people seem nicer . . . Especially in the south! Plus Philly has become too violent. You can't watch the weather without hearing about a shooting first. It gives me a headache, and I definitely don't want Mekhi in a public Philly school. It'll make him an animal, just like it did to us."

Katousha had just voiced everything Lil Man had already been thinking. Now that he knew they were on the same page, it would be easier to relocate. He had enough to buy a house in some of the nicest places in the U.S. He even thought about having a home built off of his own design. But he thought he'd better keep grinding the music out first. Baby Mekhi was another mouth to feed and body to clothe, and he'd probably be growing fast! When they arrived back home, Lil Man and Katousha focused on music together. It felt good to Lil Man knowing that he and his lady shared the same similar musical tastes and interests. When they put their heads together in creating beats, the outcomes were magnificent!

Katousha had made a track sampling 'Hush Hush Tip', an old school song by female rapper N-Tyce. When Lil Man added some finishing touches to it, they had their hands on another hit ready to be uploaded to Bad Boy's collection. Working with music was both fulfilling and rewarding. It was something else that made Lil Man and his wife grow closer. Lil Man began looking for a bigger home in just a couple of months. He wanted something that could accommodate the studio he was building. Lil Man finally came across a beautiful town house in Morrisville, Pennsylvania. It was a suburb about thirty minutes outside of Philly. The house had four full sized bedrooms and a two car garage. There was also a study, a den and other ample space Lil Man could use to begin putting the studio together. Katousha loved the house! All of the oversized windows throughout the entire home gave her a new sense of freedom, displaying a spectacular view of the landscape and neighborhood. Seeing how happy purchasing the new home had made his wife gave Lil Man a sense of accomplishment, a sense of success. He had finally picked up the piece's, and put them back together.

ONE MORE ROAD 2 CROSS

Lil Man was doing well, but he still had a problem he had been unaware of. Detectives were searching for him over the shooting in his Aunt's basement. Anytime someone is shot and goes to the hospital, detectives investigate to try and find out the exact nature of the crime . . . even if you tell them it was an accident. It's actually the doctors that notify police, and when guns are involved they get extra happy. Lil Man found out they were searching for him through an old crack head customer he had when he first started working for Stoop Head. The customer called Lil Mans phone. "Don't come back around the way. Your cousin snitched on you. Not only did he snitch, but he may have lied. The streets knew Rocky had shot himself, but he told detectives you had done it! Be careful Lil Man, they hating on you hard in the 'hood' right now!"

Damn! Lil Man was glad he never changed his phone number the way he started to. The crack head was very helpful and informative. Now all Lil Man had to do was decide what his next move would be. He decided to hire a lawyer first, and explain exactly what happened that day in the 'Lab'. He had only hired the lawyer just in case he had gotten caught unexpectedly. It was good to have a good lawyer with a heads up on your situation so they know how to fight without wasting time in jail. Lil Man would never have dared told anyone about that shooting, but he found out that Rocky was telling everybody, making it hot for himself and Lil Man!

Lil Man was against making grimy moves towards any loved ones, friends or family. But it was obvious Rocky had a chip on his shoulder that had to be shaped up. Lil Man was rationalizing with himself . . . "Rocky is out of his mind! He's just a kid. He lost two brothers, one to the system and the other to AIDS. He's on a hate mission, and had to be stopped. I love my cousin. Why is he doing this? I don't want to hurt him, but I can't ignore it either. It's always something. Can I just live? Damn!!" Lil Man sat in his office room looking at his new chrome forty five millimeter that lay on the desk. He was trying to keep from getting up and really going to shoot Rocky, the way everyone had been currently alleging anyway. Rocky had to know snitching was against the rules. He had been hustling for years. But snitching and lying, that was taking all the cake and eating it to!

When a rumor is spread in the streets people tend to run with it and spread it even more, most of the time without even entirely knowing all the facts. So Rocky had a good head start on Lil Man. There was no telling what the streets had turned this into by now, so Lil Man had to be careful who he approached for answers or for help. He decided to take his time and not make any hasty decisions. He took the truck Stoop Head had given him and got it painted blue, matching his Acura perfectly. The paint shop also did a fine tint job on the truck for Lil Man, five percent so he would barely be visible when driving or sitting in it. Painting the truck and tinting it made it unrecognizable back in the 'hood'. It was safe to drive now, the truck used to be white.

After changing the appearance of the truck, Lil Man scouted the 'hood' where Rocky lived for a few days. He bumped into a few crack heads and other people he knew to see what the word on the street was. They all told Lil Man the same thing. He was wanted for shooting Rocky. Lil Man decided to talk things over with his wife. Even though it was a street situation, Lil Man could possibly go to jail over something he didn't do. He knew Katousha had a few 'hood' connections of her own, some shady chicks who would drop their panties and rob a man in a heartbeat. Lil Man hated that this had to go on. He was ready to live a normal life and focus on a music career. Rocky's jealousy was a monkey wrench that needed to be greased. Lil Man decided to just go with Katousha's plan B. She told four of her girlfriends about Rocky and what he had done to her husband. All it would take now is for one of the girls to get close to Rocky.

As it turned out, one of Katousha's girlfriends had already been acquainted with Rocky and had been using him. Now the girl, Sharon from Logan, had a more serious motive for dating Rocky. He had done some dirt, and disloyalty would not be excused or tolerated. Katousha's girlfriends were very vindictive whenever one of them had a problem with a man. They were the 'do it yourself, take matters into our own hands' type. All Lil Man had to do now was lay low from the Police and wait to hear about Rocky's fate playing out.

Katousha was now getting phone calls about the hell Rocky was going through. Any club he went out to, his baby's mother would pop up magically with handfuls of drama. And once he escaped the embarrassment of the club scene, he would get outside to his car only to be greeted by flat tires and new key scratches. Rocky had been going through hell for months and had no idea why. The woman even went so far as to get his Mercedes towed twice, once on his own block, and again while he was out with a new lady friend. Katousha had a girlfriend who worked for the Philadelphia parking authority. Anything Rocky drove would never be safe again. Lil Man was getting reports of Rocky's agony, but wasn't sure if he was satisfied yet. He thought of the severity of Rocky's hate towards him, and hadn't called off the female wolves anytime soon.

Katousha had made a classical Hip Hop tune with a slow tempo, and told Lil Man about an idea she had for a duet. They would make the beat and write the lyrics, but didn't have to actually perform their material. Lil Man officially had taken on the position of a ghostwriter, and would get paid for his music and any lyrics as long as they were good. Bad Boy had introduced two brand new artists, completely based on Lil Man's music and lyrics. He allowed his group name 'Fokissed' to diminish, and didn't mind as long as he was getting paid. Lil Man even renewed his contract as a ghostwriter. It had been extended to four years instead of two. It was like he played on an NBA team and got paid for riding the bench. Lil Man didn't want to take on the limelight and pressures of a major star. He was 'Fokissed' on his wife and newborn son instead.

Philadelphia had virtually turned into a war zone. Shootings, robberies, carjacking's and arson were taking place all over the city. The mayor had blamed it all on drugs. Heavy drug sales and use were targeted and pinpointed as the city's main cause of murder and crime. The Police chief announced that he would be issuing bench warrants to anyone who had unpaid parking tickets to. And he also launched 'Operation Safe Streets', a city wide sting operation designed to run drug dealers off of corners using foot patrol officers that posted where drug dealers usually stood. And to make matters worse, the media was having a field day with it all. There would be an occasional home invasion robbery, and it would be talked about on the news for days. Wow! Are they trying to scare people or what? Lil Man thought of it as crime being the media's hustle, just like music was his hustle. It was a vicious cycle. But it hadn't affected Lil Man until Katousha started watching the news more often.

"Maybe we didn't move far enough away from the city Rahim. It's just a matter of time before people would discover this neighborhood and try to come and fuck it all up!" Katousha was frustrated at all the drama she would see on TV. It boiled down to her being a new mother, and thinking about the safety and future of Mekhi. But all the crime and shootings was not drug related, as Katousha would soon find out.

"Sharon and Adrienne told me to ask you if it was ok if I went out with them for dinner and drinks babe." Lil Man had liked the way she phrased the proposal, giving it a sense of consideration and respect. He had no problem with her going out sometimes, as long as she would be safe and came home at a decent hour. Whenever Lil man went out alone, he'd make sure she had gotten that same respect. "Sure babe, I don't mind. It would give me a chance to bond with the baby. It's time the men of the house 'did us' anyway! Go ahead and have a good time with the girls, just be safe and don't drive drunk."

The relationship was both loving and mature, and both Lil Man and Katousha both paid attention, respected and took into consideration what each other had said and felt. Lil Man had even thought about renewing their marriage vows and having the big wedding that they never had.

Katousha waited for a little bit and was picked up by her girlfriends around seven thirty that evening. Lil Man spent the evening changing diapers, feeding and playing with his son. He loved being a father, and couldn't wait until the infant began to speak. The baby went to sleep, all full from eating and worn out from crawling around and playing with dad. Around eleven thirty, Lil Mans cell phone started ringing. It was Katousha.

"Babe, it's about to be some shit in this club! These little funky ass bitches are in here talking shit and saying that they know you, and one of the girls is claiming she's fucking you! What the fuck Rahim!?" This is exactly the one reason Lil Man didn't condone Katousha going out alone, but he didn't really have room to deny her after all the time he spent out and about on her. "Baby calm down. You know none of them people knows me, and even if they do it probably has to be from the music or some credits on the back of a CD. I haven't even been out clubbing in months. Whoever it is is tripping. Just ignore their dumb shit and come home."

Lil Man thought it was that simple. He was wrong. "This bitch described your car and everything in it Rahim! Tell me who you been fucking with? Don't have me looking stupid in front of these raggedy hoes!" Lil Man was tempted to get the baby dressed and head to the club, exactly what a 'baby momma' would have done in that situation. But he knew whoever was talking didn't know him. Katousha was the only woman he'd been with since he came home from being away for over a year! "Babe their lying whoever it is, and their probably just jealous because you got me and they don't." Katousha had paused, as if she thought about what Lil man just said. It made sense, because the girl could have just heard about the car and never been in it. It could have been one of Stoop Head's old girls. Stoop used to brag a lot. "Just come home and we'll talk about it when you get here." "You better be right Rahim!"

Lil Man hadn't heard Katousha that upset in a long time. He wondered who was trying to start up some drama between him and his wife. The girl described his car to Katousha. That was an interesting twist, but he wouldn't know for sure until she got home and told him more about what happened. He just hoped she wasn't drunk talking out of her ass.

While Lil Man sat there confused, his worst fears were about to be reality. Katousha called his phone again. "Their shooting in here Rahim! Come and get me please!" Is she serious? Katousha had to be drunk, and forgot she had a baby at home. Why wouldn't she just duck, hide and stay out of the way until things got clear? Something was wrong. "Where you at??" "Transit at Sixth and Spring Garden! Hurry up Rahim!" She sounded serious, and Lil Man had to think fast. He got the baby dressed, grabbed the car seat and drove the truck to the club. He decided to come up from the back street so he wouldn't be noticed by anyone. Before he even got to the club, Lil Man saw that the entire block that the club was on was lit up like a Christmas tree from police car lights. He parked right where he was about a half of block away and called Katousha's cell phone back.

"Babe, I'm here! Where are you? Come out of the club and make a left, walk down and you'll see the truck across the street." Katousha came walking up looking like she had been fighting Tasmanian devils. "What the hell happened to you?" Katousha pulled down the visor and flipped up the mirror. She wasn't bruised, but her hair and makeup were through for the night. "The girl I was telling you about called herself acting bad and wanted to jump. So you know punks jump up to get beat down. Me and Adrienne stomped the bitch. We still didn't find Sharon's scared ass yet. She probably is hiding somewhere trying to sneak a ride home. Can you believe these dudes started shooting right in the club? I'm thinking how they even got guns in here! Everybody got frisked and patted down! Never again man, that shit is for the bird's for real!!"

The first time Katousha goes out by herself, she gets into a fight at a club where a shooting takes place. This wasn't Lil Mans idea of 'enjoy yourself and have a good time'. It wasn't her fault, but if he would have talked her out of going none of that would have happened. Lil Man made up his mind that there would definitely not be a next time. He loved her and the baby too much. From then on out, it was either they went out together or nobody went at all . . . Especially in a Philly club! Lil Man could tell his wife was drunk though. She was speaking angrily, and her speech was slightly slurred. She kept chanting to herself on the way home, "yeaaaaa! I whupped that bitch's ass tonight!"

"You wild babe! Don't do anything to get that pretty face scarred ok? And don't forget that Mekhi and I need you with us! Do you think the girl had anything to do with Rocky? He been getting played for a while now and word may have gotten back to him by now. With all those chicks involved, one of them was bound to slip up and talk. Whether it was over dick or a dollar." Katousha had a surprised look on her face like what Lil Man said could have been a possibility. But then she jumped to her girlfriend's defense. "Man, I seriously doubt it babe. I know some females can be grimy like that, but we sifted those out and cut them short a long time ago. It was just a lot of drunken people in there tonight that's all." Lil Man started laughing, "Tell me about it. I'm driving one home now!" They made it home and went to bed, they both were tired and luckily Mekhi had stayed sleep through it all.

The next morning, Lil Man woke up to the sounds of Mekhi crying in his crib at the foot of Lil Man and Katousha's bed. Lil Man took him out, changed him and carried him to the kitchen to warm up a bottle. When they got back upstairs, Katousha was up to and had turned the TV on to watch the news. "Three people dead last night after a shooting that took place inside a North Philadelphia night club. Four others were wounded. Police are not releasing anyonc's names as the investigation is still underway. Police have no leads, motives or suspects in the case." Katousha turned the TV back off.

"Never again! My pretty ass is staying right here with you babe!" Lil Man chuckled as he was feeding the baby. "I hear you momma. But that shooting was crazy! I'm just glad you weren't one of those seven people! Now the D's are gonna turn up the heat on anyone they think may be involved in a shooting, and that might include me! I usually don't root for the cops, but I hope they grab somebody before they grab me! That dumb shit Rocky pulled is still inexcusable as far as I'm concerned!" Lil Man and Katousha were in a position now where they didn't have to let themselves get caught up in the dramas of the hood, but somehow trouble always seemed to lurk close by.

Lil Man's mom called with more shocking news. "Your Aunt just called me. The Police arrested Rocky for a shooting at a club. Did you hear about it?" Lil Man wanted to say 'hear about it? I rescued my wife from it'. Instead he just replied "no, what happened?" His mom went on to give him the scoop, saying Rocky had been charged with three murders and four aggravated assaults when they found the gun matching the crime scene in his Mercedes. Lil Man couldn't believe it! What was wrong with Rocky? He must have really lost all of his sense and composure after Stoop Head passed away and Maze had gotten locked up. Lil Man wasn't sure what the world was coming to with all these crazy things happening one after another. But one thing was for sure, he was going to do his best to keep him self and his wife away from trouble.

Sometimes it seemed to Lil Man that no matter what you're intentions are, no matter how good you are or how many good things are in your heart . . . trouble can and will find you. It was unfortunate for Lil Man that Rocky waited until he had gotten locked up to start his singing career. "So before the shooting at the club, how did you get shot?" Some detectives are the most sneakiest and grimy people on the planet. They do not care about victims, or suspects. They could care less about your circumstances. All they want to do is solve the case. You could be trapped in quicksand up to your neck, and they will question you. If your wife chops off the main vein and you're pissing blood, they want answers. You can be choking on broken glass with your ass cheeks on fire. They'll give you the Heimlich maneuver and blast you in the ass with a fire extinguisher, just as long as they think you'll talk.

Rocky had destroyed a lot of credibility by telling different stories. First he told them that someone broke into his mother's house and robbed him. They told him there were no signs of forced entry or burglary. His next story was that he was in the crossfire between rival gangs. That story was over before it started. Then his third lie and all-time favorite, "my cousin shot me." Lil Man could not figure out for the life of him why Rocky wanted him to go down so bad. But he surely tried to make Lil Man's name hot. The smartest move Lil Man made to lay low was having everything in his wife's name who had held onto her maiden name for this very reason, and a select few of his old clientele. By using their names to register things, Lil Man was almost close to invisible to the radars.

Rocky gave the D's a lot on Lil Man. But by not having anything in his name, not even a pager or a phone, he wasn't easy to find. And Lil man's record as an adult was virtually spotless . . . besides a lot of gossip and hearsay he was a clean dude, a business oriented family man. He had started looking for another new home, somewhere away from Philadelphia all together. Lil Man decided they had better move now before getting too used to their home. Moving to another state would be an inconvenience in terms of finding a babysitter. Katousha and Lil Man didn't trust anyone with Mekhi except family members. "We have a lot of reasons to stay close by, but I have an important reason to go. I'm really trying to consider all aspects of it Toosh. I don't want to make anything hard on you."

Lil Man had set himself up for one of Katousha's aggressive sex traps. "Hard on me? MMmmm. Now that I think about it, I missed the baby shower last night." This woman would literally turn anything sexual, if she wanted it. Katousha had a way of seducing Lil Man and taking his mind away from problems. She was a self-made trophy wife, very hard to ignore. Sometimes a man would get bored with his wife, finding alternatives to stimulation. Alternatives often included watching sports, hobbies, anything to take a break from the opposition of the opposite sex. But Katousha with her soft voice and sexy voluptuous curves had no problem keeping the attention on her. And as long as she was aware and gave attention to any potential problems in their mission, Lil Man had no problem paying attention to his wife.

"Maybe we could stay here and be ok. We could just let our parent's alternate keeping the baby, and do some traveling." Lil Man had refused to look at it as if he had to go on the run. He wasn't involved with drugs anymore, even though the 'Kool G.Rap' song "On the Run" kept coming to mind and was still his personal favorite. He had rather think of it as a vacation, just some time to get away. Katousha thought of the idea of vacationing with her husband. "What do you think about birth control? I mean like a procedure or a pill. A vacation with you may cause another pregnancy Rahim." After all the drama Lil Man had been through, he decided that he deserved a great vacation. A vacation with his wife, for about a month. He and Katousha started planning it right away. They would choose four or five nice place's, and spend about a week in each.

"How do you feel about a cruise babe?" A cruise from one place to another would mean adding an extra week to the plan. They could afford it, but Katousha had her doubts and fears. "Honestly, I have never been on a cruise. But if we go away and leave Mekhi behind, I don't want to leave any room for anything to happen to us. Let's keep our vacation on land, unless we have to take a flight ok?" They planned a five week vacation. A week in Jamaica, a week in Hawaii, a week in L.A., a week in Miami and finally a trip to Paris, France. Lil Man thought he may as well revisit a few of the places he had seen while in travels with Vision Quest. Those places would be much more pleasant and enjoyable with Katousha along. Instead of drama, Lil Man began looking at pleasures and places as his 'one more road to cross'.

NO MORE DRAMA

Lil Man and Katousha were having a ball, and often on their trip she made sure that she had two. They were having more sex at the end of the night on vacation than they did back at home. It was the spontaneity of their passion for each other, on top of being able to say they had done it all over the map. The couple had really built some awesome memories, and even took some more awesome photo's to prove it. Katousha was pretty, but being on a beach in a bikini with the sun shining on her caramel complexion and palm trees in the background made her look like a model. In a lot of her photo's, she hadn't even looked American with her long and wavy wet hair and slanted eyes. Sometimes Lil Man caught himself staring at his wife like he had never seen her before. He appreciated her beauty, as well as the head on her shoulders and he felt lucky.

In Miami, temperatures were up in the nineties. Lil Man and Katousha felt like riding jet skis, just to recapture the snowmobile fun they had one before. "Would you like your own? Or would you rather ride with me on a two-seater?" Lil Man explained how a two-seater would be a much slower ride, since it was built sturdier to carry an extra person. "I'll ride my own" Katousha decided. "That way we can race!" They were having a great time on the water, and had taken more photos out on the ocean with the jet skis. After a few hours of riding, they returned to their hotel suit to start getting ready for lunch. Katousha wanted to go swimming after they had eaten. She was taking in as many water sports as she could, and Lil Man didn't mind at all. Her bikini made the view a great one.

They had a slight change of plans. After Miami came Vegas instead of L.A. Lil Man decided to give Katousha a quick three day lesson in Black Jack 21 at the Trump Taj Mahal. Until this very day Lil Man wasn't sure if he should have taught his wife those casino games and how to gamble. The lesson was supposed to make her want to stay away from casino's, but instead Lil Man played Black Jack and Roulette and wound up leaving with another ten grand. It felt good either way. He just had to explain that it didn't always go so well.

"You know I'm a lucky guy babe, look who I'm married to!!" The two stayed spoiling each other by showering one another with compliments. It was love at its finest. But while in Vegas, Katousha noticed that she weren't the only thick woman with pumps on and a tight dress with long hair. She wasn't insecure by far, but felt the need to question Lil Man's fidelity. "Do you love me Rahim?" Her question had changed Lil Man's entire facial expression from normal to confused. "Of course I do momma! Why would you ask me that?" Lil Man noticed that as she asked the question of doubting his faithfulness, there were woman walking around flirting and showing off their 'goodies' trying to get attention from different men. "I know you have eyes Rahim, and I've noticed how different woman look at you. Sometimes I just wonder if I'm enough to keep you satisfied."

Lil Man was in a position where he felt like he had to do something out of the ordinary to make a new declaration of love for his wife. "I would tell the world that I love you girl! Are you serious? Watch this . . ." Lil Man took Katousha by the hand and pulled her over to the bar in the casino where it was very crowded. He ordered himself a double shot of Hennesy, and Katousha's favorite drink which had been a double apple Martini. When their drinks came up, he handed hers to her, took his and raised his glass to the air. "Ladies and gentlemen! I'd like to propose a toast! This is for my loving and beautiful wife, who is one of the smartest and strongest women I know besides my mother. This woman has stood by me through thick and thin, and I just would like to let the world know how much I love her! But since the entire world isn't here, I'll settle for letting all of you nice people in this casino know. Thank you for your time, and cheers!"

There were ooh's and ah's and the entire crowd that had gathered for Lil man's toast had applauded and cheered for him and Katousha. He smiled, and pulled his smiling wife in closer by the waist and began kissing her shamelessly in front of the entire crowd. Katousha's heart was racing, and there was no longer any doubt in her mind that her husband had loved her. Lil Man could barely hear his wife over the applauses they had received. "Oh my god! I can't believe you did that in front of all these people." She was still smiling uncontrollably. "No shame here babe. There is no way or no one I won't let know how I feel about you! So no more 'do you love me' questions ok? Next time there's no telling what I may do so don't test me." Katousha was convinced, as well as impressed. She had a good man.

The two had another drink, and then went upstairs to wrap things up for their trip to Hawaii. They had a flight scheduled to leave at ten a.m. the next morning. Katousha could not wait to tell her mother what Lil Man had just done in the casino. She jumped on the phone as soon as they got back into their hotel suite. "Momma! Guess what!!??" Those three words were all Lil Man needed to hear to know she was genuinely excited. Lil Man was on vacation with his woman feeling like he was taking the good advice his cousin had given him before he passed away. He was living life to the fullest, and it felt good. He actually felt good enough to make a suggestion to Katousha he'd never thought he would make.

She hung up the phone, exhaled a deep breath and turned to Lil man smiling brightly. "My mom told me to tell you hello, and she said thank you for making and keeping her only daughter happy" Lil man was glad that Katousha's mother had liked him, especially after that awkward day when her parents walked in on them and she was crying. Lil Man decided to send his wife's mother a gift. "Babe, you wanna go sky diving? I think it would be fun! You'd probably love it!" Lil man had been looking over some brochures about the activities in Hawaii. Besides the beautiful beaches and hula fire dancers, they had plenty of water and air activities which included surfing, sailing, deep sea diving and sky diving. "I read over the reviews to. People say it's a lot safer than anticipated." Katousha'a entire demeanor changed, going from excited and cheerful to just plain serious.

She walked over to the chair that Lil Man was sitting in and stood in front of him. She placed her hands on the arms of the chair, and leaned down being almost nose to nose with him. But she was definitely eye to eye for sure. "Read my lips Lil man, and read them good! I WANT TO LIVE!!" Katousha had never been more serious in her life. She began caressing her body in front of Lil Man slowly from breast to thighs saying: "You see all of this?? All of this body you say you Luuvvvvv so much? Yea! This body is going to live! I'm not jumping out of no damn plane! I don't care if it's still parked on the freaking runway! No way in hell Rahim!!"

Lil Man scratched the plan of him and Katousha sky diving together, but he still wanted to do it himself. He sat at the desk in the suite, going over all the pictures he and Katousha had taken. They all looked good, even the silly faces she made on purpose were cute. Lil man then called back home to check on things with Mekhi while Katousha showered. His mom jokingly told him that the bald headed baby was doing just fine. So Lil Man, now feeling at ease, worked on some music on the laptop for about an hour before joining his wife for bed.

"I'm so glad we had a chance to do this Rahim. I can't remember the last time I had so much fun! And I know when Mekhi gets older he's going to love his fun loving dad." Katousha was still daydreaming about the stunt Lil Man had pulled in the casino downstairs earlier. She had wondered how special she really was to him and he showed it fully and boldly, publicly. A woman couldn't ask for anything more. Their pillow talk was clean and innocent, until Katousha made one of her infamous advances in the dark. "I'm glad you're having fun babe. We'll just keep doing our thing with music and we'll be able to stay on top of things. You Know?" Without thinking how perverted his wife could be at times, Lil Man had just set himself up without even noticing. He felt Katousha slip down under the covers doing a performance with the most spectacular sound effects. All she said was "speaking of 'on top of things'" and it was on from there until nearly the next morning.

They woke up still tired from the night before, but had a flight to catch to Hawaii. They rushed to finish gathering their things, packed it up, and were able to take a taxi to the airport on time. They had a first class breakfast on the flight and it had seemed like they had barely had time to finish it. The flight from Vegas to Hawaii was a short one, and when they arrived at their hotel Katousha was ready to play again. "I have a surprise for you babe" she said in a steamy and sexy voice. Lil Man didn't know what to expect after Katousha stepped into the bathroom with a bag she had from shopping in Vegas. But he unpacked their things and waited for her.

When she finally came out of the bathroom, Katousha had looked like a different woman. Her surprise was that she was wearing an outfit Lil Man suggested. He told her he loved it and thought it would look great on her, but Katousha had declined at the time and said the flimsy three piece outfit was too revealing. Lil Man's pleas and testimony's finally paid off and Katousha stepped out in the outfit with the perfect high heels to match. "Wow! You got it? You're sneaky girl! But I love it, you look great!" Lil Man couldn't wait to take his wife out and see her in the bright sun light of the Hawaiian skies. They were at a Sandal's Resort in Waikiki, Hawaii. Everything was gorgeous, especially Katousha. Her sheer floral dress with matching sun hat was perfect for the Hawaiian scenery. "Today, I guess we can take in the sights before we get all physical. I'm too sexy to be jet skiing and sailing right now."

Katousha was right. She was so flawlessly pretty and beautiful that Lil Man didn't even want one hair out of place on her head. He felt like he was married to a movie star. "What do you think about making some Hawaiian beats? We can do something with a tropical sound." Lil Man loved the idea and after they ate, they both wanted to go and work on the beats right away while the idea was still fresh. The food in Hawaii was great! Lil Man had some Waikiki chicken and pineapple with zucchini. Katousha had the Hawaiian beef fried rice, seasoned with watermelon and pineapple. They loved pineapples with everything. But Lil Man had to admit, it was delicious even on pizza!

After eating, the couple decided to go for a walk across the beach before going back to the room and working on the beat. Even though they were on vacation, they didn't mind working on music at all still. It was soothing, as well as their main source of income. Lil Man and Katousha started working on the beat and came up with something that sounded very tropical. "We have to cut it up and add something's to it. This sounds too much like 'Shyne's' "Get out" song. 'Shyne' was a Bod Boy artist who quickly became famous for having a distinguishing voice that sounded almost exactly like 'The Notorious B.I.G.'s' voice. 'Shyne' was also a platinum selling artist as well as the group he performed "Get Out" with, an R&B group named '112'.

"No problem, we should be able to slow down the tempo and add more scratches to it. Even though were using the same type of maracas, after the adjustments the two tracks will sound completely different." After working on the new track for about an hour, the beat sounded flawless. "The world is going to love this babe!" He had given Katousha a big and juicy kiss, and they listened to the beat on repeat while they discussed what they would do next. "Let's go swimming. I think I may be able to buy out the pool for a few hours." Lil Man wanted some private moments in the pool with Katousha, but the hotel management wouldn't allow him to buy out the pool for any amount of time. They said that the hotel was too crowded and that the pool was one of their main attractions. Lil Man didn't get upset. He just decided to have a pool built in the backyard as soon as he got back home.

They changed into their swim suits and enjoyed the pool anyway. Even though Katousha didn't want to get her hair too wet, Lil Man still made sure she had fun. He got her a waterproof swimming cap but she refused to wear it. "I'll look like a damn fool with that thing on Rahim!" Lil Man tried to convince her, "actually, you'd look like a smart and beautiful woman who wants to enjoy swimming while keeping her hair dry babe." She laughed and tried the cap on in the mirror. "We'll probably never see these people again babe, there is nothing to be ashamed of." Katousha gave it another thought. "Ok, let's go!" She had put the swimming cap on and wore it proudly down to the pool. Lil Man did wonders for his wife's self-esteem.

They swam with other couples in the pool, and Lil Man even wound up playing a game of water basketball with other husbands while the wives cheered by poolside drinking margarita's and daiquiri's. "That's my baby!" Katousha was getting tipsy on the sideline and had cheered louder and louder every time Lil Man had made a shot. The men in the water had taken a break and one of them told Lil Man about a beach concert later that evening. There would be singing, dancing, food and fun. It was a Luau, and Lil Man and Katousha had neither been to one before. "Ok buddy, sounds like a plan. We'll be there!"

Lil Man joined his wife in a lounge beach chair next to the pool and told her about the party. "Wow! Really? Of course I want to go! I never saw those fire and hula dancers up close before. And they might have some of that pineapple chicken there. That was delicious!" Lil Man was glad her spirits were high and she went along with the plan. He figured it would be easier to tell her about the skydiving reservation he had secretly made for the next day. Lil Man just had to try it at least once, even though his wife had major concerns about the safety issues. All she would say is "what if this, and what if that." A bunch of what ifs was not worth passing up a dream opportunity. They left the pool area and went back upstairs to get dry.

Lil Man had decided to take a nap before going out to the Hawaiian party. While he slept, Katousha had fired up the laptop and put on her headphones. She had made a whole entire beat before Lil Man woke up again. She began quietly rapping to her own beat . . . "Uh Uh, my daddy gonna love this. Ain't no one above this. A fly pretty chick putting it down. We out in Hawaii, I don't know why he thinks I don't know he messing around. Uh Uh!" Katousha voice sounded great over Hip Hop music, and she actually had the ability to write great rhymes. Lil Man heard her rhyming in his sleep and woke up listening to his woman's raps. "While he's over there sleeping, don't think I know he's creeping. Everywhere we go these other girls be peeping. But I'm the one and only, won't ever leave him lonely. He's my everything, got myself a tenderoni." Lil man couldn't help but comment.

"Girl, no one is creeping or messing around. But you sound great though!" Katousha turned around laughing. "I was just throwing words together to see how the beat was working out. Do you like it?" Lil Man couldn't hide how well the music actually sounded. He sat up in bed and began nodding his head to the bass of the track. "I love it babe! You're really becoming a pro. At this rate, we should be able to start our own production company soon! How does Fokissed Productions sound?" Even though they were on vacation, Lil Man and Katousha were still very much business minded. "Sounds good to me, as long as I'm the First Lady!"

Lil Man and Katousha had gotten dressed to get ready to go to the Luau. The flyer Lil Man took from one of the husbands said that the party would be held at the base of one of Hawaii's most popular volcano sites, Mt. Kilauea. They decided to wait around and have a couple of drinks before going to the party, allowing it to become dark outside. They then caught a cab to the famous tourist attraction.

Upon arriving at the party, they seemed to have gotten there at the perfect time. Something was about to happen that they would have not wanted to miss. There were Hula dancers everywhere, performing in what seemed to be precisely coordinated cadences. The woman in the grass skirts threw their hips around vigorously, making it look like their hips were trying to escape from their bodies under the skirts. It was so amazing that even Katousha enjoyed watching the dancers perform. The hula dancers alternated with the Polynesian fire performers. The beach was very crowded, and it seemed like the fire dancers may not have had enough room to perform properly.

One of the dancers had swung a long string of fire into one of his performing partners' backs, causing the flame to combust and ignited the heavyset man almost completely. He dropped and rolled around, but the fire had not gone out immediately. The performer had suffered first degree burns over about forty percent of his body, quickly bringing the fire portion of the show to an end. It was very rare that this type of tragedy would occur, and rumors quickly spread throughout the party saying that it was the promoter's fault for being greedy and allowing the party to overfill its legal capacity.

The crowd dispersed and made room for the ambulance and EMT's to come and get the burned fire performer. Katousha didn't want to stay after she witnessed how badly the man had been burned. "See? Bad things can happen babe. That's why I don't want to go sky diving. The last thing we need is another tragedy." Katousha seeing the burned man ruined any chances of her going along with Lil Man's planned sky diving surprise. He decided to just forget about it, and cancelled as soon as they had reached their room. Katousha overheard Lil Man making the cancellation call. "I can't believe you were still going to try and go! What's the matter with you? That sky diving crap is dangerous and I cannot lose you Rahim! Do you hear me? Mekhi and I need you!!"

Lil Man also cancelled their trip to Paris, and had scheduled to go to Niagara Falls, Canada instead. He had been there once before when he was a child with his grandparents and remembered how beautiful it was. He knew Katousha would love it, and he had plans to kill her fear of heights while in Canada. They packed up after another day of swimming and sun before heading to the airport to go to Los Angeles.

L.A was the fastest paced out of all the other places Lil Man and Katousha had visited. When they arrived there, Lil Man rented a small car so that they could get around and see all of the sites they had heard about. Two places that they were particularly interested in were Holly Wood and Beverly Hills. Katousha couldn't wait to do some Beverly Hills shopping! Beverly Hills had every shop and boutique from Armani and Burberry, to Gucci and Dolce

& Gabbana. "Let's take the first day to spend shopping and then we'll relax ok babe?" Lil Man was fine with that, Beverly Hills was beautiful. Everything from the homes to the people made Lil Man want to live there. He decided to keep that thought to himself for a couple of days, just to take in some more of its wonderful scenery before proposing the idea to his wife.

The couple had had taken a romantic walk along the Holly Wood Stars Walk of Fame. Holly Wood Boulevard and Vine streets were both full of tourists, as well as paparazzi waiting to surprise unsuspecting celebrities. Tourists in Holly Wood without a camera hanging from their necks were rare, like a rap artist without a chain or jewelry. It was easy to spot out of towner's in Holly Wood if you had lived there. Lil Man's sense allowed him to pick up on them quickly, as if he lived there for years to.

They enjoyed their days in California, and Lil Man explained the change of plans concerning going to Niagara Fall's instead of Paris. "The flight to France is going to be a pretty long one. I thought for our last trip we'd go and visit Niagara Fall's instead. That way when we're done, we'll be closer to home. Plus, I have a surprise waiting for you there. Katousha caught butterflies in her stomach immediately. Lil Man had been so romantic and pleasing during their vacation, that Katousha couldn't imagine what he had planned for her in Canada. Once in Niagara Falls, they checked into a hotel down the street from the falls. Lil Man had requested a room facing the falls, where the view was magnificent! The view was special during the night, when the falls and their mists were illuminated with multi-colored lighting. Katousha's heart fluttered with joy. She looked out of their twenty story hotel room window, and decided that she was looking upon what had to be one of the greatest sights in the world! Then she turned around to take a glimpse of the man that was responsible for introducing her to such bliss, her husband Rahim.

Katousha felt like she had fallen in love all over again. Lil Man hadn't known it, but he had his wife in a position where she would do anything in the world for him. She couldn't wait for the surprise he had mentioned back in L.A., although the views of the falls were more than enough. They rested up that night, and planned their route around the scene of the falls. Of course at the end of that gorgeous night, they made love. They made love over and over in fact. Katousha was so sexy to Lil Man that it took less than a touch to become erect again after the previous round. That first night in Canada, they had put in four rounds total, not finishing until the sun was nearly up.

That next morning, Lil Man had been knocked out cold. He was sleeping like a baby when Katousha had ordered breakfast in bed for them. Lil Man woke up smiling around eleven that morning. "Good morning my love!" Katousha greeted her man with a kiss and was so happy that everything she said sounded like a song. "Come on. Time to get up sleepy head. I ordered us some breakfast." Katousha knew Lil Man had something in store that would melt her heart and touch her soul. "Good morning babe, what did you get for breakfast?" "Bacon, eggs, toast, cereal and Danishes. There's some coffee and OJ on the desk to."

"Thanks babe, I'm gonna shower before I eat. Then we can figure out what we want to do today ok?" Katousha was cool with that. She was sure her man already had it all together and figured out already. After breakfast, Lil Man topped the morning off by laying out another fun filled itinerary. They would first visit 'Ripley's' believe it or not museum. The museum had life sized replicas of people who had been documented for achieving amazing and record breaking feats. Katousha's favorite exhibit turned out to be the world's most fully covered tattooed woman. They had taken pictures with a life sized automobile, made entirely out of match sticks. After browsing 'Ripley's' for a couple of hours, they visited the next landmark on their list. Lil Man and Katousha walked into the 'Guinness Book of World Records' museum. It was similar to the first museum they visited, but was more detailed and had exhibits of people who had done way more extremely marvelous but crazy things!

There was a man who had tight rope walked across the entire 'Horse Shoe' falls. There was another guy who had gone over the falls in a barrel. The museum had a wax figure of the world's tallest man, who stood just an inch less than nine feet tall. He had reminded Katousha of 'Lurch' from The Adams Family. Lil Man and Katousha had spent more time in 'Guinness' than they had at 'Ripley's', taking in all of the cool exhibits and sights. After leaving the museum Lil Man encouraged Katousha to try and snack lightly, leaving room for dinner. Katousha had had so much fun that she nearly forgot all about the surprise Lil Man said he had planned for her here in Canada.

They had squeezed in one more tourist attraction before eating, a two hour tour on 'The Maid of The Mist'. It was a small cruise ship with a very large deck where people had stood with rain coats on to be taken as closely as possible to the falls without going directly underneath them. Katousha had taken some of the most awesome pictures ever, and she and Lil Man had gotten other people to take pictures of them. It was great! After the cruise around the falls, Lil Man suggested that they go and get dressed for dinner. After they both were dressed, Lil Man had called a cab and told them the location of their destination. "Babe, you look great in that dress! It's time for your surprise!" Katousha's face had lit up like a kid on Christmas morning. "Are you ready?" She was so excited she could barely hold it in, like she was about to burst full of excitement juice. "Yes! I'm ready baby!" Lil Man explained that in order to be fully surprised, Katousha had to wear a blindfold once they had gotten in the cab. She agreed.

After riding in the cab for about five minutes and taking in the wonderful nightlight sights of Niagara Falls, Lil Man blindfolded his wife. They then exited the cab about two minutes later, and Lil Man held his wife's hand while guiding her to where they were going. "Ok no peeking babe, you promised." Katousha was smiling brightly with the blindfold secured over her eyes. They took steps for about thirty feet before they had reached the building. Lil Man explained that they were getting on an elevator. "Ok, how much further?" "Almost there babe, we're right there." Once the elevator door closed and began rising. Lil Man told Katousha that she could remove her blindfold now. She took it off and couldn't believe her eyes!

They were on the elevator rising up above the entire Niagara Falls view, looking on through glass in the elevator doors. Katousha was so excited and stricken with awe that she literally had to keep herself from screaming. Instead, she threw her arms around her husband and began kissing him intensely, and passionately. After the elevators decent came to a slow and smooth halt seven hundred and seventy five feet above the falls, the doors opened and Lil Man and Katousha entered The Skylon Tower revolving restaurant of Niagara Falls. Lil Man had a table reserved right next to a window so that their meal would include a non-stop spectacular view. Their meal was almost silent at first, as Katousha still couldn't believe how high they were up in the sky having dinner.

"You understand the blindfold now right? Not only did I want to surprise you, but I have a feeling that if you knew how high this restaurant was you would have said no. So I had to use my skills on you." Katousha's eyes were nearly glued to the window next to their table. "I'm so glad you brought me here Rahim! It's beautiful, and I'll never forget this!" Lil Man was a bit relieved that his wife was so pleased with his surprise. He wasn't sure if she would get along with having dinner at nearly one thousand feet in the air. The experience topped off their vacation perfectly before going back home to be loving parents to their baby boy, Mekhi.

BACK 2 BUSINESS

After all the beauty in Niagara Falls had come to an end, Lil Man and Katousha were on a plane once again, bound for Philadelphia. They had called to see where Mekhi was so that they could pick him up. He was with Katousha's parents. "Do you think Mekhi is going to recognize us? We've been away for over a month." Even though they had taken some time out to enjoy themselves, Katousha and Lil Man both secretly had the baby on their minds a lot. They avoided bringing him up as much as possible to suppress any guilty feelings they may have had about being away. "Of course he'll remember us. If not by sight he'll definitely recognize our voices. Our baby is smart."

Lil Man and Katousha couldn't wait to get to the baby and smother him with kisses and love. When they walked into Katousha's parent's house, Mekhi was in a baby walker facing in the other direction away from them. Lil Man stopped Katousha from going to grab him. "Hold up babe, call his name and see what he does" he whispered. Katousha then called Mekhi's name playfully. "Mekhi, where's my little Mekhi?" she sung towards the baby. Mekhi struggled, but managed to turn around and see both his parents standing there. The baby's eyes lit up wide and he began bouncing and cheerfully squealing, trying to make his way over to them the best he could. "Ba bo! Ba baaa!!" Baby Mekhi was trying to communicate, expressing that he recognized his parent's. He was yelling in baby talk. Lil Man had thought if the baby could speak, he'd be saying "where the hell have you two been? I was in this walker going around looking for you guys!"

Katousha picked up the baby first, and she and Lil Man had him on the couch passing him back and forth. They were complete again. Katousha went into one of her bags and began pulling out toys and stuffed fluffy animals that they had bought for the baby. He was drooling and giggling ecstatically. "Alright, you got your little bald headed bundle of joy! Now it's time to go!" Katousha's father was only kidding, but he was really tired from having the baby when it was their turn to keep him. Mekhi had kept him up late some nights, hungry or either needing to be changed. They spent some more time playing with the baby, while Katousha talked to her mother telling her about the romantic trip. She had made the vacation sound so enticing, that Katousha's mother was ready to get her husband to take her to some of the same places. "We're definitely going back to Nigeria Falls! Right Rahim!?" "Yes babe, but its Niagara." They laughed as they got the baby dressed to take him home.

On the ride home, Lil Man had stooped to check the air in the tires of his Acura since it had sat at the airport parking lot for so long. The car was ok and they went on driving home. But the wonderful time they had been having would soon be disturbed by a frightening discovery. When Lil Man drove up the street approaching his house, he noticed something all over the ground around the truck he had gotten from Stoop Head. He parked next to the truck in his driveway and got a closer look. The truck had been shot up, all over by what appeared to be an automatic rifle. "Oh my God Rahim! What the hell is going on??"

Lil Man had no answer for his wife. He had been just as surprised as she was. They took the baby and their bags into the house and Lil Man came back outside to inspect the truck. All of the tires were shot and flattened, and the rims were even shattered from being shot. Someone had really made it their business to destroy the truck and turn it into Swiss cheese.

Lil Man really had no clue what to do or no idea who to blame. He definitely couldn't go to the police. He still hadn't answered to them over his cousin getting shot, and wasn't sure if they were looking for him or not. He couldn't believe that no one had seen or heard anything, even though his house had sat alone. From the looks of the size of the shell casings on the ground and how many there were, someone had to see what happened. Lil Man had his suspicions. It had to be somebody Rocky sent. But if it were, how the hell did they know where he lived? Lil Man went inside and talked to Katousha about the ideas he had. He then asked her if she minded asking a few neighbors if they had heard anything. He didn't want anyone getting a close look at him, in case the D's had been there already asking questions.

Katousha had agreed to go and check out the neighbors. She didn't have far to go. Their house sat in the middle at the top of the encircled block, while there were only four other houses, two on each side completing the block. "Hello, sorry to bother you. But my husband and I had just returned from vacation and noticed someone had shot up one of our cars. We were just wondering if any of the neighbors had seen or heard anything." The first neighbor Katousha had spoken to had spilled every bean he had. A short elderly and balding man with glasses, he was delighted to tell Katousha everything he knew. Her dress had that effect on men.

The man told Katousha that there was a silver Mercedes parked outside their house all day, with two men inside who looked like they had been smoking. He said that they drove away and came back again several hours later. The second time they came, the guys didn't waste any time. They got out of their car and with one man on each side, began spraying the truck with bullets from machine guns. The detectives had been there asking all of the neighbors questions. Katousha with her quick thinking thanked the man, and asked him to please not contact the police. She told him that it was a life threatening matter and that they would need time to move. The man assured her that his lips were sealed and they said goodbye to each other after Katousha thanked him. She hurried back into the house to fill Lil Man in.

"Babe, the man in the first house to the left saw everything and said the cops were around questioning all our neighbors. He said two guys in a silver Mercedes shot up the truck and pulled off. What are we gonna do Rahim?" Lil Man thought for a minute. The only person he knew with a silver Mercedes was Rocky. But Rocky had been in custody about to serve life for murder. If that was his car it had to have been someone he sent, someone who worked for him hustling. And the car had to have been bought back from a police auction. Lil Man realized that he didn't have time to wait around and find out. His main concern was the safety of his family, and moving on with their lives. Lil Man had planned on getting a pool built, but now he had to move again. He started suggesting places to his wife.

"So how much did you actually like Los Angeles Toosh?" She already knew what he had in mind. "It was beautiful, but not so far ok babe? I still want us to be able to visit our families." Lil Man had to get rid of the truck. He asked Katousha to sweep up the shells, while he had gotten the truck towed to a chop shop he knew of out in South Philadelphia. The chop shop could actually repair or replace any damages to the truck easily, as long as it ran properly and the engine had not been shot. The owner of the shop offered to either fix the truck or asked Lil Man if he wanted to sell it. Lil Man had opted to sell the truck and be done with it, even though it had been a personal gift from Stoop Head. He decided to get his own in Stoops memory if anything.

After getting rid of the truck and returning home in a cab, Lil Man saw that his Acura was not there and he had several missed calls on his cell phone. He had never turned his volume back up after getting off of the flight from Canada. It was Katousha calling, and she said her and the baby left after the cops had rung the bell and she didn't answer. "I'm at your mom's house baby, and don't worry. I won't say a word. Just hurry up and get here please!" Lil Man felt like his life was being lived "On the Run", just like his favorite Kool G. rap song. Lil Man thought how weird it was that the girl in that video resembled and even sounded like Katousha so much. He even asked if it was her one day, but it wasn't. The only thing he was sure of now, is that the next time they moved it would be for good.

Lil Man received a phone call from the guy who ran the chop shop he had sold the truck to. "We thought you'd like to know that we found a tracking device in the truck. Do you have the alarm or the monitor for it?" Lil Man explained that he had got the truck as a gift, and that all he had were the keys. But he was glad now that he had gotten rid of the truck. He figured out that Rocky must have known about the device, and kept it for himself to track the truck around. He figured that Stoop Head must have forgotten to tell him about the tracker.

Lil Man had gotten got back with Katousha and the baby and it was almost like a sigh of relief. He was stressed. He wasn't sure if the shooters of the truck just wanted to send a message or if they'd return again until Lil Man was dead. He wouldn't take any chances though, he loved his family and new found musical career too much to risk his freedom or livelihood. "So, have you given any thought to where you would like to go? It doesn't matter to me. I'm just glad we hadn't spent on building a pool yet. The reps at the record label think I should be living much larger considering the hits I put out, but they don't know that I'm a simple family man now." Katousha nodded her head in unison with what Lil Man was saying, but then allowed him to keep control of the situation. "Wherever you decide to move to, you will always have my support babe. Just keep in mind that I would like for us to be in visiting distance."

Lil Man thought about it. "Planes and flights make that possible. Whether we plan to visit, or have them visit us, I don't mind paying for the flight. The west coast may just be the place to keep us drama free." Lil Man went on to tell Katousha about the tracking device that his cousin had installed into the truck. She capitalized on the new information. "Well, now that the truck is gone we definitely shouldn't have to worry about anything happening like that again. Right?" Katousha was just being herself, sweet and innocent. Peaceful. Lil Man had been thinking more strategically and militant. He wanted to get whoever was trying to get him first. And he thought it would be safer to strike from a distance.

"Let's just stay at a hotel until we make a final decision. And thank you for not mentioning anything to anyone. Lord knows we need fewer ears to explain things to." Lil Man and Katousha were on the same page. They knew that the more people they had in their business, the more drama and attention it could possibly bring. They went to the Embassy Suites hotel, where all the rooms were fully furnished like apartments. Lil Man thought it would be best to stay there, since the rooms had had a homely feel to them.

Lil Man, Katousha and the baby had stayed in the Embassy Suites hotel for nearly two weeks before they had chosen a new place to move to. "There are some Condominiums and town houses in North East Philadelphia that I think you would love babe." Lil Man was right. Katousha wasn't too fond of the Condo's on state road. She said that they gave off an enclosed apartment complex feel. But the town houses were amazing! They turned out to be nicer than the house Lil Man had previously purchased. "Baby! I Love this house! Get it, get it, get it!!" Lil Man had pondered over the location for a while, and decided that they would move there.

He wanted to start all over. He was still doing music and loving his wife and son, but he felt his appearance had to change. Lil Man spent about an hour feeling his head, trying to determine if it were round enough to get a baldy. He said what the hell, and shaved his wavy hair from front to back. The next change he had made on his appearance was selling the Acura. The dealership had given him twelve thousand for it, when Stoop Head initially paid seventeen thousand. They said because of the rims and the moderations to the interior, the value had depreciated. That was bullshit, the first dope dealer to see that car is probably going to give up close to twenty thou cash, easy! But it didn't matter to Lil Man anyway. He was thinking about nothing but safety, and trying to shake a troublesome past. He bought a Steel grey Range Rover from the Land Rover dealer and left it plain except for the windows . . . They were tinted down to twenty percent instead of the usual dark five percent.

Lil Man was kind of wishing he had held on to his Mercury for Katousha, but he quickly realized that she wouldn't want to drive that is he was driving a Range Rover. Another royalty check had just been deposited into Lil Man's account from the record label, so he decided to take Katousha to the Lexus dealer and let her pick out her own car. She really had wanted the SC 400, but it was a coupe. No matter how pretty she would look in that car, she still thought about her family. So she settled for the GS 300, the one featured in Jay Z's "Dead Presidents" video. It was even the same color as the one Jay Z had driven, pearl white with the Steel grey bottom to match Lil Man's Range Rover. Katousha was happy with the car, and promised Lil Man she would take care of it. He hadn't minded her getting around on her own since she had her license.

Lil Man purchased the town house, and after Katousha met some movers over at the other house to get their things he put that one up for sale. The new home was in his mother's name, and both of the new cars were in his wife's name. Lil Man had felt comfortable again, but still unsettled about the thoughts he had about his cousin Rocky. Lil Man decided to make one more move towards

Rocky's favor, and he would finally be at ease. He called his Aunt. "Hello Auntie, its Rahim. I didn't quite get all of the equipment from your basement and wondered when it would be ok to stop by . . ." His Aunt had told him that he could come by any time before nine P.M. That's usually when she'd go up into her room for the night.

Lil Man then told his Aunt he would come and get it out of the way now so that he wouldn't bother her again. When he arrived at his Aunt's house, Lil Man parked in the back at the 'Lab' door and walked around front to ring the bell. His Aunt let him in and he kissed her cheek. "I'll be very quick Auntie. I'm not going to cut into your tea time." His Aunt instructed Lil Man to take his time, and to holler upstairs when he was finished. She would be in her bedroom. Lil Man went into the 'Lab' and went straight for the safe. Jackpot! It was still in the same place where Stoop Head had it all these years. Lil Man wasn't worried about it catching up with him. Rocky had gone crazy and wouldn't bring it up, and Lil Man felt like if Stoop were looking down on him that he'd understand. Lil Man lifted the three by three cube up and out the back door to his truck with a towel covering it. He then gathered the few studio items that where left, which had only been a couple of microphones, a set of speakers and a headset and put them in the truck to.

Lil Man let his Aunt know that he was done, and they said their goodbyes. Lil Man hadn't told Katousha what he had done until they had gotten home. "Do you ever think that bad things happen when you do bad things Rahim?" He knew she wouldn't understand. "Baby girl, I have been a good person to everyone I know. And I didn't get where I am by sitting back and hearing or taking crap from people. In this world, when you want something you've got to go and get it. Where just coming back from getting it, so what's the damn problem?" Katousha had to laugh from the way Lil Man had put it, but her facial expressions let him know that she was serious. "You know what I mean Rahim, and I like our new house. I don't want to move again. Mekhi has to grow up in a stable home!" Yup, she was serious.

Lil Man had stopped at a hardware store and bought a sledge hammer, a blow torch and some safety goggles. Everything he needed to work on the safe a crack it open. He drove home and parked his truck inside the two car garage so that he could unload it in private. After he got the safe and other things out, he backed the truck back out into the driveway so that he would have room to work on the safe. Katousha had ordered delivery food since the kitchen had not been fully set up for cooking yet. After they ate the Stromboli and Buffalo wings she ordered, Lil Man went out to the garage to get busy on the safe.

Lil Man stayed up working on the safe half the night, while Katousha waited curiously. She worked on music, trying to keep from being too bored without her man in the bed with her. But the patience finally paid off, and Lil Man had gotten the safe open a marveled at its contents. Another six hundred thousand in cash, a forty five millimeter handgun and a thirty inch twenty four karat gold chain with a lion's head with ruby's for eyes. Lil Man carried the safe to his bedroom to show his wife what was inside. "This is the final move I had to make to feel even with Rocky. This would have gone to him somehow if I hadn't taken it." Katousha wasn't at all impressed with the safes contents. "But didn't these things belong to your other cousin? How is this getting even with Rocky?" Katousha had a point, and Lil Man knew she was right.

But somehow he still felt a little justification from taking the safe. It was sweet. He thought to himself, 'this is what Stoop would have wanted'.

The next day, Lil man drove the safe to a junkyard to have it crushed. Once he was sure that the evidence was gone, he could finally put the situation behind him. Lil Man felt like he was well-off now. He hand handled all of his business in the streets and had caught up with his musical deadlines. All he thought he had to do now was be a loving father and husband. But as fate would have it, Lil Man wasn't quite out of hot water just yet. He was still wanted for questioning. He thought it may have blown over. But what happened next let him know that police don't stop their search until the wanted are found.

Lil Man was on his way home from the junkyard on Roosevelt Boulevard, when he had been pulled over by highway patrol. He hadn't even waited for the officer to come and speak to him. He called his wife right away. "Babe, I just got pulled over on the Boulevard. I was almost home to, damn! There's a good chance that they may take me in for that thing with Rocky, so I'm going to keep you on the phone so you can listen. So if they do arrest me, pick somebody up so you can come and get the truck. It doesn't need to go to any police impound anywhere. And call my lawyer, he knows about the lies Rocky told already and will know how to get me out. Hold on, here comes the officer . . ."

"Good afternoon sir. You have any idea why I pulled you over today?" Lil Man had some great acting skills. He put on the innocent unaware face before he answered the highway trooper. "No sir, I have no idea." The trooper leaned forward looking around inside of the truck, as if to be surprised that it was so clean inside. "Your temporary tags are not filled in correctly. I could barely see the numbers or the state. Do me a favor and go ahead and get out your license, registration and insurance for me would ya?" The trooper had spoken with a deep southern accent. 'This is Philadelphia! What the hell is this guy even doing here?' Lil Man thought to himself. He handed the paperwork and his license to the trooper in confidence that everything was legitimate. "Ok fella, gone ahead and sit tight for me and I'll be right back witcha."

Katousha was still on the cell phone listening. "Damn, was he profiling or what? Let's just hope for the best baby, the truck is clean and legit." The officer returned to Lil Mans window and handed his paperwork back to him. "Here you go, put that away. And sir I'm afraid I'm gonna have to ask you to step out of the vehicle." Lil Man gave Katousha the signal to go ahead and make the lawyer call and to come and get the truck from Roosevelt Boulevard and Grant Avenue. "Who is Katousha Johnson?" Lil Man was aggravated from being cuffed. "That's my wife, and I'm not answering another question until you tell me why I'm being arrested." "You're wanted for questioning. According to our system, you have had a warrant for your arrest for at least two months. Take a seat in the back of my car and sit tight. Is there any drugs or weapons in the vehicle that I should be aware of?" Lil Man was being as sharp as he possibly could with the officer, knowing that his lawyer was already on the job. "I'm pleading the Fifth Amendment and for the record you do not have permission to search my vehicle." The truck was as clean as a whistle, and so would Lil Man's case be if the officer had searched his truck against his will. When Lil Man called Katousha, he activated the recording feature on his cell phone.

The trooper had requested backup and when the second car arrived, the officers had begun searching Lil Man's truck together. They drove Lil Man to police headquarters in downtown Philadelphia, where he had been processed and waited for the detectives or his lawyer, whoever would show up first. Lil Man was allowed a phone call and called his wife. She informed him that she had spoken to Neil Patrioni, Lil Man's attorney. "Neil said that you had to be fully processed, and would be charged with weapons violations and aggravated assault for shooting Rocky." Lil Man couldn't believe. He was sitting in jail over a lie from a jealous person, and what made it worse was that the person was family. "Its cool babe, I'll get through this. How is the baby?" Lil Man tried to make conversation that would put Katousha's mind at ease. "The baby is fine Rahim. But your lawyer also said that even if you post bail, you will not be released until you are interviewed by detectives about the shooting."

Lil Man had spoken with Katousha for ten minutes before he was put back into his filthy cell. The cells in the "Round House", which was the nick name given to Philadelphia police headquarters, had to be the most trifling facilities on earth! You would rather be in a concentration camp than in there. It was barely breathable. There were feces in all of the corners, sometimes it was mixed in with throw up. The sink slash toilet ensemble was filthy and broken. It was like every person who ever tried to use the toilet missed on purpose, getting their fudge colored waste all over the cells. There was hardened cheese all over the walls and ceiling that had cracked from being old, and would cut you if you weren't careful.

What made the conditions worse for Lil Man is that he was not even supposed to be there. If he had gotten caught for a crime, he would have no problem sitting and doing his time as long as his wife was maintaining and taking care of their child. But he was sitting over a lie, and would clear his name up without even adding anything negative to his cousin's situation. Lil Man couldn't see himself stooping as low as Rocky had, lying to put a case on somebody. It had gone against the grain. It had broken all the laws and codes of the street and normally, Rocky's action would have been punishable by death. But these circumstances were slightly different. Rocky was locked up, and it would take some time before Lil Man could get to him. Not only that, but Rocky was family. A first cousin. And Lil Man still had some feelings about that. He knew Rocky would get what he had coming to him eventually, and when he did Lil Man vowed to put it behind him as if Rocky was just another guy on the street. He had to think like that, the guy had put a gun to his head for Christ sakes!

It took Lil Man the full seventy two hours to get processed, the maximum time allotted for staying at the district jail before being transported to prison. The judge had set his bail at half a million dollars and Lil Man were to post ten percent in order to be released. It took fifty thousand dollars just to see his wife and kid again. To Lil Man, it was worth every nickel. His lawyer had promised to get that money back once the case was over with. Lil Man had been taken to the Curran Fromhold Correctional Facility on State Road in Philadelphia, otherwise known as C.F.C.F. He didn't think he'd be going there, but the detectives that wanted to interview him were obviously taking their time. No matter how much money a man had, when you're behind those bars, you're on their time and no longer your own. The system was a monster that ate huge chunks of time away from your life.

When Lil Man went through the prison's process of intake, he had seen all sorts of familiar faces from when he had hustled. A lot of those faces were from high school, and he was reluctant to speaking to anybody because he hadn't known what type of damage Rocky's rumor had caused. Technically as it stood he was sort of in Rocky's house right now, and had to be careful how he moved and spoke to people. Rocky had money and power, just like Lil Man had. But Rocky was more in touch with the streets. He was stuck on a hustler's mentality and no matter how much money he had made the streets were all he ever cared to know. That was what separated him from Lil Man. Lil Man's plan was to get out of the 'hood', and when he got paid that's exactly what he had did. He even tried to leave most of the attitude behind as well, but was glad some was still in him for times like this one.

"Hey man! I know you! You're Rahim Bowman! Remember me? It's Pete man!" Lil Man couldn't believe his eyes. It was Pete Mason, his friend from grade school he had once helped save from a terrible beating after school. Lil did Lil Man know, Pete would be a lot different know. He was in jail for robbery and burglary, and had nearly totally lost his mind due to a crack cocaine and PCP addiction. "What's up Pete? What bring you to such a lovely place?" Pete laughed. "I got caught with a gun. I mean I had my gun on me, in the liquor store. And they said I tried to rob the place just because I had my gun out and took some bottles without paying. Shit man! I didn't ask them for any damn money! I was just thirsty, so how is that robbery?" It was safe to that Pete was truly crazy. He didn't belong in prison. A psychotic ward would have been the place for Pete. But Philadelphia was so overrun with crime, that the city's police were just throwing everybody together in the same place, not really caring what their problems were or what circumstances they had. The system was nuts.

Lil Man saw that Pete's state of mind had not really been that of a normal person, so he decided to try and jar Pete's memory to see how much he truly had lost. "Do you remember Veronica?" Lil Man knew if Pete could remember Vernie, then he'd probably remember the time Lil Man had saved his butt. "Veronica, Veronica, Veronica" Pete whispered the name over and over until it came to him. "Oh yeah! Veronica! She was the sexiest red bone in our whole school man! Remember how those dudes jumped us over her?" Lil Man wanted to say, 'No, they jumped you and I saved your ass. I got jumped separately on a different occasion due to the prettiness of our classmate'. Instead he just went along with Pete's version. "Yeah man, they were surely some wild days we had. So what's your situation? Are you getting out of here anytime soon?"

Lil Man thought that if he made Pete feel like he owed him, he could send him to take Rocky out and his cousin would never even see Pete coming. "I'm not going anywhere man. The judge set my bail four months ago. I ain't got no damn money!" Perfect! Lil Man spent hours befriending Pete. He was basically recruiting his 'hit man'. Lil Man told him about the situation with Rocky, and told him how he needed Rocky to meet his maker. Lil Man assured Pete that if he had gotten close to Rocky and put the work in, his bail would be paid and he would get another payment once he had gotten released. Pete agreed, and Lil Man took his info and saved it on an envelope.

Lil Man had stayed at C.F.C.F for nearly two weeks before he was finally released. Come to find out the lead detective on his case lost the file and was unaware that Lil Man was in custody. He hadn't been released until his lawyer contacted the judge and formally had gotten the guess dropped, without even going to court. Money well spent. Lil Man was so pleased with his attorney's work that he split the bail refund with him as a bonus, twenty five thousand dollars. "Take the wife somewhere special" he urged his attorney. Lil Man promised he would never see those cells again, even if it meant he had to make himself a blind mind. Having your freedom stripped was one thing, living in those types of fouls conditions was a totally different ballgame. Once he had gotten home, Lil Man greeted his wife with the biggest hug and kiss she had ever felt. He promised her that he would never leave again.

He then went over and picked up Mekhi, who had been inching over in his walker to greet dad anyway, and promised him the same thing. "I'm sorry Mekhi. Da da had a little bit of business to take care of, but it's all over now! He spun around in a slow whirl while holding Mekhi and felt like a brand new man! There had been one more phone call Lil Man was waiting to receive, but he tried not to think about it. He would get it whenever the job was done.

"Money doesn't always bring happiness, but happiness will bring money!" Those words from Stoop Head had resurfaced in Lil Man's mind all of the time. He always found some old memories of Stoop that made him day dream and think about how great life could be, or how short it could be. Lil Man felt blessed. He had a beautiful wife and a wonderful baby boy. He had a beautiful home, and a bank account that allowed him to do anything he wanted to do. He was in good health, great shape! He was earning money doing something both he and his wife had enjoyed. Lil Man thought to himself . . . 'What more could a man ask for?"

About two or three months had gone by, and Lil Man and his family had spent time bonding and adding furniture to decorate and make their house into a home. Katousha had found an arts and crafts shop nearby, where she bought vases, plants and framed art work. Lil Man had gone to a pottery barn out in New Jersey and purchased two concrete life sized lions to put on either side of the walkway leading up to their house. It was beautiful what they were doing to the place. And seeing Mekhi scramble around in the bright green grass was just the icing on the cake.

One afternoon while they were on the patio in the back of the house, the phone had rung. It was Lil Man's mother. She said that Rocky had been stabbed to death in prison, and no one had seen or heard anything about who had done it. Lil Man had to do all he could to act surprised. He hadn't told Katousha about his hired help on State Road. He decided to wait a few days to let things die down, and then Lil Man went and paid Pete's bail. Lil Man was very nervous about bailing Pete out and being connected to Rocky's murder somehow. But he had no one else to send, he kept his word.

A few days after Lil Man had paid the bail, he then called the number Pete had given him. "Pete! What's up man? I just wanted to thank you, and we could meet up anytime for you to get paid aight?" Pete hadn't told Lil Man yet, but he had some news that could very well come back and bite Lil Man in the ass later on. Lil Man checked the magazine of his thirty eight millimeter to make sure it was fully loaded. He had to be cautious, he was going to meet a broke crack head who had murdered someone to get out of prison. You really have to be careful with a triple threat like that.

When Lil Man pulled up into the gas station where they chose to meet, Lil Man saw Pete begging people for change and offering to clean the windows of cars for food. He was dressed in filthy clothes. It looked like being in prison was actually better for Pete. He had a way to stay clean, a place to sleep and food to eat, more commonly known as 'three hots and a cot'. Lil Man pulled over near Pete and cracked his window while blowing the horn. He wasn't letting Pete get into his new Range Rover.

"Heyyy! Lil Man! You are looking good baby, looking real good!! Say listen man, I'm sorry I didn't handle the job but thanks for getting me out man! I would have been in that bitch forever if it weren't for you!!" Hold up, Lil Man was extra confused. "What you mean you didn't do the job?" Lil Man was trying to get Pete's story straight. He had to listen carefully because people high on crack spoke fast and didn't make any sense unless you were paying extra close attention, not to mention Pete also had smoked angel dust. He was very jittery when he talked. His eyes were wide open like he had seen a ghost. "They didn't let me get close to your man. I never made it to his cell block." Another thing about people who were as high as Pete had been is that they tend to tell the truth. Sometimes they can't even help it. Telling the truth makes them feel like they still have a grasp on reality. Everything else is just a hallucination or figment of their imaginations.

Lil Man was prepared to give Pete a nice amount of cash. He had counted out twenty thousand in cash to pay for the hit on Rocky. But after Lil Man saw Pete's condition and Pete told him he wasn't even the one who had done it, Lil Man changed his mind and kept the money. He figured Pete would just take the money and smoke it up. As a matter of fact, Lil Man had actually wondered if he had hurt Pete by bailing him out of prison. Pete would have been better off in there, safe and away from his crack demons. Lil Man decided to buy Pete some food. He told Pete that if he tried to find a job and really clean himself up by laying off the drugs, that he would help him. Lil Man would get Pete a haircut and some decent clothes, if he really wanted to help himself.

Un-Focused

Lil Man was back to being steadily concerned only with his family and career. He would never find out who had murdered Rocky, but he was sure that no more hits or tampering would be coming from him in prison. Lil Man had thought that Rocky's death had stemmed from one of the people he had shot at the club that night. Lil Man kept finding himself in a daze daydreaming about all the drama he had been through. From struggling to get along with his family, to fights in school, being arrested, hustling and police. Lil Man looked back at it all and decided that Katousha and Mekhi were the best things that ever happened to him. He also thought of all the love he used to get from Stoop Head, but often wondered if Stoop would have been so generous if it hadn't been for him being sick and near death.

Lil Man and Katousha would have some very deep and intimate conversations whenever they weren't working on their music. And Katousha noticed something more and more about her husband every day. Lil Man would go from one extreme topic to the other, as if bouncing back and forth between conversations and constantly changing the subject. Sometimes she never understood why and had just dealt with it and had gotten used to it. She just summed it up to being 'that's just how he is'. But it seemed that the more often Lil Man had done it, the more concerned his wife had become. She decided to try and find out what was going on with her man and sought for professional help while they could still afford it.

Katousha called a doctor and consulted with him over the phone about Lil Mans worsening condition. The doctor told Katousha that she should bring Lil Man in to talk with him. She agreed, but first she had to figure out a way to convince Lil Man to go. She wasn't sure if voicing it just once would be enough, he may possibly just change the subject again and blow the whole situation off. But Katousha had to try. It was for the sake of her family. Katousha had poured two glasses of chilled wine after putting Mekhi down for an afternoon nap. She then set the wine out on the patio in the rear of the house and asked Lil Man to join her outside.

"Rahim, I wanted to talk to you about how strangely you've been acting lately. When we have conversations, I catch you drifting off into a daze and then you snap back with a different topic like nothing ever happened. It's scaring me, and I'm worried about you." His wife was being very serious, but Lil Man's sense of humor had gotten the best of him and he sarcastically made a comment to lighten things up a little. He sat that for a moment after Katousha had finished speaking and then finally responded. "Did you see the Eagle's game last night?" Katousha wanted to laugh because she knew her man was being funny. But she was really hoping to get him to go and see the doctor that she had found.

After discussing the attention span shortness's for about a half an hour, Lil Man agreed to make an appointment with the doctor. Katousha had informed him that she had saved him the trouble, and made the appointment already. It was in two days at one thirty pm. "Wow, so you didn't waste any time huh babe? It's like you have my entire life figured out right?" Katousha had anticipated Lil Man getting a little upset, but she was still pushing towards him getting some help. Even though he had his sense of humor and was still taking care of her and the baby, Katousha couldn't help but notice that the daydreaming would progressively last longer. The attention spans were getting shorter, and she was in fear of losing her relationship. Lil Man was losing his focus.

They drove to the doctor's office out in Bensalem, Pennsylvania, right outside of Philadelphia. Katousha hadn't told Lil Man what type of doctor he'd be seeing, but he would soon find out. They had reached Dr. Levy's office, and went inside and waited to be seen. Lil Man was quiet, and Katousha had wondered what was on his mind. Damn! Even at the doctor's office, he was still drifting off into space and Katousha couldn't snap him out of it for a while. She was eager to tell the doctor in person what was going on. After a few moments of flipping through magazine's and a couple of trips to the water cooler, the doctor finally came out and introduced himself to Lil Man and Katousha.

"Hello. My name is Dr. Levy and I am the therapist who will be assisting you this afternoon. Ms. Katousha Johnson and Rahim Bowman, Is that correct?" Katousha had begun speaking first, since she had initiated the appointment. "Yes, that is correct." Katousha spoke while Lil Man had went into one of his spacey spells, right in front of the doctor. And when the doctor had called Lil Man's name, he hadn't responded at first. The doctor then suggested that he consult with the two on a one on one basis. After interviewing each of them individually, the doctor rescheduled them for treatment sessions that would extend to six months before making an official determination or diagnosis. After that day Lil Man had begun visiting the therapist's office once, sometimes twice a week. Lil Man had given the doctor permission to search his medical records in the midst of him being treated by the therapist. The doctor actually was nearing a diagnosis and wanted to see if Lil Man would have been allergic to any medications.

After discovering that there were several physical ailments as well as mental and hereditary issues, the doctor felt it safe to rule and diagnose Lil Man with a.d.h.d. 'Attention Deficit Hyperactivity Disorder'. Dr. Levy first informed Katousha of his findings, and began interviewing her about her husband's behavior as far as sleeping habits and mood swings. After the doctor had broken down and explained the true meaning and characteristics of Lil Mans disorder to Katousha, she had thought that everything overall had sounded pretty normal. "Dr. Levy, I don't mean any harm at all. But can't anybody go through that? No one has a good or great day nonstop, do they? I mean, I had visited a club not too long ago and was as happy as ever until some chick got disrespectful with me. That's a pretty normal reaction where we're from."

The doctor had pretty much agreed with Katousha as far as the circumstance she described, but then explained that Lil Man's situation was hereditary and mental. Katousha started not to like the doctors' prognosis herself, and the whole thing was her idea! The doctor was painting Lil Man out to be a real nut case. 'Oh well' Katousha thought. 'I love my crazy man. I'll just take my nut case home and deal with him the best way I can.' For six weeks' worth of visits, Lil Man had paid about forty five hundred dollars and had been called a nut by the doctor. It had bothered

Katousha so much that she was ready to pay for a second opinion, but had refused to waste any more money on it. They would just live with the advice the doctor had given about plenty of rest and remaining as stress free and less excited as possible. The doctor had mentioned that sleep aids could help with any anxiety attacks at night, and could help counter the effects from the disorder.

Katousha was concerned for Lil Man's actual health, but all Lil Man had gotten from the experience was another reason to be upset at his dead beat father. He had passed down a hereditary disorder. 'Thanks a lot, dad!!' he thought to himself. Lil Man and Katousha had driven home and discussed some of the things the doctor had mentioned. "You know what babe? Maybe I should have just told you this before you dragged me to a shrink, but I have had a lot on my mind lately. When I daydream, it's not that I'm lost out in space, I'm actually concentrating on a thought that I don't want to lose. And I'm not pointing the blame anywhere either, but ever since Mekhi came in we have had less time to reflect on personal thoughts. And that's perfectly fine, I love sharing my time with both of you. That's all it is baby, just a moment of reflection on the past and counting all the blessings that we have today."

Katousha was not buying that for one second. She knew Lil Man better than that. Katousha had noticed a change in her husband and swore to find out what it was all about. She had a feeling it had something to do with the streets. Her intuitions had pointed to things a doctor wouldn't even understand. She apologized to Lil Man for making him go to that doctor and she left it at that verbally, but Katousha would definitely be doing her own investigation on her man to find out what was going on. She started by going through his cell phone. There was nothing questionable to find in it. Then in the middle of the night while he slept, Katousha went out and searched the Range Rover. It was good that she knew how to open the secret compartments that were nearly invisible. She had never had time to get a good look in them before now. She first went through the glove box thoroughly. There was nothing in there except one of Lil Man's guns and the paperwork for the truck. She then searched the invisible console on the floorboard between the two front seats. In it she found another gun, and a bottle containing a golden liquid. Katousha thought it could be cologne, so to be sure she took off the top and smelled it.

Katousha hadn't known it, but she had just taken a whiff of one of the most powerful and dangerous drugs on the street. It was PCP, and it was so strong that the whiff she had just taken could have easily gotten her high and twisted her entire thinking pattern. She screwed the top back on and closed the compartment back. She then went back upstairs and got in bed with Lil Man. She wasn't sure why, but Katousha could not sleep. She thought she would be dead tired, but actually wound up being the exact opposite. The chemical she had just smelled would never let her get any sleep right now. She had to wait at least an hour before the effect had worn off. She decided to take advantage of her energy and began fondling her husband in his sleep. She had become so horny and wet that she even had forgotten to question Lil Man about the bottle like she had planned to. Lil Man woke up and went along with his wife's flow. He jumped up out of his sleep and flipped her over to her knees in the doggy style position, and began pounding away at her love box until she woke the baby from uncontrollable squealing.

'One down, now just one more to go.' Lil Man had rocked his wife to sleep without even trying. But Mekhi was a different story. To Mekhi, it may have sounded like mommy was getting hurt. But after some warm milk and cartoons, the baby was off to lala land right along with his mom. Now Lil Man was up and wide awake. He decided to look around the house to see what he could go out and buy tomorrow to add to decorating their home. Plants and paintings were his favorite touches, as long as the plants were in vases. And not just any vases, they had to be a floor model sized. Katousha was a fan of wicker, but Lil Man said wicker was more of an outdoor thing. So their patio and deck in back of the house wound up looking like a jungle with the wicker furniture complimenting the spider plants and the bamboo shoot torches.

After surveying the house for a while, Lil Man had gotten back into bed after checking on the baby again. He was in a dreamy state from the intense sex and had been picturing an exotic aquarium he could put together. He couldn't fall asleep right away. He began to wonder what made Katousha wake him up at two in the morning for sex. She was freaky at most times, but this move had been totally out of her character. Lil Man decided to just ask her about it in the morning. The next morning, he had woken up to the smell of breakfast cooking. He sat up to see inside of Mekhi's crib. The baby was downstairs with mom. 'Wow' he thought. 'They've got the drop on me early today huh?' When Lil Man walked downstairs and into the kitchen, Katousha was still cooking and Mekhi was happily racing around on the smoothly waxed hardwood kitchen floor in his walker.

"Da Da!!" Mekhi made an effort to call Lil Man when he saw him, grabbing Lil Mans and Katousha's attention, who hadn't known Lil Man was standing in the kitchen doorway. "No snitching Mekhi. You are blowing Da da's cover!" Lil Man walked up behind his wife who had seemed to be undistracted at the stove, and put his hands on her waist, kissing her neck. "Good morning babe." Lil Man immediately saw something on the counter that was not supposed to be there. It was the bottle from Lil Man's truck containing the golden colored juice. "Good morning Rahim. I have a confession. I have gone out and went through your truck. What is that in the bottle Rahim? And don't lie to me ok?" Lil Man hadn't felt busted. He had a perfectly reasonable explanation for the bottle being in his truck. "It was in the safe when I first opened it babe, I put it up in the truck so it wouldn't be near you or the baby. It's wet. We used to sell it back when Maze was still out. There was also a Kilo of cocaine in the safe along with that bottle and the cash. It should be in the garage, or did you move that to?"

It had been nearly a year since Lil Man had sold drugs. He no longer had to. But his sense of hustle wouldn't allow him to hold on to that much product and not get rid of it for a decent price. He decided to get rid of it wholesale for a package price, that way he'd be over and done with it for good. Lil Man made some calls from his old 'hustle' phone to talk to a few smokers and see if he could figure out who had enough paper to take a key of coke off of his hands. Lil Man knew that the coke was pure and should be sold at top dollar, because it used to belong to Stoop Head who had only dealt with the best. But Lil Man decided to give somebody a sweet deal, just to go ahead and get rid of the stuff.

Lil Man received a phone call back from Benny. Benny was a crack head who bought crack from everybody. He didn't care as long as he could smoke it. Benny said that he had two guys who were going half, and would be putting their money together as long as the stuff was pure and un-cut. Lil Man said cool, and that the price would be twenty four thousand for everything. Benny called back an hour later and said the guys were ready to meet him. They discussed the meeting place and Lil Man told Benny to make sure the dudes were on time. He would be meeting someone in a red van in a Home Depot parking lot off of the Boulevard.

Lil Man wrapped the goodies up and stashed them away in his scent proof compartment along with his chrome three eighty. He told Katousha what was going on, and assured her that he would be right back and that this was the last time he'd be doing anything like this. They kissed and Lil Man left to go and meet with the buyers in the red van. Lil Man was sure everything would run smoothly because no one had known what he was driving.

When Lil Man reached the parking lot he spotted the van quickly, an old and rusted red Dodge Caravan. He decided to cruise the parking lot for a second and pretended he was looking for parking, while he was checking out the scene. Once he felt comfortable, Lil Man pulled up and parked right next to the red van. There were two guys in it, and Lil Man rolled down his passenger side window to communicate. They didn't have to say too much of anything, both parties had identified each other. Lil Man signaled for one of the guys to get out of the van. A young guy, probably in his late teens had gotten out of the van and walked around to come and join Lil Man inside his truck. Lil Man wasn't showing anything until he saw the money. The boy pulled out five rolls of money wrapped in rubber bands. "This is twenty four" he said nervously. His hands were even shaking as he passed Lil Man the cash. Rahim sensed something was wrong, but didn't have time to figure out what. The best way to make these sorts of transactions was quickly, smoothly and calmly with a cool head.

Lil Man went into the scent proof box and pulled out the bag containing the key and the bottle of 'juice'. Just when he tried to hand it to the guy he noticed a silver Mercedes pulling up on the other side of him in a hurry. It was a set up. The first thing Lil Man had faced was his passenger pulling out a gun demanding the bag and the money back. Lil Man had to think fast. Being trapped by the other car, he didn't have time to jump out nor was it even possible because the Mercedes had been parked so closely. He decided that the only thing he could do was floor the gas pedal, sending the Range Rover head on into a car parked about twenty feet ahead. The impact had sent Lil Mans passenger flying through the windshield into a bloody mess out onto the ground of the parking lot. Lil Man saw the Mercedes approaching again and decided to deal with them once and for all. He stooped low into his seat so it would look like they had both gone through the windshield. Lil Man waited for the silver car to get close and when it did, he opened fire into the tinted Mercedes windows emptying the three eighty and sending both occupants to hell.

Lil man had been banged up pretty badly from the crash, but knew he had to hurry up and get out of there. The Range had stalled the first two times Lil Man had tried to start it. Then the engine finally turned over. The front was smashed terribly and Lil Man knew he wouldn't be able to drive it far. He had to get off of the scene and ditch his truck somewhere until he could get it towed to the chop shop. Even though Lil Man was extremely hot at the moment, he knew that if he could get out of sight he would be set. He had gotten rid of the dudes who were looking for him that had shot up his cousin's truck. And on top of that he still had his product and the twenty four thousand bucks. All he had to do now was make it home safely.

Lil Man parked the truck in someone's driveway, gotten all his things out and put them all in a bag and walked away from the truck. He didn't want to call a taxi to get home. The airwaves would probably be listening out for someone trying to flee that area. And he couldn't get on a bus or a train with twenty four thousand and a key of coke, the scent was too strong. He had to call Katousha. "Baby, drive down the Boulevard and pick me up. It's an emergency. The truck is gone. Just hurry up babe!" Luckily they had only lived about five minutes from the Boulevard, and once on it Katousha would have reached Lil Man in no time.

Lil Man spotted Katousha's Lexus coming towards him on the opposite side of the Boulevard. He waved his arms so she would stop, and he darted across the Boulevard and jumped in the car with his wife. "Babe! You won't believe what they hell just happened to me girl! Them dude's tried to get me! One of them may still be alive, I doubt it though. But the guys that Rocky sent after me are gone for sure. Oh, and I made twenty four thousand and still have my stuff . . ."

Lil Man was still catching his breath while explaining to Katousha what had happened. They went to go and park so that he could stash his goods and gun safely before driving around 'dirty', meaning having illegal goods in the car. Katousha's Lexus had a compartment in the trunk, similar to the one in the Range Rover. Lil Man had wanted to check the scene since he was in a different car now with darker windows. When they drove by the Home Depot, there were cops everywhere! And no ambulances meant there was no one in a rush to get saved. The dude who had flown out of Lil Mans windshield was a goner to, along with the goons in Rocky's silver Benz.

Lil Man was sure his street troubles were over now. His stalkers were gone, and their sender was gone. Lil Man just had to cope with the fact that he was responsible for killing three people. It was going to be hard to live with, but he just kept telling himself . . . "It was either them, or me!" Lil Man called his friend at the chop shop and explained that he had an emergency tow job for him. He told him where the truck was parked, before surveillance videos began flashing all over the news. With three dead bodies and no suspects, the media was sure to broadcast anything they could find out to try and capture a suspect. Lil Man instructed the chop shop to crush the truck, getting rid of it as it was sure to be evidence. He told them they would be getting paid if they hurried and picked up the truck. The sooner Lil Man received a call saying the truck was gone, the more money they'd be getting.

The police scoured all over Philadelphia in search of Lil Man's truck. Luckily for Lil Man, from the angles of surveillance they didn't have a clear shot of him or the trucks' plates. He was in the clear. But this type of situation would definitely turn up the heat all around the city. Lil Man was debating on whether to contact his lawyer or not. No one had a clue that Lil Man was involved in the shooting deaths. He decided not to fill his lawyer in just yet.

Lil Man and Katousha were on their way home. Before they reached the house, Lil Man had gotten the call that the truck had been picked up and was on its way to being crushed. "Thanks Frankie! Listen, I'm going to stop by tomorrow and straighten you up real nicely ok?" "Alright man, no problem! We know your word is good here . . ."

Lil Man and Katousha didn't go straight home. Instead, they went for pizza and had taken Mekhi to a local park. Katousha kept a stroller in her trunk, so they just strolled around the park for a while after eating and killed some time until Lil Man felt comfortable enough to go home. The sun started to set and it began getting dark outside. Lil Man picked up Mekhi out of his stroller and placed him in his car seat while Katousha put the stroller away in the trunk. All day since the Home Depot incident, the couple had noticed heavy amounts of police activity everywhere and things weren't any different during their drive home. Katousha and Lil Man noticed police cars zipping back and forth in all directions, pulling people over and chasing down vehicles that resembled Lil Man's truck. "They are following a lot of false leads. That's good for us" Lil Man told his wife.

They went home and tuned in to the news to see what was being said to the public. "Another violent day in Philadelphia's 'Frankford' section as gunfire erupts leaving three men dead. The police have no leads, no suspects and no motives . . . . Stay tuned as we hope to bring you more in this developing story." Lil Man was glad to hear that the authorities were clueless. And as long as he had stayed off of the street for a while, he'd be ok. While lying low, Lil Man just worked out in a room he had set up with gym equipment. The rest of the time he'd be working on music, eating or making love to his wife.

After a while Mekhi was crawling faster and even walking a little on his own. They had to keep a close eye on him. He was bound to wind up anywhere if you hadn't kept a close eye on him. One day while Katousha was cooking breakfast, she noticed Mekhi had gotten quiet on the other side of the kitchen counter. When she went to check on him, Mekhi was already half way upstairs. "Just where in the world do you think you are going little boy? Huh!? There's nobody up there. Are you trying to leave your momma downstairs all alone? Huh? Your daddy is in the workout room. You looking for your da da? Rahim, come and get your son. He keeps slipping away while I'm trying to cook!" Lil Man came into the kitchen shirtless, sweating all over with chest and arms bulging. "You should've just put him in his walker babe. But anything for my babies!" Katousha was overwhelmed by Lil Mans sweaty and shiny physique. She didn't even have an answer, and if she did it would have come out sounding shaky. All she could do was watch him interact with the baby while biting her bottom lip, nearly burning the eggs that she was cooking. She was turned on. Lil Man was a distraction, as well as an arousal for Katousha.

Lil Man laid low for months before he went out and bought a new car. Staying in and collecting checks from music, he felt it was time to treat himself. Katousha's car was already beautiful, but he decided it was time to upgrade her as well. It was an early Saturday morning when Lil Man decided to get a new vehicle. He knew he had to stay away from the Land Rover dealership. It was out of sight out of mind with them as far as he was concerned. Lil Man thought about getting something exotic, but he didn't want to be too flashy. That morning, they went to a rim and tire shop and had some twenty inch chrome wheels put on Katousha's car. Lil Man said they were for her birthday, which would have been in a week. He would still have something else in store for her to, but today was about their cars.

After the car was driven out of the garage from the wheels being put on, Lil Man and Katousha looked at how beautiful the car had become. "Wow! That thing is pretty girl! You mind if I get your phone number and maybe we can go out later?" Katousha loved when Lil Man flirted as if they had just met. He made sure he kept his woman turned on. Lil Man saw how sexy the car had looked and felt it was only right to get something to keep him in the sexy class with his wife. "Let's go to Jaguar baby. There happens to be one near our house on Grant Avenue." Before leaving the wheel shop, Lil Man had inquired about wheels that would fit a Jaguar. The owner of the shop had given Lil Man a pamphlet containing wheels that fit on foreign cars, especially Jaguars.

They headed toward the highway to get a feel of the new wheels while heading toward the Jaguar dealer. "How does it feel baby?" Lil Man could tell Katousha was proud of the new look of her car. She had already been glad to be driving a Lexus, but Lil Man was spoiling his wife. It was partly because he had felt so guilty about the drama he involved her in. But Lil Man thought that if it weren't for some drama, life could very well much be boring. "It feels great baby, and I can feel the car sitting up a little higher. It feels smoother." Lil Man thought he had better give her some basic rules and guidelines to having and driving on custom wheels. "Toosh, just for future reference you cannot typically drive the way you're used to driving. You have to slow down crossing tracks and going over potholes. The main reason being is because the tires are thinner, and the chrome is sort of fragile. If you hit something hard while going too fast, you can crack the rim and will get an instant flat. It could get worse. You could actually shatter the entire rim and of course that would lead to a serious crash."

While Lil Man was telling Katousha about the delicate wheels, he could feel her slowing down as he spoke. The more he spoke, the more nervous she became. She started feeling like the car was riding on light bulb glass, soft and easy to break. But Lil Mans plan was working. He wanted his wife to become a defensive driver, more careful and taking care of her wheels. "One last thing babe. These wheels are much heavier than the ones that came off. So the studs that held the other wheels on are now supporting more pressure. You really have to try and not hit any big bumps or potholes." When you pay a huge price for something expensive, you tend to appreciate it more. Lil Man was trying to pass the sense of appreciation over to his wife, without her having to pay anything. The notion could pertain to many things. Jewelry, children, anything that was yours you would care for more than others. In this case, it was chrome rims. Lil Man knew that once Katousha had gotten used to driving on the delicate wheels and tires, that she would eventually become a better and safer driver. "What are studs?"

Katousha's question let Lil Man know that she was paying attention. He loved that about her, always curious, always inquisitive and thirsty for knowledge. She had a real head on her shoulders. "Studs are the four or five bolts that hold the rim onto the car. Sometimes they can snap from hitting a pothole with heavy wheels. They can even snap with normal wheels, but it's less likely because tires with more air will absorb more impact." Lil Man had explained everything to a tee, and Katousha wasn't the type that needed important things drilled into her head. She would definitely remember. They arrived at the Jaguar dealership and took Mekhi's stroller from the trunk. They went inside and shopped the showroom of all the latest models.

"I think I want to go with green babe. What do you think?" Katousha didn't really want to interfere with Lil Mans decision making in selecting a vehicle. She left it completely up to him because she realized that cars were his thing, and he had known a lot more about them than she did. But she was confident that any questions she had, her man would fill her in thoroughly. "I think you would look good in anything daddy. But green is a good look. I think green or white if we're talking Jaguar colors." Katousha calling her husband daddy let him know that she was probably horny. He took his focus off of the cars for a moment and concentrated on her freaky tendencies. He and his wife found themselves frolicking around in the dealership like horny teenagers all over again. "Alright, alright babe. Stop, I gotta buy a car." She had gotten Lil Man worked up, and would definitely pay for it later that evening . . . her entire plan of course.

No matter if you are rich or poor, healthy or sick, no matter your age, race, color, or creed. If you are in a serious relationship, listen to your significant other. Make them feel wanted, let them know that they matter and you can easily reap the benefits of true love. You can constantly renew the reasons you fell in love with your mate in the first place, just by simply listening to them. You will always find something new. Lil Man and Katousha's relationship consisted of constant revision. The revision wasn't necessarily always for correction, but was there for fresh perspectives. Their love's flame was far from dying out, due to constant revision. They were never bored with each other.

Lil Man was doing the paperwork on a 2003 Jaguar S-type, forest green. After everything was finalized, he and Katousha left the dealership to go and eat. "I still need you to follow me from the rim shop babe. I don't need any cops jumping behind me with these temporary tags. Remember? That's why that one trooper stopped me last time." Katousha agreed and they left and went to Friendly's for lunch.

Once they were seated inside the restaurant, the waitress brought over a high chair for Mekhi. Katousha had a disposable camera that she kept in her purse to capture cute moments of the baby. "Let's give him his first French fry! Not let him eat, just hold one and take a picture."

Lil Man wanted to see his boy grow up so fast that he was ready to feed him fast food just to speed up the process. "If we give him a French fry he is not giving it back! That baby has a death grip on food!" Katousha was always surprised at how strong her baby was. His powerful grips and aggressiveness with food turned her off from breastfeeding. "That baby? Let's not forget that he came out of you babe. Maybe he gets his power from your thighs, I know I do!" They laughed, and Katousha smashed up a French fry to softness to see what Mekhi would do with it. They knew he would try to eat it, but whether or not he would like it was the issue.

The first French fry turned into two. And the two turned into four. It was official, Mekhi loved fries! Katousha had to stop. Mekhi would start demanding bigger portions each time. But the couple took some great photos with the baby smiling with fists full of smashed French fries. After they ate, they drove the two cars back to the rim shop.

Lil Man ordered some twenty two inch chrome wheels that resembled flowers. They fit perfectly on the Jag and looked magnificent. They drove their cars home, and Lil Man parked his in the garage so that he could put some finishing touches on it and added a few accessories. The week had started out with Katousha damn near getting Lil Man committed just because the man had daydreamed. Now she was the one all dreamy, unable to take her eyes off of her man. She studied Lil Mans movements and listened to his voice. They were under each other's spell, but now it had seemed that Katousha was the one who was un-focused.

WORLD TOURING

Lil Man had a lot of time to get deep into his music, and he had been coming up with some huge hits. He was submitting two albums worth of tracks just about every two weeks. That was almost double what some artists could do in a month. It was worth it, the CEO of the record label had been paying him very well. Lil Man had finally gotten rid of the key of coke he had and the bottle of wet. It was almost twenty five thousand dollars' worth of stuff, but Lil Man had to finally get rid of it once and for all. He knew that he could get anything he needed done from the guys at the chop shop after making the drop. He passed the stuff to the owner with no exchange in return. Lil Man technically owned their operation now. He and Katousha left the chop shop and everyone inside was extremely happy and told Lil Man to call if he needed anything . . . and they meant ANYTHING!

On the way from the chop shop, Lil Man had received a call from the record company. It was Diane Vander' perch. She said they needed extra hands to accompany a few artists on a thirty day tour. Lil Man agreed and discussed the matter with his wife. He explained to Katousha that he agreed in advance so he wouldn't ruin the positive flow he had going on with them. The checks were coming in heavily. Touring had been in Lil Mans contract, but he didn't get to do it too often because he was 'behind the scenes'. The tour consisted of assisting three artists while on tour, basically being the sharp level headed person while they had gotten drunk, high and tended to their groupies. There was a huge bonus percentage Lil Man would get from each show just for being there. He loved the whole idea, and he would get to see some of his very own songs performed live.

Katousha hated that Lil Man had to leave, but she understood it was about work. They had a week before he would meet the touring artists at the company's office in New York. Lil Man just spent as much time as he could, playing with the baby and conversing with his wife. "The company is collaborating with artists from other labels on this tour, that's why they want to send as many people as possible. Larger numbers represent us better, makes us look stronger. But I have an idea. While I'm gone, you could be planning another trip for us including places we can take Mekhi." Katousha loved that idea, and it had already given her something to do while Lil Man would be away. She wanted to surprise him with great places, the way he did for her while on their vacation.

"These thirty days are going to fly by babe, trust me. Our first stop will be in Tokyo, Japan. Then we'll be working our way back from there, France, Europe, Italy and places like that. I'll send you as many pictures as I can through our cell phones, and I'll keep my eye on some beautiful spots that we can revisit together. How does that sound?" Katousha's entire attitude had now changed about her husband going away. He had already proven to be a great trip planner, and she had gone from hating to see him go to not being able to wait to send him on his way. "Sounds great daddy! I would love to do some foreign country traveling with you!"

The day came for Lil Man to leave, and his wife drove him to the train station. They kissed and said their goodbyes. Mekhi had been knocked out in his car seat from the ride. Lil Man kissed his sleeping son on the forehead and left for the train. Katousha decided to stay at her mother's house while Lil Man was away. She didn't want to be alone, even with the three eighty Lil Man had left her. Their house was large and she'd have a lot of ground to cover alone. Staying with mom was the perfect excuse for abandoning ship. Katousha decided that another good way to surprise Lil Man was by finding work. Even though she was contributing to the music and was good at it, she decided to search for a nine to five job. She knew getting out of the house for income would be more fulfilling than networking at the computer in the house. Not to mention, Katousha had watched Lil Man spend hundreds of thousands of dollars. She felt anything to contribute and add to the pot would help, or at least be commendable.

"Your Aunt Susan has her own cleaning service. All she does is straighten offices downtown in one of those lawyer buildings on JFK Boulevard. Give her a call and see if she has a spot for you. It would be perfect for you if you're just trying to make some extra cash and give Rahim's pockets a rest." Katousha's mother had given her the best inside tip ever. Katousha called her aunt, and she would be able to start working right away. "Thanks mom! I just got off the phone with Aunt Susan, and she said that I could start Monday! Lil Man is going to be so happy I bet!" Katousha was excited. She had landed her first job ever since being out of high school and with her husband. She and Lil Man had been talking about Katousha getting a job, but she had no idea what she wanted to do. She had a lot of experience in braiding girls' hair and sewing in weaves, but she was shy when it came to the business. Katousha didn't interact well with strangers. In fact, she often wondered of herself, how was she so bold to approach Lil Man when they first met? 'I must've been high' she thought to herself. Whatever the case may have been, she was happily married with a good husband. Her baby had a great father. She wouldn't have traded it for anything!

Katousha's first week as a professional cleaner went smoothly. She caught on to the routine quickly, and before long her aunt began leaving her alone and didn't have to check behind her so much. Whenever her aunt went to get lunch, Katousha would call Lil Man's cell phone and begin sharing her excitement about the great day that she was having. Lil Man was relieved to hear his woman so happy back home while he was on tour. One of his biggest worries was that she would get bored, and go outside of the fidelity box. But Katousha's calls and joyful voice soon put an end to those insecurities. Even though Lil Man knew he had given his woman the world, sometimes a man just wonders . . . "What if." 'What if' was a terrible monster that could haunt your mind whether it was day or night.

But one afternoon while at work, Katousha's once peachy and creamy job wasn't so pleasant at all. She was cleaning on the twenty seventh floor of a center city high rise when she noticed blood leaking from an air duct. It grabbed her attention immediately. At first she was upset, thinking some drunken secretary had spilled wine on the carpet. But after taking a closer look, Katousha saw that her problem was much bigger than a wine spill. She called her aunt's cell phone. "I'm in suite twenty seven forty two, and I have a major problem in here! Please hurry!" Katousha's sense of urgency prompted her aunt to come bursting into the suite in a hurry. "What's the matter Toosha!?" Katousha had been crying, and could barely speak. She just pointed toward the air duct behind the huge office desk. "What in the world!?" Aunt Susan was just as shocked as Katousha had been, and immediately called the police.

When police arrived, officers had quarantined the floor Katousha had been working on and detectives began questioning her and her aunt. They removed a body of a man in his fifties from the air duct. He was a lawyer, and had been beaten and shot to death. Questioning Katousha hadn't done the detectives any good. She was new, and barely knew the building let alone anyone who had worked there. Her Aunt however, had been in the business for at least fifteen years and had become familiar with a lot of the staff who had come and gone from the buildings she worked in. "Mrs. Mason, how many buildings do you clean on JFK Boulevard?" The detectives were asking Katousha's aunt general questions, trying to find any leads or possible motives that they could about the murder. The killer was counting on the buildings super cold air to freeze the body and stop the bleeding. But someone had shut the air off on the top fifteen floors that day, another detail they were determined to find out about.

Aunt Susan was reluctant to answer any questions at first. She didn't want to become a target for snitching. But a detective pointed out that if she didn't cooperate she would be obstructing justice, and could even be viewed as a suspect. "You can go right ahead with the obstructing of justice bullshit officer! If I don't know anything, you cannot make me know anything by threatening me. Now would you please go and get another officer who is compassionate enough to conduct this interview without harassing me!? You're lucky I won't have your badge for breakfast!" Aunt Susan had picked up a lot of legal mumbo jumbo from working around lawyers and hearing them talk. She also watched 'CSI' and 'Law and Order' faithfully almost every night. In fact, the only time she missed the show is when she fell asleep from being too tired from work. And even then, she would wake up mad as hell at herself for missing an episode.

After Aunt Susan snapped on the detective, he and his partners were convinced that she didn't know anything about the murder. They left her alone, but urged her to call if she had remembered anything. After that, the lawyers who worked in the building had to work some magic just to get things from their offices. But they were all suspects. A lawyer has to be the most difficult suspect the law could be against. Lawyers knew too many tricks and bridges to fill in the gaps of the law. And if one was sharp enough, he could very well literally get away with murder. The Philadelphia Police department was a persistent one though, it would take a lot of skill and maybe some luck to pull a fast one on them.

The investigation of the murdered lawyer would take months. Forensics, evidence analysis, common sense and perhaps a forthcoming witness or two would definitely be necessary. The boys in blue had their work cut out for them. Some of the detectives were the same ones who responded when Lil Man shot his would-be robbers in the Home Depot parking lot. They were supposed to be 'hot stuff', a term police used for top cops who had a lot of convictions and arrests under their belts. The 'hot stuff' would be called in to any district to help the local departments solve crimes that needed special attention. The lawyer's death had become a high profile case, and had been repeated over and over on the news right along with Lil Man's situation at Home Depot's parking lot.

Katousha and her aunt were forced to focus on other buildings when it came to work. Their main building was crawling with investigators, and they were making everyone uncomfortable who had worked there. The murder of the lawyer was so wild and random, that it had inconvenienced the lives of dozens of people. Either by being unable to work in their own offices, or by being interrogated with the investigation that had affected anyone who had worked closely with the deceased lawyer. "Don't worry about it sugar, all my other buildings have just as much work. And hopefully there are no more bodies to discover." Katousha's aunt had found herself offering a lot of consolation. Katousha had been very shaken up about discovering the crime and she had never seen a dead body before the lawyer had been stuffed inside of the air duct.

"It's not your fault or anybody else's Aunt Susan. I probably won't be fully comfortable again until my husband is back at home. Right now he's out of town on tour, and ever since he left I have felt a little less strong. But I can handle it. He's just my everything, that's all. Katousha's aunt had never met Lil Man before, but she could tell he had taken very good care of her. Just simply from the way Katousha's entire demeanor had changed whenever she had spoken of her man, aunt Susan knew Lil Man was a good guy and wanted to meet him. "Your mother told me you guys had gotten married. Are you going to have a formal wedding the families can enjoy with you?" Katousha was glad her aunt asked that question, it had been eating her up not to discuss it. "We talked about it, but we think the wedding will be a small one. We want to get married on a Jamaican beach, and all of our guests would have to be flown there. The more the merrier, but since he insisted on paying for it I told him I didn't mind keeping it small."

Katousha's aunt was proud of her niece. She had a prince charming on her hands, and while working together she had given Katousha a lot of tips on how to keep her man. Most of the tips were sexual, but Katousha didn't mind. She loved the way her aunt kept things so real. "When you give him head, be sure to caress his balls and give him eye contact. Girrrrrrrl!! That shit drives a man crazy! That little secret alone could empty bank accounts all over America if done right!" Sometimes Aunt Susan had gotten sidetracked and had forgotten Katousha was married, but Katousha knew it was just 'girl talk'. Aunt Susan would often change the subject to keep her mind off of her deceased husband. He died of cancer a few years back, and she had never dated again since his passing. Work had become her new man.

"So what do you think about our sleeping friend in the air vents over at the other building?" Katousha had been secretly trying to forget about the dead man, but she decided that maybe engaging in a conversation about it would help her. She was trying to be stronger without the constant comfort of her man around. "I don't know. Maybe he had ruined somebody's case or something. Maybe he lost a huge settlement, or sent the wrong person to jail. Who knows? I think lawyers are sneaky, like human snakes. They get paid to be convincing liars, always masking the truth somehow and manipulating people." Susan was impressed with how mature and intelligent her youngest niece was. She loved talking with her at work and had hoped to keep her around for a long time, even though she was paying six hundred dollars a week for her time.

After Katousha wrapped up the work day, she went back to her mother's house to unwind and be with Mekhi. She had decided to wait until Mekhi was fast asleep before calling Lil Man. She had plans to curl up on the phone and talk to her man as long as possible. She was missing him. "Oh my God Rahim! You will never guess in a million years what happened to me at work today!" Katousha told Lil Man about the dead lawyer. "Whoa! Y'all gonna have the feds all over y'all asses for this one!" Lil Man told her over the phone. "That's some serious shit babe! And best believe no matter how innocent you are they will be watching you. And if their watching you, they'll damn sure watch me when I get back. Damn! You should've just cleaned the blood and left his old ass in there!" They both laughed over the phone, but Katousha knew her man was right. He advised her to try and not talk about what had happened so much. Lil Man also told Katousha to watch what she says over the phone. If the feds were involved, which they were, there was no telling whose phone could be tapped. They would be listening to everything trying to pick up clues, locking unsuspecting people up for crimes not even related to why they tapped the phone in the first place. The feds were deep!

"See? You're gonna make me want a new phone Rahim!" "I'm just telling you what I know to keep my babies safe, that's all. Now pipe down before I come spank you, calling me at four in the morning like you're crazy!" Lil Man was in Europe, and Katousha had forgotten about the time zone differences. "I'm sorry daddy, but momma been missing you." Katousha had said the magic words, and knew exactly how to stimulate her man over the phone. "Babe, chill out! We only have a couple weeks to go." Katousha insisted on moaning in Lil Mans ear, and touching herself while on the phone. Phone sex wasn't Lil Man's style, but he let his wife do her thing. The most he could participate was only listening though.

Masturbating in Europe while on the phone with his wife just wasn't in the plans. Lil Man would wait, letting the tension build up and releasing it once he returned. "But its soooo warm and wet daddy, I don't know what to do." It was torture. Katousha was having one of her freaky spells and Lil Man was half way around the world. He had to say something to kill the mood and temptation. "I know what you can do, take your ass to sleep! You killing me girl." Katousha ignored him and continued with her motions, giving her man an earful that could've made him go AWOL on the tour. "I'm sorry daddy" Katousha giggled erotically. "I just baked you a very warm and gushy cream pie, don't you want it? Its soooo warm!" Lil Man could hardly take it anymore. He was tempted to hang up on his wife. She was doing her job of being sexy a little too well at the time.

Lil Man finally convinced his wife to calm down, promising that he would take care of her every need when he returned home. Meanwhile, he had some news to share with her to. "We had a couple of label mates get into a fight on one of the tour buses. They had gotten extra drunk, and started going at it like they never even knew each other. One of the artists wound up being arrested and couldn't perform. We almost had to cancel the tour. The people were mad as hell that all the artists weren't there. We had to pay promoters extra to cover it up and still make the shows sound good enough to attend, which wouldn't be hard to do. Each show was only a few tickets away from selling out."

Katousha began yawning over the phone. Lil Man's story was boring, compared to Katousha's dead lawyer and the ocean flowing between her thighs. Lil Man was just discussing work, and Katousha wanted to be excited. "I'm boring you right? Well babe, you did wake me up in the middle of the night and sort of caught me off guard. But here's an idea, why don't you take some pictures for me of you right now. And when the lights come back on in this bus, or when its daylight I'll take some for you ok?" It wasn't exactly face to face, but at the time Lil Man and Katousha loved sending each other picture messages. Technology had come a long way and was advancing at a rapid rate. But it definitely came in handy for times like these, when couples were away from each other.

"Babe, do me a favor today. Find a place that builds pools and see how long it would take them. Ask them about a kidney design, fiberglass and be sure to mention that it will extend from under our patio and deck." Katousha hadn't known the first thing about inquiring about a pool. She tried to change the subject. "You sure I can handle that boo? I have all the pool you'll ever need right here." Katousha just kept teasing Lil Man over the phone. She knew if she had said half of those things around him she would barely get through the night with being constantly stroked, over and over. She needed her man to come and make love to her.

After they hung up and Katousha had gotten a few hours of sleep, it was time to meet Aunt Susan for work. They would still be inconvenienced by the murder investigation, so Susan had them working in an office building closer to West Philadelphia near the Amtrak train station. It would be an easy task. The offices were freshly renovated and mostly just needed dusting. Katousha had caught herself staring out of the large ten by ten foot glass windows down at traffic and pedestrians walking around commuting to and from work. From the thirty fifth floor everything looked tiny. People looked like ants running around. Being up that high had reminded Katousha of the restaurant in Niagara Falls, the Skylon Tower.

The work week went by fast because they were switching from building to building. In another one of their new buildings, Katousha was cleaning an office on the sixteenth floor when she heard a knock on the glass which came from the outside. It was a window washer, and even though he was dangling from the side of a building he was persistently flirting with Katousha. She ignored the man realizing that she had all the man she needed, hurried up and cleaned the office and left to another one. The man had actually maneuvered his scaffold to her next office and continued trying to get Katousha's attention. Frustrated, she held up the back side of her hand waving her one and a half karat three stone diamond wedding band Lil Man had bought her. The ring shone so brightly, it nearly blinded the man when the sun hit it. Katousha's ring was kryptonite for would be Super Man flirters.

Katousha was glad to know other men were still interested in her. She had been with Lil Man for a long time. But their attention only meant to her that she still looked good enough for her man. Neither she nor Lil Man had any interest in seeing anyone new. Even while on tour Lil Man had faced temptation when the artists had thick girls in bikini's trotting on and off of the tour buses. He would even feel guilty looking sometimes. It was torture, and Lil Man couldn't wait until the tour was over.

The tour Lil Man was on had ended a week early. An outdoor pavilion had closed due to thunderstorms and the show could not be done. The staff on tour was now headed back to the United States to continue promoting their new music, but Lil Man and a few others were allowed to go home. Once in the United States the record label had started using their own security guards and managers again. Lil Man couldn't wait to surprise his wife and son. He was given a check, and took a taxi home while Katousha was at work.

Lil Man had gotten home and realized his wife hadn't been staying there. She had a gun just in case, so Lil Man didn't understand what her worries were about. But it didn't matter, he was back home now and was about to plan a new surprise for his lovely lady.

COMING BACK 2 AMERICA

Lil Man wanted to do something creative for his wife for when she had gotten home and he surprised her. He decided to treat the day like it was Valentine's Day and bought dozens of roses, about six of them. Some of the roses would be given to Katousha in whole, but the others would have their petals plucked, marking significant trails around the house. Lil Man couldn't find a bucket of pre-plucked rose petals anywhere, they would've been perfect. But he felt like his wife was worth any extra effort in plucking the thorny flowers himself.

The first trail was made from the front door and leading to the kitchen table. The table had been decorated with a dozen roses as the centerpiece, two candles lit, two wine glasses and a few other petals sprinkled around the table top. It was beautiful! The second trail of petals had gone from the kitchen table, up the stairs leading to their bed. After Lil Man plucked petals from four dozens of the roses, he had to be careful not to use them all. Katousha would have a dozen in the kitchen, and he wanted to leave some for their personal bathroom which was connected to their bedroom. With just four single roses left Lil Man had arranged three of them on the bed, two on the pillows and one in the center on the comforter. He left one rose to hand to her personally along with her gift.

After arranging the roses in the house and setting the kitchen table, Lil Man went back out and headed to the jewelry store that his cousin Stoop Head had taken him to. He remembered seeing a heart shaped diamond pendant necklace set with a matching charm bracelet that he knew Katousha would love. Katousha had become a bunny rabbit, and Lil Man was feeding her plenty of karats. On the way from the jewelry store, Lil Man called Katousha as if he were still out of town. "Babe, after work do you mind going home and checking on the house? We have some expensive things there and I'd feel safer if you made an appearance or two, just to make sure our presence is felt ok?" Katousha agreed, and would be headed home after work. Now all Lil Man had to do was prepare the meal. He didn't have time to cook, so he called several caterers who delivered to see what they could prepare the quickest.

Lil Man ordered his wife's favorite fish, Tilapia seasoned with lemon juice and asparagus tips. Everything was setup perfectly, and now Lil Man just had to hide out in the garage until his baby arrived. He chose the garage because he could see out of it, and Katousha always had used the front door. About thirty minutes and two cigarettes later, Katousha finally pulled into their driveway. Lil Man popped in a stick of double mint chewing gum and let Katousha take in all the sites of the roses. Once she saw the kitchen table, she had known Lil Man had to be there, and she had gotten so excited! She read the note on the kitchen table, it said: 'Surprise mommy, come upstairs . . . .'

Katousha was excited, but cautious at the same time. She went back outside into Lil Mans Jaguar and took out the loaded three eighty he had left it in and cocked it back before going upstairs. She wasn't taking any chances after all the weird things that had been happening. With gun in hand, Katousha followed the rose petals up the steps and to the bed for another note that read: 'wanna shower with me?' There was still no sign of Lil Man, so she took out her cell phone and called him. "Man! Where are you?? You got me all nervous in this big house by myself, stop playing!" Lil Man didn't want to spoil the surprise and reveal his location yet, he just quietly crept out of the garage and upstairs towards the bedroom.

Katousha was in the bathroom of the bedroom when Lil Man walked in. His figure startled her and she turned around in a hurry squeezing the trigger of the hand gun on impulse. The shot grazed Lil Mans shoulder and hit the bedroom wall behind him. "Damn baby girl! That's how you feel? I missed you to!" Katousha put the gun down on the bathroom sink and ran over to her husband. "Oh my God!! Baby, I'm so sorry! I didn't mean it! You scared me! You told me to shoot first and find out later!" Lil Man was glad that his woman had it in her to squeeze a trigger, but he second guessed the advice he had given her about shooting first and asking questions last. She had almost shot him in the face. "It would help to identify the target first babe. Other than that, great job. You held down the fort!" Lil Man was bleeding from his shoulder with lots of skin missing and it was burning a lot. Katousha had gotten some hand towels and ran cold water over them for his wound.

"It'll be fine. So how was your day?" Katousha was surprised and amazed at her husband's manly response to getting shot. Even though he had only been grazed, he still hadn't shown any signs of pain or anger. He was too happy to see his lady. "How the hell are you asking about my day? I just shot my own husband!! What kind of day is that?" Lil Man had to calm his wife down on top of stopping his own bleeding. "It could've been way worse babe. Imagine if you had better aim. I would be a goner." Katousha knew he was right, but she still managed to feel bad. "I'm so sorry Rahim. Baby just name it and I'll do anything for you!" Lil Man would have liked to think that it would have gone the same way without her shooting him, but there was no telling now. The trigger had been pulled. "No more guns for you until you practice at the shooting range. If I had been an intruder, that shot should have hit my forehead, right in between the eyes. You see how this arm graze hardly hurts me? That's how you know you have to try and take out your target with every shot. If that had been your last bullet, you would be in trouble."

Katousha felt better after she saw that Lil Man wasn't at all mad at her. He seemed to be more upset that she hadn't killed him. He was making his wife tougher, just in case he wouldn't be around one day. After Lil Man had his arm wrapped nicely in the towels, they began kissing and caressing each other. "That bullet is going to cost you. It's going to have to come outta your ass girl! My wife can't shoot me and then not give me all the ass in the world." They both laughed, and proceeded downstairs to check out the Tilapia dinner. "What time are we picking up Mekhi?" After the mistake she had just made, Katousha knew she would have a busy night ahead of her. "He can stay with my mom until tomorrow. She has his baby bag with plenty of milk and diapers."

Lil Man and Katousha ate their candle lit dinner, but then had to go for a ride. He needed gauzes and some ointment to properly wrap up his arm. In the back of his mind he had really felt better knowing his wife was willing to protect herself and their home. He had wondered about it, but his new scar on his shoulder had erased any and all doubt that. After re wrapping his arm with the gauze, the couple went for a stroll by a lake near their home. They had lived near a yacht club, and some of the yacht's had made Lil Man want one. But he never went so far as to get it. They were extremely pricey and even though he could probably afford it, he figured his money would last longer without it. 'Maybe a fishing trip would do just fine' he thought to himself, constantly trying to convince himself that he didn't need a yacht. He felt like he had bad luck with those sorts of things. 'All I need is for my wife or son to jump over board and I have to jump in after them, and probably shoot it out with a shark. No yacht for me' he thought. He was being silly thinking of weird scenarios. After all he had been through, just about 'anything was possible' he thought.

Katousha and Lil Man had talked about where they wanted to take Mekhi. She had done her homework while he was gone, and had come up with an itinerary including Sesame Place and Disney World. The places sounded great to Lil Man and he would make the reservations right away. In the meantime, Katousha had more immediate pleasures in mind for them two while they were still alone. Night had fallen during their romantic stroll, and Katousha's horny bug had bitten her unexpectedly. She had caught Lil Man totally off-guard. "Let's do it out here, like we did a couple years ago . . . remember?" Lil Man was shocked. They were out in public and Katousha had started demanding sex. "Take me baby, I don't have on any panties." Lil Man knew that as she had gotten hotter, his chances of making it home without giving it to her were decreasing. He found himself looking around for a spot where they could go at it un-noticed. But Katousha didn't even care about that. Nothing could compare to her sense of spontaneity.

She had reached a point where she didn't give her husband too many more moments to speak or think about it. As he kept trying to walk and talk and make his way back to the house, she cut him off, unbuckled his belt and jeans and dropped down bouncing to a squat position while performing fellatio like a porn star. It had felt so great that Lil Man could hardly catch his breath from the images of his gorgeous wife and what she was doing and how it felt. Lil Man remembered Katousha telling him that giving head actually had turned her on even more. He hadn't touched the cookie yet, but he knew his wife would be soaked. "Baby, the house is only like three blocks away. I'm not trying to get any grass in my ass. We're grown up now." She ignored him, and actually went harder and deeper on her husbands 'package'. He soon realized that she wouldn't let up anytime soon.

Lil Man was tempted to use his bruised arm as an excuse, but decided he may need it for another time. Making love to a gorgeous woman wasn't so bad at all anyway. They were near a pond on the side of one of the large houses and it was nearly completely dark. Katousha maneuvered and worked her magic until Lil Man was on his back in the grass. Katousha's sound effects made him no longer care either. They were shooting an entire scene without the camera. She had rotated her position while keeping the 'package' secured in her jaw, placing the cookie jar smack dab in Lil Man's face. He wouldn't be coming up for air either, not until Katousha had been finished squirting during the 'sixty nine 'position.

Their outdoor episode lasted for about forty minutes when Katousha realized she wouldn't finish the job until they had gotten in bed. Lil Man was enjoying himself and had been holding back on purpose. "Let's go home so you can throw me a baby shower!" Katousha had all types of codes and names for sexual acts. A baby shower was one of the few that were probably self-explanatory. Once they had gotten home, the two had finally taken their real shower together that Lil Man suggested in one of the previous notes before getting to the 'baby shower' that Katousha had wanted. They could both tell they had been longing for each other while separated. The sexual tension had been intensified very much. Katousha was having orgasm after orgasm, almost entirely soaking their mattress. When Lil Man finally released, they had both had almost passed out but quickly got up to go and sleep in the guest room due to the wet bed.

The next morning Katousha had gotten up early and cooked a huge breakfast, thanking her man for a wonderful night. She had served Lil Man while he was still in bed, and she went to get showered and dressed for work while he ate. Lil Man had mixed feelings about Katousha working. On one hand, he wasn't used to her leaving him in the house alone. And on the other hand, he had commended her for having ambition. But Lil Man always thought that if he made enough money that maybe his wife should never have to work. Katousha had mentioned a woman she had spoken to while they were out in Beverly Hills. The woman was draped in diamonds and pearls and spoke of her mansion with a driveway filled with Rolls Royce's. She told Katousha that a good man wouldn't allow his wife to work. Katousha didn't believe in what the woman was saying, because at the end of the day there was nothing like your own and building together with your partner.

"Babe, I'm going to be working on music while you're at work. But I've been thinking of a new project. We'll talk about it some more once you get home ok?" They kissed for about three minutes before Katousha finally left out of the door for work. Lil Man had already been secretly working on his project. He had been keeping a journal, just sort of keeping account of all the up and downs he had gone through to get where he is. He was pleased to be earning a living through music, but a part of him wanted to share some of his life's highlights with the world in a different way.

Lil Man had a fresh new concept he was using while making music. He would sample different snippets from old songs and compile them together making a whole new song. Many other producers were making remixes, but Lil Man's compilations were so hot, that artists had started remixing his remix and making enough money for everybody. The music was flying off of the shelves, giving him time to put into his other projects. He put the finishing touches on two of his latest songs, and began taking inserts from his journal to see what direction his project would go in. He wanted to write a screenplay for a movie . . .

Katousha had gotten off of work, and had picked up Mekhi before returning home. "There's my little buddy! Where you been man!" Have you been hiding from me!?" Lil Man and Mekhi were both ecstatic to see each other. Mekhi had the cutest smile, grinning from ear to ear with his baby gums bearing no teeth. He would smile and get excited every time he had recognized his dad after a period of time. It was beautiful. Katousha and Lil Man had done some more talking about where they wanted to take the baby. Katousha would explain to her Aunt that she would be going away with her husband, she had become known for that throughout the family. But more importantly, Lil Man wanted to discuss his new ideas with his wife and see what type of input she had to inspire him.

"Babe, I've been jotting down certain events in my past and keeping them together in my journal. Do you think I should send them to a producer who does movies? Great films make a lot of dough, and we'd be set for a while!" Katousha pondered for a moment before responding. "Babe, anytime you didn't spend on the street was time spent showing your talents. You've proven that through all of the marvelous music you've made. I think you can do whatever you focus on and put your mind to! I will say this though. I have a bit of a confession." Katousha had made Lil Man slightly nervous when she had said the word confession. It was like one of those awkward Jerry Springer moments. "Spit it out baby, there nothing to it but to do it."

Katousha took a deep breath before spilling her beans about the trust she may have betrayed by her husband. "I have been snooping through some of your things behind your back. I wanted to know if you were being true to me, but there's no doubt in my mind that you are now. Anyway, I have read some of the entries in your journal on certain dates that we have been through some crazy things. Especially dealing with your wild ass cousins! But my point is, that maybe you should consider writing a book. I think if you told your story about going from hustling to making music, you could inspire a lot of people. And your book definitely would have a happy ending after all of the drama, you know with me and Mekhi in your life and all the love we're sharing. It's just an idea babe, give it some thought."

Katousha was right. Lil Man did have a good story on his hands, and it would definitely have a great ending. "Thanks babe! You may have given me the best idea yet. Between our music and my book, we may possibly be able to show people that anything is possible. I'm going to pray about it, and give it some extra thought. If I put our lives into a book, people may view us differently. But my mission is to inspire. I love you girl!" Lil Man began flipping through his journal to see what parts he would put into a book, and what parts he'd leave out. He couldn't incriminate anyone but himself, everyone else had died or been killed. He decided not to waste another moment. He looked back at all the negativity in his life and was glad that is was over. Taking a deep breath, Lil Man began putting his journal entries into story form. He tried remembering as much as he could from being a toddler to growing up in school, and wrote about that to. After naming the main character Lil Man, he then had a drink to come up with the perfect title for his Novel. The drink turned into two, and two turned into three until his vision actually started to blur and his speech began to slur as he struggled to regain his focus. "I got it!" he shouted. "I'll title the book 'FO-KiSSED' after my rap name! People will love it!"

Lil Man was excited about the idea and began writing right away. He would stay up late nights trying to get as much written as he could from the journal to his computer. Writing about his life wasn't the most pleasant idea, he had stirred up a lot of painful memories that he wanted to forget. But he also remembered that a lot of people had viewed others' pain and turmoil as entertainment.

And when it came to entertainment, Lil Man was a great writer and musician . . . A personal message he would like to share with the world is "Stay FO-KiSSED!! And if you can dream it, you can achieve it!"

To Be Continued . . . .